The Confessions of
Gonzalo Guerrero

Being a true and accurate account of Gonzalo Guerrero, a citizen of Castile, his shipwreck, his capture by the Mayans, his efforts to survive in an unknown and heathen land, how he came to adapt, his union with a Mayan wife, his children, and how he came to take up arms against his former countrymen.

By John Reisinger

i

The Confessions of Gonzalo Guerrero

Copyright 2014, 2018 by John Reisinger
www.johnreisinger.com
Glyphworks Publishing, 2018

ISBN-13: 978-0983881889
ISBN-10: 098388188X

To Barbara, for her help, support, and patience

"So it was that I decided to take up arms against my former countrymen; to stand with the Mayans against the Spanish conquest that threatened to devour them.... I had been forced to choose between the country of my birth and the woman of my heart. I made my choice and have never doubted I made the right one."

Gonzalo Guerrero

Foreward:
The Mendoza scrolls

Gonzalo Guerrero is one of the great mysteries of the Spanish conquest of Mexico. Shipwrecked in the Yucatan years before, Guerrero apparently led, or at least aided, the Mayan resistance to the Spanish conquerors. On two occasions, the Spaniards were able to contact him, hoping to entice him to return, but were refused. Until the discovery of Guerrero's confessions, however, little was known for sure about his life or what role he might have had in fighting the Spanish invasion.

The documents now called the Confessions of Gonzalo Guerrero were discovered in five Mayan pottery jars owned by the Mendoza family of Madrid since 1548. The jars, all with tight fitting lids sealed with resin, were almost forgotten in a display cabinet in a back room of the family villa in the Madrid suburb of La Moraleja.

In 2010, however, a visitor, an assistant curator at the Museo Nacional Del Prado, noticed the jars and arranged a loan of them to the museum for an exhibition. Noting the sealed condition of the jars, the museum X-rayed the jars and discovered that there were cylindrical shaped objects that appeared to be scrolls packed tightly in all five jars.

With the Mendozas' permission, the jars were opened. Inside were scrolls made of sheepskin, covered on both sides with writing. Most remarkably, however, the writing was in Spanish. Due to the dryness and lack of air in the sealed jars, the scrolls were intact, but a concentrated effort was necessary to completely unroll and record the writing.

To the astonishment of the curators, it soon became apparent that these scrolls appeared to be the hand-written memoirs of the mysterious Gonzalo Guerrero himself.

Although written in Spanish, the style of the writing is narrative and more free flowing than was the rule at that time. Some have dismissed the papers as a forgery, saying that no 16th century Spaniard would have written this way, but the

Confessions were written after Guerrero had lived with the Maya for over 20 years and become one of them. His writing would have no doubt reflected his altered outlook and philosophy. Analysis indicates that the resin that sealed the jars is over 400 years old, as are the scrolls themselves, so a modern day forgery seems unlikely.

Here, then, is the translation of the Mendoza scrolls; The Confessions of Gonzalo Guerrero. The narrative has been left as written with a few exceptions. For some Mayan words or place names, the more familiar modern term has been substituted, and some historical notes have been added.

Most accounts written at the time either viewed the Maya in an idealized way, or spoke in horror of idolatry and human sacrifice. Gonzalo Guerrero views the Maya with an impartial eye. He points out the brilliance of the civilization, but he also the human sacrifices, incessant warfare, and brutality. Where the Confessions deal with known facts, such as the fighting at Chichen Itza, the details follow the historical record closely, indicating that Guerrero was accurate in his reporting and observant of the world around him.

Guerrero also seems to have been completely candid in his confessions, including more examples of his shortcomings than his heroics. When his actions were self-serving or venal, he duly records them that way. When he is torn by indecision and conflicting loyalties, that too is noted. The picture of Guerrero that emerges, blemishes and all, is very different then the image of him that the Spaniards saw.

Guerrero was a man of 16th century Spain, thrust into an alien world. He was at the mercy of people who spoke a language he didn't understand and thought in ways that were different than anything he had ever experienced. It was as if an astronaut had been stranded on a distant planet and found a fully developed alien civilization there. As a result, Guerrero was forced to go to great lengths and make agonizing choices to adapt and to survive.

Here, then, is the story of an ordinary man who found

himself in an extraordinary place at an extraordinary time in history.

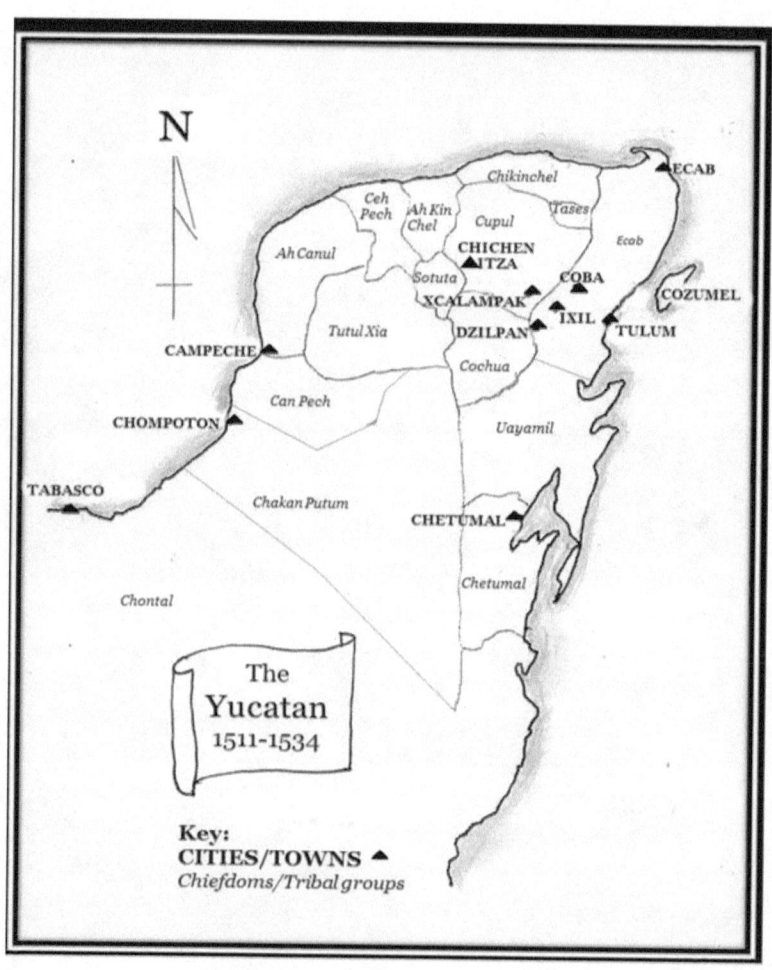

THE PEOPLE

(Note: The languages spoken by the various Maya peoples in the Yucatan varied from place to place with many variations in vocabulary and usage, so that there can be several different words that mean the same thing.)

AVILLA and SEVILLE, Spain

Gonzalo Guerrero------------author of the Confessions
Hectore Guerrero------------his brother
Uncle Fernando
Don Arbenza-----------------a judge of the Inquisition
Consuelo Arbenza------------his daughter

The SANGRE DE CRISTO

Juan de Valdivia--------------Captain of the expedition
Jeronomo de Aguiller---------expedition member
Brother deAngelo-------------expedition member
Eduardo Perez----------------expedition member
Jorge Ortega-----------------expedition member

SANTO DOMINGO, Hispaniola

Hernan Cortes-----------------adventurer

IXIL, Yucatan

Chan Oc (Maize Boar) --------Batab of Ixil
Box Naab (Shell Water) ------wife of Chan Oc
Zazil Ha (Clear Water) -------daughter of Chan Oc
Chac Pacal (Great Shield)----elder
Ah Kin Mu (Macaw Priest)---chief priest
Cuac Caan (Rain Sky)--------senior leader of warriors
Balam (Jaguar)----------------junior leader of warriors
Ix Kutz -------------------------wife of Balam

5 Cimi---------------------------daughter of Balam
2 Ahau---------------------------son of Balam
Can Pec (Snake Dog)----------Jaguar warrior
Akbal Dzib (Night Scribe) -----keeper of sacred books

DZILPAN, COBA, TULUM, COZUMEL, ECAB, CHICHEN ITZA, Yucatan

Pom Tzec (Copal Skull)---------Batab of Dzilpan
Akbal Ek (Night Star)---------Halach Uinic (chief) of Ecab Maya
Tolotl----------------------------Aztec merchant

CHETUMAL, Yucatan

Nachan Can----------------------Batab of Chetumal
Zotz Bacal-----------------------leader of Chetumal warriors
Cab Mut (Honey Bird)--------- cousin of Nachan Can

Chapter 1- The Expedition

In which I escape the Inquisition and depart for the New World

Greetings to any who find this message, and to the people of the Kingdom of Castile in this, the year of Our Lord 1534.

My name is Gonzalo Guerrero. I was born a Spaniard, but will die a Mayan. I am recording my confessions so that my actions, and the reasons I became a Mayan warrior and took up arms against the country of my birth will be better known and understood by the people of Spain, who no doubt think of me as a renegade and traitor. So for the sake of my family in Spain, and for the sake of my immortal soul, I will relay the truth of the events that brought me here.

Many years have passed since I last wrote Spanish words on a scroll, and the quill feels awkward and unfamiliar in my hand as it slowly scratches its way across the blank surface. As I write, strands of hazy white smoke from the burning incense on the pyramid temple of Kukulcan drift over the treetops like twisting serpents. The sweet smell mingles with the scent of wood smoke from the cooking fires, and the damp mists of the forest. These smells are familiar to me now, and sooth my heart, despite their association with blood and death.

To tell my story, I must tell you of the past. The Maya believe time runs in infinite repeating cycles, so unless you look to the past, you can never understand the present. My story does not begin in the land of the Maya, or even in the New World. My story begins in a bedroom; the bedroom of the Señorita Consuello Arbenza.

In the year of 1511, I was like many other hot blooded young Spaniards living near Seville, longing for adventure and riches in the mysterious and exciting new world across the great ocean.

Along with my sister Maria and my brother Hectore, I grew up on our family's farm when Castile and Aragon were still recovering from over 700 years of struggle against the Moors.[1] After all the death and destruction, the invader had finally been driven from our soil in the wars we called the *Reconquista*. With my brother, Hectore, I would pretend I was a brave soldier of Castile fighting off the Moorish invaders. We would battle each other with swords and spears made of sticks, our harmless combat raging furiously across fields, streams, and woods. Our Uncle Fernando was a master swordsman, and spent long hours teaching my brother and me the art of fighting with the sword and the pike. By the time I was 14, I was defeating the best of the local fencing school.[2]

As I grew older, I became increasingly restless to escape my dull life on the farm. My head was filled with the tales I had heard of the Indies, and the island of Hispaniola where Admiral Colon had started his colony.

"More expeditions are going to the New World," I would moan, "and I am missing all the adventure and riches. While Spain is marching to glory, I march behind a plow!"

Even Hectore, who was usually the most patient and understanding of men, sometimes grew weary of listening to my laments. I recall one exchange that was typical.

"Before you sail for adventure, *Senor Conquistador*, you still have that manure to spread," he said one day. "Perhaps you will find something valuable in it."

"Come, Hectore," I replied, brandishing a broomstick, and knocking a bucket out of his hand, "fence with me so I will be ready for the new world." I took up the dueling stance.

"You may battle all the buckets you wish, Gonzalo," he

laughed, "but you will never leave Avilla."

He might have been right, but in that year of 1511, my life suddenly changed forever. I still talked of seeking my fortune in the new world, but dallied at home courting a woman named Consuelo Arbenza. She had black hair and a nature as voluptuous as her body. Consuelo was hot blooded as I was, and I would court her in the traditional way, with a chaperon and a guitar during the day, but come to her room in the night. She lived with her father, but he was often away performing his duties as a judge of the Holy Inquisition. Many an evening, while Don Arbeza was consigning heretics to the flames, Consuelo and I would spend hungrily grappling in her big canopied bed giving full rein to our youthful passions. Although I love my wife dearly, I will always have a special place in my heart (or perhaps my loins) for Consuelo Arbeza and those soft velvet nights in Spain.

But the priests say the pleasures of the flesh are dangerous, and so it proved with me. One night, Consuelo and I were just at the point of fumbling with each other's clothes, when I stopped. I thought I faintly heard the click of boot heels on the tile floor of the corridor outside her room.

"What was that sound?" I said, suddenly alert. "Could there be someone else in the house?"

"Father is presiding over a trial of heretics in Seville. No one will be home for hours yet," she said, running her hand up my leg and pulling off my doublet in one deft motion.

At that moment the door burst open and there, black in the corridor light behind him, stood Consuelo's father, Don Julio Arbenza, with a sword in his hand and blood in his eyes. What happened next took only a few seconds, but seemed to go on forever.

"Seducer! Fornicator!" he bellowed, raising the sword. His oaths mingled with Consuelo's screams and seemed to fill the room as I scrambled over the bed and toward the open window. With the bed sheets tangled around my ankles, I tripped and knocked over a table as the figure of wrath crossed the room and bore down on me. With all the pent up strength I had been saving for Consuelo, I managed to hop over to the window and roll out an instant before the Toledo blade was thrust quivering into the windowsill behind me. I fell into a rose bush and frantically made my escape through the darkened garden while picking thorns out and trying to put my clothes back on.

I will spare you the details of the scene that ensued when I arrived home. Suffice to say, it involved a good deal of shouting, recriminations, and panic, and in the end, my family decided I must flee to Seville before I wounded something other than my dignity. As a judge of the Inquisition, Don Arbenza had the power to make my life extremely unpleasant.... and short.

So while Hectore watched with tears in his eyes, my father sent me off with some gold coins and an ivory handled dagger he had carried in the war with the Moors. The dagger was a thing of deadly beauty; its rich carvings and cold blade glistened in the soft firelight.

"Gonzalo," he said in exasperation, as he bundled me out the door, "your life will be a short one if you don't learn discretion where women are concerned. A judge of the Inquisition...*Madre de Dios*!"

My uncle Fernando went with me to Seville, and, as our horses' hooves echoed in the quiet blackness of the Spanish night, listened patiently as I complained about how unfair the world had been to me. He then said something I was to remember ever after.

"Everyone complains of the injustices of life," he said philosophically. "It is true the world can be a terrible place because some of the people who are in it seem determined to make it so. But you don't have to be one of them. If you

4

cannot make the world a better place, Gonzalo, at least do what you can to keep it from getting worse."

The waterfront of Seville was a riot of noise and bustling motion, crowded with merchants, adventurers, soldiers, priests, beggars, prostitutes, and officials of all types. On the docks, there were rough looking seamen from everywhere; Catalonians, Moors, Italians, Greeks, Arabs and many more whose pedigree was uncertain. The only thing they all seemed to have in common was a love of drink and a hatred of bathing. But within this untidy mass of humanity were an air of excitement and the heady feeling of unlimited possibilities.

A man in a tavern took me to a Captain Juan de Valdivia in a ship named the *Sangre de Cristo*. They were to leave for the New World the next morning and had room for another man. I hastily bought a second hand sword and breastplate from an armorer and departed Seville at dawn, one step ahead of the vengeful Don Arbenza and the Holy Inquisition.[3] It was the last I ever saw of the land of my birth.

I had never been to sea before and soon learned that it was not as wondrous and romantic as I had thought. The only way to travel in less comfort is to be dragged behind a horse. The first surprise was how small the vessel was. Even at the dock, the *Sangre de Cristo* had looked puny; about 70-80 feet long and about half as wide. Into this space were crammed 50 men, and all their equipment and provisions. There were no beds or comforts of any kind. When you needed to sleep, you bedded down on some sacks or straw if you were lucky, or in some damp corner if you weren't. Not that sleep was easy or relaxing on a ship underway; between the dampness, the violent motion, and the incessant banging, creaking and groaning of the hull and the rigging, it was enough to keep a corpse awake.

In spite of the discomfort of our travel, or perhaps

because of it, everyone was eager to get to the New World. To say we were all fortune seekers is to oversimplify. Personal gain may have been the most important factor, but it was by no means the only one. Religious fervor was high, and many felt they were part of a holy crusade to spread the true faith among the heathen and to carry the cross to the far reaches of the earth. Exciting possibilities indeed, but I almost didn't get there.

One night, I was at the top of the main mast, trying to untangle a violently flapping sail during a blinding rainstorm. There was a sudden lurch of the ship and to my horror, I found myself losing my balance and about to plunge to the deck far below. Suddenly, as I teetered between life and death, a hand came from nowhere, grabbed my collar, and jerked me back to safety. My savior was Jeronimo de Aguiller, a lay brother who intended to become a Franciscan monk after having proved himself worthy by saving the souls of the Indians. He was somewhat shorter and thinner than I was, but apparently strong enough when he had to be.

When I was back on deck again, cold, wet, and shaking, but alive, I turned to Aguiller.

"Jeronimo, you saved my life up there. I could have been killed and taken you with me."

"It was my Christian duty," he replied simply, "You would have done as much for me."

I wondered if he was right. Would I? Although I was not to know the answer until much later, we became friends from that day onward.

Another devout traveler was Brother deAngelo. He was young, idealistic, and hell bent on lifting the Indians to civilization whether they liked it or not. He believed he would be instrumental in their spiritual salvation. But he was a good-hearted soul who seemed constantly amazed and disappointed at the world he saw around him.

Eduardo Perez was a different sort altogether. He was a

burly, evil looking man who had fought in Italy and spoke of killing Spain's enemies ruthlessly and without mercy. He seemed to relish the thought that he would soon get a chance to spill blood in a holy cause, and practiced fencing with anyone he could find. To relieve the tedium of the voyage, I sparred with him several times, and we were able to teach each other a few new tricks that might be put to good use one day. But for all his skill, Perez seemed impulsive and reckless. And I wondered if he might not be almost as dangerous to his comrades as to the enemy.

And so the *Sangre de Cristo* and its mixed crew of missionaries, dreamers, adventurers and opportunists slowly made its way to the fabled land called the New World.

One morning, when it had begun to seem as if we had been at sea most of our lives, we finally heard the cry we had all been waiting for; "Land ho!"

We all crowded the rail and strained our eyes. There, shimmering on the horizon was a dark smudge; Hispaniola, the outpost of Spain in the New World and staging area to wondrous lands waiting to be claimed and exploited.[4]

As the bulk of Hispaniola steadily grew larger, everyone prepared in his own way; de Aguiller and brother deAngelo prayed, Captain Valdivia consulted his charts, Perez sharpened his sword, and I stood by the bowsprit dreaming of gold and glory.

Chapter 2- The Wreck of the Sangre de Cristo

In which I am shipwrecked on an unknown shore

Hispaniola's capitol, Santo Domingo, was mostly a scattering of shabby wooden structures lining dirt streets among the palm trees at the mouth of the Rio Ozama. There appeared to be a large central square almost bordering the river, and a few more stone or wooden buildings were under construction. On the river side of this square a fine stone building, the Alcazar of Diego Colon, was almost completed. This massive two-story structure was to be the home of one of the sons of Cristobal Colon, himself. Nearby, they were laying out the foundation of a cathedral.

Most of the town was surrounded by a palisade wall down to the water, although sections of this stockade were being replaced with stone fortifications. Santo Domingo had very little wharf space, so the *Sangre de Cristo* dropped anchor in the river and several of us headed for shore in one of the longboats.

By the time we stepped ashore, the mid afternoon sun was blazing high in the sky. The damp heat, heavy with the smell of sewage and rotting vegetation was almost overpowering. The streets and buildings of the town seemed to shimmer in the stifling haze, and after a few steps, we were all dripping with sweat. It almost seemed an effort to breathe in that tropical furnace.

"Look," said de Aguiller, suddenly pointing to the dock area, "those must be Indians."

He indicated several figures hauling crates and barrels between the ships and the weathered looking warehouses nearby. Someone said they were Arawak Indians. The Indians were short and brown skinned; they mostly wore only ragged loincloths, and perhaps sandals. Their long black hair hung down in their faces or stuck to the sweat on their shoulders. They all had a dispirited and resigned look about them, as if they saw only hardship and death in their future but were helpless to do anything about it. De Aguiller grew pale, visibly shaken by the Indians' condition, but I had other, more pressing concerns.

"This heat is unbearable," I complained, "Come, Jeronimo, let us slake our thirst and renew our strength. There is a tavern over there. We will drink to our success in the New World."

The tavern wasn't much of a place; a few crude tables on a dirt floor under a thatched roof held up by poles with the bark still on them. Inside, it was almost as hot as the street, but at least it was shady. A bald, greasy looking barkeep was speaking to a man with a sword at his side. The man had a black beard and the air of someone who knows exactly what he wants and will stop at nothing to get it. His eyes reinforced that impression, for they seemed to burn with single-minded determination. If he hadn't been here, I thought, this rascal might well be back in Seville helping Consuelo's father burn heretics at the stake in an *Auto de Fe*.

The man's name, we learned, was Hernan Cortes.

Of course, I had no way of knowing at the time of the effect Cortes would have on my life and on the lives of millions of others. I would like to say that I had a feeling about him and sensed danger, but I really didn't. Oh, he was an impressive figure; confident, decisive, and well spoken. Even so, I could never have imagined where destiny would lead him.

"*Buenos dias, señors*," he said with a nod of his head. "I regret I cannot join you, but I merely stopped in for a quick refreshment. I am on my way to make arrangements for my

9

expedition to Cuba."

In spite of his formidable appearance, Cortes seemed amiable enough, and as he drank his ale, he spoke of his plans.

"The new world is a land of unimaginable potential," he said, "Wealth beyond measure belongs to whoever is bold enough to seize it. We stand at a time in history that is unique. A modern world is encountering a rich but primitive world that is unknown. Think of the possibilities, *señors*! Here, there is always another, richer land just over the horizon, and new worlds to conquer! For a brave man of Castile, there is no other place to be."

We were spellbound by this man. He refreshed our wilted spirits far more than the ale. Wealth beyond measure.....

"Well, my friends," said Cortes, slamming a now empty tankard down on the table, "I must beg your leave. Cuba awaits." He flipped a coin to the barkeep, and was gone, back out into the glaring sun to conquer his new worlds.[5]

"I can't stop thinking about those Indians," said de Aguiller, as we raised anchor the next morning. "They are being kept in miserable servitude. The Captain said it is called the Repartamiento system and is supposed to teach the Indians about the Holy Faith in exchange for their labor. The Indians have no choice, of course, but even so, could this be the consequence? The Indians have been reduced to slaves in their own lands and they are dying in large numbers as a result. I understand a Dominican brother named Fra de Montesino preached a sermon last week condemning the Castilians for their treatment of the Indians. 'God's children' he called them." De Aguiller shook his head slowly; deep lines of worry and confusion furrowed his brow. "Surely all this can't be God's will."

"Who can say?" I shrugged, "Perhaps the Repartimiento system is teaching the savages about Heaven by sending them there."

"But if they are God's children..."

"Come Jeronimo: what does all this have to do with us? We are not Indians! Let us speak of pleasant things!" I tried hard not to think about the Indians too much.

But de Aguiller still looked troubled.[6]

In a few days' time, we reached Jamaica. The island resembled Hispaniola with white sand beaches all around and palm trees waving and bending in the warm breeze. A thick green canopy of forest covered everywhere else. We dropped anchor in the clear blue water and sent a party of men to explore. They returned two days later with reports of scattered villages of naked savages, a few miserable native crops, and absolutely nothing resembling gold. This was repeated twice more as we made our way from east to west along the southern coast. Finally, on the last expedition ashore, I was taken along. Here again, I saw naked Indians living in pathetic huts of sticks and leaves. In each village we came to, we assembled the occupants and read them a proclamation that they were now subjects of Spain and had to become Christians. This was usually met with blank stares since none of the Indians spoke Spanish.

We also searched the huts for gold and found none. As I looked into one hut, I interrupted a grunting Perez ravishing a naked Indian woman on the dirt floor. She didn't appear to be struggling, just waiting sullenly for it to be over. I was uneasy about what I saw, and just stood there in the doorway without speaking. Although I had laughed at de Aguiller's sentimentality regarding the Indians, I saw no need for such callous brutality.

"Eduardo...." I started to say. Perez noticed me and interrupted to say he was finished.

"Come, Gonzalo," Perez leered over his shoulder, "have a quick poke to keep up your strength. Most enjoyable, too, if you don't mind a few scratches and the smell of wood smoke." He stood up and pushed the woman aside. She was silent, but looked up at me with a burning hatred that made me uneasy. Perez continued to leer, waiting for me to take my turn. As I stood, paralyzed by my confusion and revulsion, a gleam of light reflected off an object Perez wore around his neck, and I saw it was a crucifix. The tiny figure of Our Lord seemed to look at me accusingly.

"There is no time," I lied, "We must return to the ship."

"Well, never mind," Perez shrugged, "there will be others."

I paused in the doorway as I left and looked back at the woman. Her eyes still glared at me, and I made a hasty retreat.

"Prepare to get underway!" shouted Valdivia, when we had returned, "We have spent enough time in this poor place. We sail to the south!"

A cheer went up from everyone. Soon we would be in the rich lands of the south, where we could go forth and trade the cross of Christ for the gold of the Indies. I put the image of the Indian woman out of my mind and looked forward to the great adventure ahead.

The next morning dawned gray with rain. Whitecaps were forming at the tops of the waves, and being blown off by a rising wind. The *Sangre de Cristo* plunged and rolled like a seagoing drunkard.

"A storm is building," said Valdivia, sniffing the air, "Take in the sails and lash down the cargo. Step lively; this could be a bad one."

As if slapped by a giant hand, the ship lurched with the force of the storm. The winds howled like all the lost souls in hell and waves like foaming grey mountains slammed into us. The *Sange de Cristo* rose up one side of each wave and slid down the other. Massive gray green walls of water broke over us, and the ship shuddered like some living thing. We prayed for the storm to abate, but it seemed to grow in its fury.

Soon, pieces of rigging were carried away, then with a loud crack, the mizzenmast went, crashing across the stern in a tangle of ropes and splintered wood until another wave cleared it off.

The next wave took the mainmast down, crushing two more men as it fell, and tearing off most of the starboard rail. By now, we had given up trying to steer the ship and devoted our efforts to just keeping the *Sangre de Cristo* afloat.

"Jeronimo," I shouted, "Help me brace the bulkhead. It's ready to collapse!"

We worked frantically shoring up the splintered timbers. Others were working the bilge pumps, but water was coming in faster than the exhausted crew could pump it out, and the ship started wallowing lower in the water.

Soon, all the masts were gone and the battered hull was taking on water between planks that had been loosened or broken by the pounding of the waves. As de Aguiller and I wedged a brace in place to try to strengthen the splintered side of the ship, I looked down and saw I was standing in water. The *Sangre de Cristo* was dying.

"Everyone into the longboats!" shouted Valdivia, who, like the rest of us was now so bedraggled as to be scarcely recognizable. "Launch from the starboard side; it's already under water. Be quick about it!"

As we floated clear, only the stern of the ship was still above water, as if reluctant to meet its fate. In a few minutes, though, it sank beneath the waves, and the *Sangre de Cristo* was gone with only a few shattered planks of wood and pieces of debris to mark its grave.

With the next dawn, the storm was gone and we took stock of our situation. Two longboats with 24 men between them were bobbing on the clear blue waters without any land to be seen.[7]

"Each boat has charts, compass and quadrant for

navigation, and fishing gear," said Valdivia, "We have two barrels of water and a barrel of biscuits. We have sails, but the masts have been carried away in the storm, so will have to row."

Before the storm, Valdivia had taken a sighting and determined our latitude. He estimated we were 60 miles southwest of Jamaica, but couldn't be sure how far the storm had carried us. We only knew we needed to go northeast back to Jamaica, but a strong westerly current was taking us further away by the minute. We would have to row 10-12 miles a day just to stay in the same spot. If we stopped to rest we would lose what we had gained. Finally, Valdivia made the only realistic decision he could make.

"We will row with the current. With any luck, we will be carried to the western part of Cuba. If we row steadily, we will make 22 miles each day."

"And what if we don't find Cuba? Will we row forever?" A man named Ortega challenged the decision. He stood up in the boat and pointed at Valdivia. "I put it to you, Valdivia; how long do you expect us to row?"

"Until we either find land or die," the captain replied coolly, "And it's CAPTAIN Valdivia. Now sit down before you swamp the boat."

Ortega glared at him for a moment, then sat down.

So we turned about and headed into the unknown. We could never have made it back to Jamaica against the current, and the faster we could travel, the more likely we would find another land before we died.

So we took turns rowing while the others held the sail over their heads for protection from the sun. As the food and water diminished, though, our rowing became less effective. We caught some fish and ate them raw, but after 10 days, we were thirsty and famished. The sun had burned us, and our hair and beards were wild and tangled. On the thirteenth day, Jesus Hernandez, who had been delirious with fever for three days, died in his sleep.

In the tropical heat, the water was the biggest problem. We used the sail to catch rainwater and directed it into the almost empty barrels, but it was not enough. Day followed endless day. The sun blazed mercilessly overhead, sweating out what little water we had in our bodies. By the twentieth day we were all too weak to row more than a few strokes. Valdivia estimated that we had come over 300 miles. Where was the land?

Brother deAngelo, his mouth parched and his tongue swollen, prayed faithfully for God's deliverance and mercy, but found neither. Perez had saved his sword, only to use it to cut up the occasional fish. Ortega still grumbled, but his protests were feeble, and no one was listening. Even de Aguiller's optimism was sorely tried.

"This can't be, Gonzalo," he would say, looking at the endless expanse of sparkling blue water, "I feel so strongly that God has some plan for my life."

I couldn't be much comfort. "Perhaps he planned for you to die in an open boat with hungry, thirsty and foul smelling companions," I said sarcastically.

"I too have a destiny;" chimed in Perez, "to be the conqueror of new lands, and the scourge of the Indians. This sword is thirsty for blood that does not come from a fish." He tapped the hilt of his sword with a meaty forefinger.

"We all have a destiny, my sons;" said brother deAngelo "to bring the word of God to these lands. God is testing us so that we will emerge stronger for the trials that await us."

"With all due respect, brother deAngelo," I said wearily, "if God doesn't stop making us stronger soon, he'll kill us all."

After 25 days, we were down to 18 hungry, thirsty, sun burned scarecrows drifting in a state of despair and delirium. In a few days, we would all be dead; hope was finally gone. On the night of the 25th day, another storm came up and drove us relentlessly to the west through the darkness. With our last remaining strength, we bailed to keep the boats afloat out of sheer force of habit rather than any thoughtful effort. But we soon lapsed into an exhausted unconsciousness one by one, and let the winds carry us as they wished. We were beyond caring.

Slowly, through a blurred haze of sleep, I awoke. My eyes were still closed, but I sensed something was different. There was no motion of the boat. And there was a sound. It was familiar, but I couldn't quite identify it. With my eyes still closed, I strained to remember the sound. Then, with a start, I recognized it....surf.

My eyes opened and were almost blinded by the glare of the morning sun reflecting off of a white sand beach. The boat was firmly grounded above the surf line where the wind and storm had driven it. The other boat was nowhere to be seen. Slowly, I looked up the beach and saw blue skies, waving palm trees, and miles of white sand. I also saw something else.

Standing on the beach surrounding the boat were ten Indians with bows and arrows, spears, and war clubs motioning for us to get out of the boat and come with them.

Chapter 3- The Land of Blood

In which I encounter the mysterious Maya...and sudden death

"Where are we, Gonzalo?" De Aguiller had also awakened and crouched wide-eyed beside me. "And who are those people? They look different from other Indians."

Different indeed. Instead of naked Indians, these were dressed in elaborate loincloths made of good quality cloth dyed red and black. They also wore short jackets and large, complex headdresses made up of wide headbands and long green feathers. Some of them wore a short cloak tied over one shoulder and under the opposite arm much like the garments worn by the ancient Greeks. They had sandals and wide bracelets of jade or some similar material on their wrists and ankles. Even their physical appearance was different. They were short and brown skinned like the Arawaks, but stocky and more muscular. Each had a broad band of black painted across his chest and face. And what faces! They had flat, elongated foreheads that seemed to accentuate their noses, and several of them were cross-eyed!

Even their weapons seemed better fashioned than the others we had seen. The clubs with which they were motioning us out of the boat were not just pieces of tree limbs, but were finely carved and lined along two edges with pieces of sharpened stone to form a cutting edge, almost like a sword. These people were far more formidable than the Arawaks on Jamaica, and were worlds away from the poor specimens remaining on Hispaniola. The Spaniards and the Indians silently regarded each other across a gulf that was far wider than the few feet that separated them.

The Indians' leader, who also wore discs in his earlobes

17

and a necklace of bone, motioned once again, and this time, they all took a step closer. I had a feeling their patience was short, and they would not ask a third time, so I started to get out of the boat.

"No!" came the deep voice of Perez. He had already gotten out with his sword in his hand, walking slowly toward the Indian leader. The Indian, although he was a good foot shorter than Perez, viewed him with curiosity, not alarm.

"No heathen savages have the right to give orders to Castilians. You take us to your chief, you brown swine, or I'll see the color of your insides! Do you hear me? "

The Indians still made no move and said nothing, but stood there waiting for the rest of us to follow. For a few tense seconds, the only sound was the rumble and hiss of the surf and the whisper of wind in the palm trees. This enraged Perez even more and he advanced on the leader.

"Very well, you will all taste Toledo steel." With that, Perez raised his sword to strike. Suddenly, almost too fast to see, the leader swung his club in a fast, vicious arc. There was a sound like a melon dropped on a stone floor and Perez crumbled dead on the beach with his skull smashed. Red splatters of blood stained the white sand. His body twitched once, then was still.

"*Santa Madre de Dios,*" whispered de Aguiller hoarsely.

In stunned silence, we all got out of the boat and followed the Indians into the jungle. Each of us looked in horror at the still form of Perez as we passed. Several flies were on his face and the blood had soaked into the sand.

It had all happened so fast; day after day in the boat monotonously drifting under the hot sun, a stormy night, then a landfall followed by capture and the violent death of Perez. Perez. I couldn't accept the fact that he was gone. Not Perez. Our strongest, bravest man who fought like a demon and spoke of killing hundreds of Indians had been felled by a single blow. What hope did the rest of us have?

The Indian who had killed Perez walked slightly ahead of me in an easy, confident gait. I was sickened to see that his club had a smear of blood and strands of hair along one edge.

As we walked, I looked closer at the cloak the leader was wearing. It had an intricate pattern, perfectly rendered. On his upper arm, the same Indian had a bracelet with an odd looking carved ornament. Looking closer, I was appalled to see that the ornament was a human jawbone. These people seemed to be a strange blend of sophistication and savagery.

We trudged on in a single file along a barely discernible track. The Indians spoke to each other occasionally in a guttural sounding language that was unfamiliar to any of us. At first, we tried to talk to either our captors or each other, but the Indians spoke sharply to anyone who made a sound and we soon fell into a gloomy silence. Our captors had loosely tied us together with loops of rope around our necks, but hadn't searched us, so I still had my father's knife in my boot. Even so, it would be of little use against these well-armed killers.

To fight back a rising sense of panic that made me want to bolt and run for my life, I speculated as to who these people were. They were certainly not Arawaks, or even Tainos or Caribs. So who, I wondered, were they? Then I remembered a tale a drunken sailor had told me in a tavern in Seville; about how Colon had once sailed far to the west and come upon a large trading canoe full of Indians dressed in woven cloth and carrying trade goods. Part of the cargo had been green feathers; the same as those worn by these Indians. I was weary, but I strained to recall the details of the story. What was the name of this land? Yupa...Yuca....Yucatan. That was it. And what did these people call themselves? Oh yes; then I remembered; the Maya.

Onward we trudged. The jungle wasn't nearly as thick and tangled as it had been on Jamaica, consisting of fairly short trees and scrub. Another curious feature was an almost total

19

lack of surface water. We walked for almost a full day and never saw a stream or a pond.

Just when it seemed we would all collapse from exhaustion, we started passing cultivated fields of beans, squash, peppers, and corn. I noticed that the fields had crops planted in mounds rather than rows. Apparently, these people didn't know the plow. Near the fields, I saw huts made of sticks with thatched roofs similar to the ones we had seen in Jamaica, except that each one was sitting on a stone masonry platform about a foot above the ground. This method seemed to be a very effective way of keeping the floors dry in the heavy tropical rains; more evidence of sophistication.

Just then, the road made a slight turn, revealing a startling sight. We were approaching a town, laid out as straight and neat as any in Spain. A central square was flanked by buildings of fine stone masonry on three sides, and on the fourth by a stone pyramid as tall as a tower! We were astonished. What manner of people were these Maya? They could kill without hesitation or mercy, yet they were apparently skilled weavers and builders as well.

As we approached the central square, the huts were closer together and we could see children at play and women grinding corn, preparing meals, weaving, or nursing babies. Unlike the naked Arawak women on Jamaica, these all wore dresses of brilliant white with flowered trim, and regarded us with curiosity. Taking a closer look at the babies and small children, I saw the reason for the flat foreheads and crossed eyes we had noticed. Many babies had wooden boards strapped to their foreheads to flatten them. Others had a bead suspended from a thread in front of their noses that caused them to cross their eyes. These features must have been considered marks of beauty. Again I wondered; what kind of people are these, and what sort of alien world had we stumbled into?

In the square was a large milling group of people in an open-air market. They were trading in cloth, feathers, corn, squash, peppers, skins of animals, turkeys, pottery, jewelry, clothing, and weapons. The men wore at least a cloth loincloth and sandals, and many of them also wore cloaks and impressive feather headdresses. Men's hair was pulled straight back and tied. The women were dressed in the white cloth dresses we had noticed earlier, and wore their hair either straight or braided. The scene was lively and prosperous looking as people bargained furiously.

As we were marched through the square, we could get a better look at the pyramid at the far end. The structure was somewhat taller than the mainmast of the *Sangre de Cristo*, about 50-60 feet. A flat area was at the top as if the pointed cap had been sliced off. On the flat area was a small, flat roofed building. Access to this building was up a long and very steep stairway that scaled one face of the structure. The building and the stairway were painted a brownish red color while the rest of the pyramid was white. On each of the four corners of the flat area, a thin column of smoke rose straight into the still air. The effect was alien and unnerving. I glanced at de Aguiller and wondered if we had all drowned and were in hell.

After passing through the square, we came to a stockade with a small gate. The leader motioned us inside the gate, and when we had entered, closed it after us. Once inside, we could see that the stockade had a roof made of a grid of poles lashed together. We were in a cage.

"They are safe! Praise God," came voices from the shadows on the other side of the enclosure. The men from the other boat were already there, or most of them, at least. I was glad to see them until I noticed Ortega was there.

They had had a similar experience to ours, but had lost more men to the storm and the fever. Between our two groups we had but 12 men left; 12 men out of the 60 who had left

Seville ready to conquer the Indies for God and for gold. Instead, most of them lay at the bottom of the sea or in the jungle, and the dying was not over yet. My gloomy thoughts were interrupted by the arrival of two Indians bearing large bowls of a thick yellow porridge that proved to be corn ground up with some peppers. Being near starvation, we plunged our hands into the bowls and ate greedily.

"I wonder what they want with us," said de Aguiller, licking the last of the corn from his fingers. "Are they fattening us up for a cannibal feast?"

The same thought had been at the back of my mind as well, and I found myself wishing I had stayed away from Consuelo's room that night in Avilla.

In spite of our weariness, we slept little that night, jumping at shadows and starting at the eerie sounds of forest. I sat dejected on the dirt floor with my back against one of the stockade supports. The lower part of the wood was worn smooth; apparently many others had been kept there before us.

At dawn, an apparition materialized out of the mist. Under a huge headdress was a large, brutish looking man. He was more richly dressed than the others, heavily weighed down with necklaces, bracelets and feathers. A wide black stripe was painted across his face, making him look like the devil's brother. The other Indians treated this figure with a mixture of both respect and fear.

Small swirls and eddies of mist were stirred up as the figure moved toward us, intensifying the impression of some horror from another world. The man stopped directly in front of our cage and looked at us impassively, his broad brown face seemingly made of stone. He was obviously their chief, for he moved with an air of arrogance and command. An atmosphere of graveyards hung over the man like the morning haze that surrounded us. The other Spaniards in the cage eyed him warily in silence, but I looked him directly in the eye with a look that could perhaps be considered insolent. When he came to me, the brute returned my stare as if noting every detail of my face so that he could remember it later, and I felt as if I were staring into the face of death itself. The warriors referred to this man by a name I would later learn well: Pom Tzec.

Finally, he passed me by and looked at the others in turn. With a grunt and a quick gesture, he indicated Ortega, and three Indians instantly dragged our shipmate out of the cage and took him away. In spite of our terror, we tried to stop them and shouted protests, but were beaten back. The chief paused for a moment, then looked directly at me once more before leaving. Ortega screamed as he was dragged away, then all was quiet once more.

Our cage was situated in such a way that the upper half of the pyramid was visible over the top of an intervening building. We had speculated that the pyramid must be the royal palace because of its size and height, although the building at the top seemed much too small for such a purpose. So we were given new hope a few minutes after Ortega was taken away to see him, along with two others climbing the steep stairway to the top.

"Look," said brother deAngelo, "There's Ortega. They must be taking him to meet their chief. God be praised."

While we were talking, the three figures on the stairway were nearing the top. When they were at the top step, they were met by five other figures like the one in the white robe. For a moment, the group stood still. There was no movement except the four trails of smoke slowly rising from bowls of incense on the corners of the flat area. Suddenly, five of the figures in white robes seized Ortega, one on each wrist and ankle, and one with a noose around the throat. They pulled him down on his back across a waist high stone block at the head of the steps. The other figure stood over Ortega and

23

raised a knife in the air! With a practiced deliberate motion, the Indian stabbed Ortega in the chest while the others held him firmly in place. Then, as we watched, repelled and fascinated at the same time, the Indian reached into the wound with his hand and pulled out Ortega's heart! He then lifted the heart up to the sky, then turned and walked into the building with it. Meanwhile, Ortega's now lifeless body was being tossed bouncing down the steep steps, the arms and legs flopping grotesquely. It had only taken a few seconds.

Chapter 4- The Slave

In which I am forced into a terrible new life in a dangerous land

There was stillness in our cage for a long time as each man crossed himself and tried to come to terms with the horror of what he had just seen. Finally, the silence was broken by low murmuring voices; every last man was praying, "Holy Mary, Mother of God, pray for us sinners now and at the hour of our death......"

I interrupted de Aguiller's fervent prayers and took him aside. "Jeronimo, we must escape before they kill us all."

"Escape?" He almost shouted the words, pointing toward the distant forest. "Escape to where? We are in an uncharted land with no friends, no weapons and no ship. Jungles infested with murderous Indians surround us. There are only eight of us left and three have the fever."

"What you say is all too true," I reluctantly admitted, "but it seems we must choose between the likelihood of death out there and the certainty of death in here. I see no other choice; we must go tonight. If you believe in the deliverance of God, this is your chance."

As we waited for darkness, the hours dragged on in a haze of damp heat, buzzing insects, and nervous apprehension. The guard didn't move; we didn't move. People passed by intermittently, as slowly as time itself.

"I can't understand it." said de Aguiller, shaking his head in bewilderment. "These Indians seemed almost civilized compared to the others."

"Civilized?" I raised my eyebrows in surprise. "Because they weave cloth and build in stone? They are murdering savages that have learned a few tricks; nothing more." I spat for emphasis.

"They are God's children, all the same," said de Aguiller. I couldn't tell if he was trying to convince me or convince himself. "God will deliver us from this evil. You will see, Gonzalo."

Late that night, with my father's knife, I cut the ropes that held several of the poles of our stockade in place and slipped away with de Aguiller. The others were to follow at about ten minute intervals so we would not attract too much attention if anyone saw us. We planned to head east for the sea and freedom.

There were a few people about, but we kept in the shadows as we carefully made our way east, our footsteps crunching in the still night. We reached the square, and saw the pyramid in its entirety. As we got closer, the pyramid grew in both size and malignancy in the pale moonlight. Hideous intertwined snakes were carved in low relief on the stone walls by the bottom of the stairs. Most of the pyramid's massive bulk was covered with intricate carvings and designs of the most unnatural and unsettling nature, featuring lions and giant birds eating human hearts. The alien repulsiveness of the designs made the pyramid even more ominous and forbidding. Looking up to the top of the steep stairway as we passed, we could see the altar stone, still glistening with blood.[8]

Soon we were out of the town and in the surrounding forest. Using the moon as a guide as best we could, de Aguiller and I pushed through the brush until dawn. Finally, we stopped to rest and wait for the others, but there was no sign of them. We slept for an hour or so, then continued. All that day we pushed on, seeing no one. We slept along a trail that night, half dead with fear and exhaustion.

"Do you think we'll ever see Spain again?" De Aguiller's voice was a whisper as we sat jumping at sounds in the night.

"If we don't see any more savages first," I replied. "We must be miles away from that accursed place by now. Maybe we have a chance after all."

At that moment, everything went black.

When I awoke the next morning, I had a sore spot on my head. When I tried to rub it, I found my wrists were tied together, and Indians surrounded me once again. Our escape attempt had failed. There were five Indians this time. I didn't recognize any of them, but they ordered us to march just as before. De Aguiller looked like a man who had seen all his hopes destroyed as we trudged along. If anything, this march was worse than before, because we knew what fate awaited us. I still had my knife in my boot, but, with my hands tied, couldn't get to it. I racked my brain desperately trying to think of a way out of this death march.

Late that afternoon, we started to see the same signs of a nearby city as we had before; cultivated fields, houses, children, but something was different. De Aguiller noticed it first.

"Gonzalo," he whispered excitedly. "This is a different town!"

He was right. The layout and arrangement of buildings was different. We were in another city altogether. We had escaped to captivity in another place, but whether we were better off or not we couldn't tell. At least we were far away from that hideous being they called Pom Tzec.

Soon we came to stone buildings, including, I was sorry to see, another pyramid. Two such cities only two days march apart seemed incredible. We came to a stone building near the main square and were separated. De Aguiller was taken off and I was told to remain. We were untied by now and I was able to shake his hand.

"*Vaya con Dios*, Jeronimo." I said. "I don't know what's in store for us, but it seems we are good at survival. Keep your

27

optimism and your faith. They have served you well so far."

"Goodbye, Gonzalo. I believe you will be good at survival also. I will pray to God for our deliverance."

Then they took him away and I was alone; thousands of miles from home, and among people who cut out human hearts. Once again, I wished I had never met Consuelo Arbenza.

A gruff voice from behind me grunted an order in a language I didn't understand. When I turned, I saw another Maya, old and dignified, with white hair and a broad, wrinkled brown face. He was short and stout, and richly dressed with an elaborate headdress, jacket and cloak. His face was expressionless, but he looked wiser and less malignant than most of the others.

He pointed toward a broom made of sticks; apparently he wanted me to sweep out the building. Knowing better than to argue, I picked up the broom and started my task. Now I knew I was not going to be sacrificed after all.

Apparently, I was going to be a slave.

So I swept the leaves, scraps of food, dead insects, stone chips, scraps of cloth, pieces of feather, sticks and other assorted debris from the stone house. I felt relieved that I was not to make the fatal trip to the top of the pyramid, and that I was one of only two survivors of the ill-fated expedition of Captain Juan de Valdivia. After all that had happened, just being alive was reason to rejoice. Still, I kept thinking that I had left Avilla because I wanted to avoid drudgery, find riches, and escape danger with the result that I was now a slave, had no prospect of riches and was in more danger than I could have ever imagined.

Now that the immediate threat of being sacrificed seemed to have passed, I would somehow have to find a way out. Meanwhile, I could only bide my time, perform my duties, and try to stay alive.

My days soon became predictable and routine. I would

start a cooking fire at dawn with wood I had gathered the day before, then carry two large jars on a pole to fetch water. Then I would be sent to the fields to help with weeding or hauling wastes for fertilizer. I was fed reasonably well, with meals of corn mostly, but with other vegetables as well. Every day or two, there would be some meat mixed in with a stew. The meat was mostly turkey, which the Maya domesticate. Turkeys, in fact, seemed to outnumber the people and could be seen roaming around everywhere. Meat was also provided by deer, wild boar, and a breed of small, hairless dog bred for food.

Drawing water was the part of the day I looked forward to, because it was then that I sometimes saw de Aguiller, who had similar duties for another master. Water was drawn from a deep pond called a cenote, a few hundred yards from the square. A crowd of loincloth-clad slaves stood three deep around the cenote in the mornings.

"After a few weeks, I finally saw de Aguiller at the cenote, and I asked him if he was well.

"Yes, praise God, but the work is unceasing, and I fear I will meet God before I ever get to save souls for him."

"If you wish to save souls, Jeronimo, be sure you save your skin first," I said, looking around cautiously. "Do what they want and gain their confidence. One day soon, we will escape together."

"Yes," he said hopefully, "or perhaps the Spaniards will arrive and rescue us. Let us pray for that day."

I was glad to be able to talk to someone again, for I was only able to learn the Mayan tongue a little at a time.

As we spoke, I noticed we were attracting the disapproving looks of the other slaves, especially a huge, shaven headed one with a fat, ugly face. If he hadn't been a slave, he could have been an executioner.

"Look at that one, Jeronimo," I said, indicating the big slave. "He thinks we're talking about him. Watch this. He

29

doesn't understand a word of Spanish."

I smiled my most ingratiating smile and waved to the suspicious giant. *"Buenos dias, senor*! You are a sack of donkey manure. You remind me of a pig I had once." I said this in such a friendly manner that the giant grunted and turned away.

De Aguiller and I then drew our water and went our separate ways, happy that we had survived another day.

After a few months, I began to learn more of the language, at least the commands. I could even form simple sentences. The Mayan language had a different rhythm and pattern than Spanish, partly because almost all words are accented on the last syllable. One peculiarity was their habit of making a word plural by adding ob instead of s. Sometimes I wondered if some of the Maya's language rules and construction could be the result of their practice of pressing infant's skulls.......... or should I say skullob?

With slow, but constant progress in learning the language came more knowledge of my surroundings. I even learned a few of my masters' names. The old man I served was Chac Pacal, an elder of the town. The town itself was named Ixil. Names seemed to follow no set rules, and to make things even more confusing, if that is possible, most Mayas change their names at least once! A baby is named for the day he was born. Only near adulthood is he given his permanent name. No wonder these people cut the hearts out of strangers, I thought; to them it must make perfect sense.

I didn't see de Aguiller every day, but there were always assorted other slaves drawing water. This was a constant occupation since the cenote was the only source and water was used for cooking, cleaning, washing, and for the steam baths the Maya seemed to love. Sometimes, I had to fetch water several times a day. Life on the farm in Avilla began to look like a life of ease in comparison.

I saw the big slave with the scar on his face most days, and took pains to avoid him since I could tell he was trouble. Every group has its hierarchy, I suppose, even slaves. No matter how small the dung heap, someone will want to sit on top. The big ugly slave's name was Tzec, which means skull. This is actually a fairly common name among the Maya, so I'm not sure if this was his actual name, or some sort of descriptive term because of his bald head. At any rate, Tzec always claimed the right to be first to the water, and often picked some hapless slave to fetch his water for him. I was too new and too foreign to challenge the status quo. So I avoided contact and continued to look for de Aguiller.

When I was sent to work in the fields, which the Maya call milpa, I would toil for hours under the blazing sun planting, weeding, or picking the corn, beans, peppers, or squash. I noticed that the land seemed to have no large animals that could be domesticated. Without draft animals a plow would have been useless, so the mound system was used, or a forest area was cleared by burning and the ashes used as a fertilizer. Planting was done by making a hole in the ground with a sharpened stick and dropping in several seeds.

Great religious significance is attached to the raising of corn. I found this out one day when I stood up from weeding and was startled to see three of the same hideous, white robed priests who had almost dragged me up the pyramid to cut my heart out when I was captured. For a moment, I held my breath, thinking they had finally come for me and I was going to the sacrificial stone. As it turned out, however, they were there to bless the crops; and they did so in a most peculiar way.

After chanting some rambling prayer, one of the priests took out a large thorn and stuck himself in the earlobe, drawing blood. He leaned over and let a few drops of blood drip on the ground, then moved on to another field. Blood on the altar; blood on the cornfields. This land seemed to swim in blood; I only prayed it wouldn't be mine.

Chapter 5- Cimi

In which I make a friend, struggle to adapt, and meet an extraordinary woman

Other than de Aguiller, I had few other contacts. Most of the Maya treated me with indifference, speaking only to give orders. My trips to the market gave me a chance to practice the language and within a few months, I could carry on at least a basic conversation, but no one took any real interest in me. Until one day, as I was stooping down to build a cooking fire, someone finally spoke to me in a high-pitched voice.

"What's the matter with your face?" Startled, I looked up and saw a little girl, about six years old standing in front of me. She was looking at me in that frowning, inquiring way that small children have when they are demanding that adults explain themselves. My inquisitor had thick black hair cut in bangs that hung above her big eyes like a curtain hanging over a pair of windows. She was wearing a white dress with embroidery at the neck, similar to those worn by the older women, was barefooted, and held a wooden doll in one arm. Since I was still squatting, our heads were at about the same height. I didn't reply because I was so surprised, and also because I didn't understand the question.

"You have hair all over your face," she said, without the least embarrassment or attempt at diplomacy. Facial hair was not unknown among Mayan men, but a thick beard like mine must have been a strange sight.

"My uncle has hair on his face," she continued, "but not like you. My grandfather has no hair at all. Hair should be on your head, not on your face. When I am bigger, I won't have hair on my face. This is Ix Chan." She was indicating her doll when she said this, apparently forgetting her original

33

question.

"Uh....Yes. Hello." I said, not knowing what else to say. By now, my Mayan was reasonably understandable to most people, though my accent was still awkward.

"You talk funny," she said, cocking her small head suspiciously. "My mother says people from far away talk funny. Are you from far away?"

"Yes, very far," I sighed.

"Someday, I would like to go far away, too. And you know what? I'm taking Ix Chan with me. Ix Chan goes everywhere I go. One time I went way over to Izamal. We are going again soon."

A few months ago, I would never dream of holding a conversation with a six-year-old, but after being ignored for so long, I was thoroughly enjoying her stream of babble. She paused for breath, distracted by a cricket that was crawling over her foot, then said her name was 5 Cimi, after her birth day. She wouldn't have her adult name for years yet.

"Hello, Cimi. My name is Gonzalo Guerrero. I am honored to meet you." I bowed slightly.

Her face screwed up into another inquisitive frown. "Gonalo Gurererero? What kind of a name is that? "

"It's a name for someone who comes from far away," I said defensively, thinking that at least I was called by a name and not a date.

She shook her head rapidly. "Gonlo Gzorer...it's no use, I can't."

"You can't remember it?"

"I can't even say it! I think your name should be Dzul."

This was a word I was not familiar with and I asked what it meant. She said it meant someone from far away. Later, I found out that it actually meant foreigner, a somewhat more sinister connotation. Dzulob is another name for enemies.

"All right, Cimi," I said, "Dzul it is! You are welcome to come talk to me anytime. And Ix Chan, too."

So Cimi and Ix Chan said goodbye and promised to come see me again. I was actually looking forward to it.

As I finished building the cooking fire, I thought about my beard. Maybe Cimi had a point. My beard marked me as a foreigner even more than my skin, which was getting brown by now anyway. Maybe if I shaved it off, I would fit in better and wouldn't have to depend on children and wooden dolls for companionship. A bare face might also make me less noticeable when I escaped. That night, using my knife, which I had kept hidden, I shaved off my beard. I certainly was cooler, but I couldn't tell how I looked.

The next day, a ceremony was held in the main square in front of the pyramid. I was brought along to carry water and to hold a large woven fan over them to keep the sun off. A huge crowd was present, and as I looked around, I could see a sampling of the entire society. In the front ranks were the elders and the nobility, dressed in the most fantastic and complex finery you could imagine. They all had huge and elaborate headdresses, far bigger than the heads they sat upon. The crowd resembled a swaying, multicolored forest spreading out from the base of the pyramid. In addition , the nobles and elders all wore cloaks of brilliant colors and were weighed down with an immense amount of jewelry, including ear plugs, and ornaments hanging from arms, ears, noses, and lips. As the distance from the pyramid increased, the crowd grew progressively more plain, until, at the edges of the throng, were farmers and commoners, called the mazehual, wearing only loincloths. At the sides of the crowd were Mayan warriors bearing wicker shields, spears, and the nasty war clubs with the stone edges that had struck down Perez. The warriors wore helmets that resembled animal or eagle heads, and quilted cotton garments that probably acted as a kind of armor. In all the tales of adventure I had read, I had never imagined such a colorful and dazzling pagan spectacle.

35

The pyramid had bowls of burning incense at each corner at the top and bowls burning at intervals along the stairway. The columns of smoke rose in the air in parallel streams that almost looked like giant columns in the still air. At the very top was a larger bowl in which a fire was burning. Everyone sat in the sun for a good while, then rose and looked back up a center aisle that had opened up, almost like a wedding. A procession was making its way toward the pyramid. First came musicians, if you could be so generous as to call them that. They were pounding on drums, blowing on flutes, and banging away on other instruments of the percussion type. The din was both incessant and aggravating.

Finally, a parade of nobles followed, accompanied by four of the nightmare priests in the white robes. With them was a figure in the most brilliant and elaborate regalia in the entire square. He had an intricately carved headpiece topped with a towering cascade of long green feathers. On his body was a heavy embroidered cloak with more feathers and plumes sticking out in all directions. He looked like a human peacock, and from what I could hear around me, he was their Batab, or king.

When they reached the foot of the stairway, the Batab and the priests stopped and turned toward the crowd. The priests then removed the Batab's ceremonial robes revealing a long white priest's robe underneath. They then turned and ascended the stairway. As they climbed, the devil's orchestra started up again and the crowd chanted. When they reached the top, the group turned again toward the crowd with the Batab in the center standing next to the bowl of fire. One of the priests then brought out what looked like a crumpled piece of white fabric and stood by the Batab. There were a few more chants, then an astonishing thing happened; the Batab pulled back the folds of his robes revealing he was naked underneath! No one else seemed shocked in the least, however, even at what came next. The Batab produced a long thorn like the priest had used in the milpa to bless the crops, and pierced his male member until it bled! All the while, the priests were wailing away as if stabbing your manhood were the normal thing to do. The priest with the white cloth knelt before the Batab and let the blood drip on the cloth until it was spotted with red. He then raised the cloth for the crowd's inspection, and threw it in the fire! I had once heard that being a king was difficult because of the responsibilities of the office, but this was a duty I had never imagined. Blood, always blood. Who could understand these strange people?

As the crowd slowly made its way homeward I wanted to ask my master, Chac Pacal, what I had just seen, but he was too preoccupied with greeting almost everyone he passed. The crowd was in a festive mood, as if a great entertainment had just occurred. After we turned off the main plaza and came to the elevated stone house of Chac Pacal, I had the chance to speak to him.

"Chac Pacal, I would ask permission to speak," I said, with eyes downcast.

He looked at me and nodded languidly. The old man was enjoying the shade under a thatched canopy; a welcome relief after the sticky heat of the plaza.

"I am a stranger, here, a dzul. But I wish to know more about your people. What is the purpose of the blood on the milpas and today at the pyramid?"

He frowned. "Didn't you have hair on your face?"

"Er...yes, but I cut it."

He nodded slowly. "Yes, I thought so. Why?"

"I wanted to look more like your people. My hair made people avoid me." I wished he would get back on the subject, so I returned to blood letting. "Uh,...the ceremony today?"

"Many Gods dwell in the 13 levels between the underworld and the sky with different aspects and powers. Itzamna (Lizard House) is the father of the gods, though he too has a father, Hunab Ku. His wife is Ixchel (Lady of the

37

Rainbow), the goddess of the moon and of pregnancy. Some gods, such as Chac the god of rain and Kukulcan (Feathered Serpent), the god of wisdom and learning are benevolent gods. Others, such as Ah Kinchel are good and evil at the same time. Ah Kinchel is the sun god during the day, but becomes the god of the underworld during the night.

The gods nurture and support all life in this world, but the gods require nourishment. Blood is the food of the gods, and the gods require constant feeding to assure rain, harvests, childbirth, and even the rising of the sun. All Maya sacrifice to the gods, but the more noble the blood, the greater the power of the sacrifice. The ceremony was for the ruler to publicly sacrifice both as an offering to the gods, and as an example to the people. Most men sacrifice with blood from the ears, or the male part; some women, with blood from the tongue. Blood dripped on a cloth as you saw today, can be burned so the sacrifice reaches the gods sooner. Sometimes, captives or .....others are chosen to be messengers to the gods. The priests at the top of the temple sacrifice them. Their hearts are cut out and fed to the gods."

I was both astonished and appalled. Now I knew why Ortega and the others had been killed. And why did Chac Pacal pause and say others? Did he mean slaves? Did he mean me? My determination to escape became greater than ever; there had to be a way. I had to get away from all the blood before the blood was my own.

A few days later, I was pulling up some weeds that were growing in the joints between the stones of the low wall that surrounded Chac Pacal's house. Most of the buildings, though substantial, were not well maintained, and crumbling mortar thick with weeds was everywhere. Nor was there much evidence of any new building. The people seemed to be living in a place built earlier by someone more advanced, or, at least more energetic. I wondered if this was a civilization in

38

decline. Not only was I a slave, but a slave of a dying empire, I thought ruefully.[9]

"Now you look better," said a familiar, childish voice. Cimi had come by for another visit. I was glad to see her because she was incurably cheerful, a quality I was in dire need of at the moment.

"Hello, Cimi," I said, "And hello to Ix Chan also. Where have you been for the past few days?"

"I was in Izamal with my mother. She has a sister there. I was playing with my cousin, 2 Imix, when there was a terrible accident, and Ix Chan's head fell off! I cried until my uncle fixed it. My uncle makes pictures in the memories of the ancestors where they live. Do you think Ix Chan's head will come off again? I hope my head doesn't fall off. Why are you pulling up those flowers? We have lots of flowers at my house. My father is coming back from a raid today. He's a Nacom, you know. Can a girl be a Nacom? What is a Nacom, anyway?"

Something in this cascade of words and thoughts struck a chord in the back of my mind. What had she said about making pictures in memories?

"Cimi, what are pictures in memories?"

"What?" She had obviously passed well beyond that thought and wasn't used to backing up.

"You said your uncle made pictures in memories?" I had heard the word for memories before, and thought I must have heard Cimi incorrectly. "How do you make a picture in a memory?"

"He paints and uses a brush to make the pictures. He can make gods, kings, or anything. I tried to paint a picture of Ix Chan once, on a rock. The paint all ran together and it didn't look like anything. Ix Chan was so disappointed. One time...."

"What is a memory, Cimi? How can anyone paint on it?"

"A memory is a whole lot of flat white pieces tied together. You can look at the pieces and remember what happened before because of what is painted on them. They keep them in

39

a big room near the plaza."

I could hardly believe my ears. She was describing a book. The Maya had books! If I could find the books and learn to read them, I might find a way out of this place. They might even have maps! At last, I saw a glimmer of hope. There might be a chance to return to Spain after all.

"How do you understand the memories, Cimi?"

"You're being silly," she giggled, "I'm just a little girl. Only men understand the memories. Even my mother doesn't know how. What happened to the hair on your face? You don't look like a dzul anymore, but you still talk funny. Look, I scraped my knee. I was running after my cousin and I tripped over a stone. My knee got scraped because it hit something hard.....It hit Ix Chan's head. That's when it came off."

"Thank you, Cimi," I said, laughing. "You and Ix Chan have given me a great idea."

For the next few days, I varied my route on my daily rounds to explore more thoroughly to find out where the books were kept. Finally, I found it; a low stone building off to itself behind the pyramid. I watched to see how much activity was around and was pleased to see there was almost none. Well, with reading restricted to so few people, it wasn't surprising. I had to be careful, because the books might be considered sacred. In any event, I was sure they were not meant for slaves. I could see that priests sometimes went in and out, but never after noon, so I decided to enter the building and look for information in the books each afternoon on my way to fetch water.

The night before my first attempt, I could hardly sleep I was so excited by the possibility of escape. The Maya were obscure, superstitious, illogical, and frequently violent. If I did not find a way out, it was only a matter of time before I wound up at the top of the pyramid with a knife in my chest. I would find de Aguiller and we would escape together. With the exception of Cimi, I wouldn't miss any of these dangerous lunatics.

The next day, I slipped into the building with the books. In the cool, gloomy chamber were wooden shelves with books stacked on them. The books consisted of thin plaster pages stitched together at each end so they opened like a folding screen. The first one I opened was a disappointment. It was covered with dense hieroglyphics and garishly painted pictures of what appeared to be demons from hell. Understanding these would be harder than I had thought. I was so engrossed, I didn't hear the footsteps approach behind me.

"What are you doing here?" a voice echoed off the stone walls. I spun around, knowing I was trapped and tried to think of a way to talk myself out of trouble.

In every man's life there are a few moments in which he can sense that his whole world is about to change. On these rare occasions, a man can feel the hand of fate touch him on the shoulder, and he somehow knows that everything that happened in his life up to that time was merely a prelude; for he is looking directly into the face of destiny. Such a moment happened to me when I turned around to face the source of the voice.

There, framed by the stone entrance, stood the most beautiful woman I had ever seen. The hot sunlight, streaming in the doorway, framed her with radiance like an angel from heaven. She was tall and slender with skin of creamy tan and long, straight black hair that framed a perfect, delicate face. Her deep brown eyes had a softness that captivated me. She wore a white dress with a red border at the neck and hem. Beyond her beauty, however, was an alertness and intelligence that I had not seen among Mayan women before. She held herself with poise and regal bearing that Queen Isabella would have envied. I was utterly and hopelessly entranced. Whatever excuse I had prepared evaporated from my mind, and I just stood there with my mouth open soundlessly, drinking in the sight of this extraordinary creature.

"Answer me. What are you doing here?" The angel spoke again, this time more insistently.

I couldn't think of a plausible excuse, so I decided to tell the truth; well, most of it, anyway.

"I...I meant no harm, my lady. My name is Gonzalo Guerrero, and I serve the house of Chac Pacal. I am from a land far away, and I merely wish to learn more about the greatness of the Maya." I had hoped she would be flattered by my interest.

She wasn't. "What land?" she demanded.

I was amazed. No one had ever asked me that, not even the ever-curious Cimi. Here was a woman with an intellect to match her beauty.

"The land is called Castile, and it is many days from here to the east across..." I hesitated, realizing that I didn't know the word for ocean-perhaps there wasn't one. ".....across the waters."

"Cozumel is only three days journey," she said coldly.

"Please pardon my poor pronunciation. The land is Castile, and I journeyed over 40 days across the great water."

Her eyes narrowed with suspicion. "Forty days across the water...to become a slave?" I had to admit it didn't sound too convincing.

"That is not why I came. I simply had some.... misfortune."

"Then why did you come?" Her tone was sharp and insistent.

I had to be careful how I answered this innocent-sounding question. If I said I sought riches and conquest, I might be shipped off to the sacrificial stone as a dangerous invader. At the very least, I would be viewed with suspicion, and that would make my life even harder.

"My people have a great thirst for knowledge and for trade. We wish to learn of these lands and have commerce with them."

She gave no indication whether or not she believed this highly idealized version of my original mission.

"If you truly wish to know more about my people, then know this: the sacred books are only for the priests and the ruler. Anyone else will be put to death." She paused. "Now, go."

As I made my way past her as she stood in the doorway, I couldn't help gazing directly into her eyes. If you say that it was a foolish and dangerous thing to do, I can only reply that you have never seen those eyes. They were deep, soft and a rich brown in color. To look away from them was impossible. To my surprise, she did not look away or show anger, but returned my gaze, her head turning as I passed close to her. I felt a thrill of excitement as I brushed by.

I reluctantly started to walk away, but had to turn for a last look. I was pleased to see she was still looking at me, but whether out of interest or merely to make sure I didn't return, I couldn't tell.

Chapter 6- The Instructor

In which I improve my status but make a powerful enemy

I was in a state of confused excitement as I made my way to the cenote. All I could think of was this enchanting and exciting woman. Who was she? Where did she live? Was she married? All these questions swirled about in my mind as I joined the crowd of slaves by the cenote. I was oblivious to the commotion around me, thinking only of her. She could have had me punished, or even killed, but didn't. She had beauty, intelligence, and compassion. But one question kept returning, seeking an answer I couldn't provide: if the books were only for the priests and nobles, and women were banned from them, what was she doing there?

As I pondered this question, a sound was growing, and gradually intruding into my preoccupied mind. It was the sound of a crowd in a state of excitement. Something was going on closer to the cenote. Slaves milled about, and the air was thick with a cloud of choking white dust stirred up by their bare feet. I heard someone say that Tzec had been insulted and was going to punish someone. I pushed through the crowd and saw what they were excited about.

Tzec was beating some hapless soul with the pole from his water pots. The victim was putting up a gallant fight, fending off blows and rushing Tzec with a pot in his hand. Even so, Tzec clearly had the upper hand, and blood had begun to appear on his opponent. Suddenly, through the mud and blood, I recognized the victim; Jeronimo de Aguiller! At that moment, Tzec noticed me, pointed in my direction, and said "When this one is finished, you will be next!"

Fighting an impulse to run for my life, I grabbed a pole

44

similar to Tzec's and took a few steps closer, praying that I had learned enough from Hectore and my uncle to survive.

"Why wait? I am here now," I said, holding the pole in the ready position, "or are you afraid?"

He stood for a moment, torn between his haste to get at me and his desire to finish off de Aguiller. I decided to goad him to get him away from de Aguiller, and possibly lash out carelessly. If Tzec was as slow as his size would indicate, I might be able to hold him off. The sweat from my palms made the pole feel sticky in my hands as I nervously awaited his response.

"Why do you hesitate? Are you stupid as well as ugly?" I shouted. I could hear the crowd gasp. This was an insult that had to be answered.

With a bellow of rage, Tzec forgot all about de Aguiller and charged at me with his pole. Fighting to keep my knees from shaking, I feinted to the left, then sidestepped to the right. As he went plunging past me, I swung my pole and swatted him squarely in the stomach. The pole made a satisfying slapping sound as it struck home. As he doubled over, I smacked him on the back of the skull. He stepped back, rubbing his head, and looking confused. Before he could recover, I went on the attack.

By now I could see that Tzec had no real skill at fighting. Like many big men, he had always gotten his way through his sheer size and had never needed to develop any finesse. Well, he would need it now. A few more parries and thrusts and soon, Tzec was at my mercy, while the other slaves were cheering loudly. Now that I was in control, I was determined to make him pay for his attack on de Aguiller. I walloped him until his entire body was covered with blood and bruises. His defenses became more and more feeble until he actually collapsed. In a final gesture of contempt, I threw my pole down across his chest as he lay in the dirt.

I got de Aguiller up and helped him away. Looking at us

with a new respect, the other slaves cleared a path for us. De Aguiller was not hurt as badly as I feared, but if I hadn't intervened, he surely would have been.

"Thank you, Gonzalo," he said as we walked away. "I seem to have gotten in over my head."

"You are fortunate you still HAVE a head," I replied. "What happened?"

"A slight disagreement, I'm afraid. He demanded that I fetch his water for him. I pretended not to understand, and started to walk away. Apparently the combination of ignoring his wishes and turning my back on him was considered highly insulting, so he started beating me with that pole. I couldn't get to a suitable weapon. Then you came along."

"That just proves that everything is backwards here," I said. "I'm supposed to be the one that makes everyone angry."

At the edge of the crowd, we passed under a large tree. In the dappled shade beneath the tree stood a warrior. He was wearing the usual feathered headdress and mantle, along with various bracelets and ear plugs, and at his side was a war club tucked into a broad green sash. He was tall for a Maya and had a muscular build. From where he stood, he must have seen the whole fight.

As we passed the tree, the warrior stepped in front of us. I stopped abruptly. A high ranking warrior could kill any slave who displeased him, I was sure. If this one was a friend, or perhaps master of Tzec, I was finished. The warrior looked at me intently and placed his hand on the handle of his war club.

"Who are you?" The deadly looking figure nodded in my direction.

"Gonzalo Guerrero, servant of the house of Chac Pacal," I replied, trying to look innocent.

He looked at me suspiciously. "I saw what you did to that slave just now. What land were you taken from that you know how to fight that way?"

"The land of Castile," I replied. "A land of warriors many

46

day's journey from here."

He nodded, then indicated I was to follow him. I had no doubt I was in deep trouble, though getting in trouble for helping someone else would be a new experience.

"I am called Balam,"(Jaguar) he said. "I am the younger Nacom of the warriors of Ixil. Tell me your name again."

"Gonzalo Guerrero."

I didn't say so, but suddenly remembered that Cimi had told me her father was the younger Nacom of the warriors. Apparently, that was Balam. Balam nodded and looked thoughtful.

"You fight well. Our warriors are brave and strong, but we are few in number compared to people around us. Presently, we are allied with Dzilpan, but the alliance is weak and we could be at war at any time. We must be able to defeat greater numbers in order to survive. If you possess skills that would help us, I want you to teach those skills to the others."

We had walked about a quarter of a mile when we came upon a walled-in plaza with lines of huts along two of the enclosure walls. Inside the plaza were groups of warriors, and I felt a momentary twinge of panic at the sight of so many feathered killers like the ones who had first captured me. Some were practicing archery at straw targets, others were engaging in sparring with war clubs and heavy padding, and still others were resting, talking, or checking weapons. Except for the feathered headdresses and the brightly colored sashes and loincloths, it could have been a military camp in Castile.

"First you must look like a warrior," said Balam, ushering me into a small building. "Our men cannot learn from one who looks like a slave."

So I was given a sash for my waist, a feather headdress, a necklace and wide jade bracelets for my wrists and ankles. Finally, I was given a padded jacket and a pole with a padded end. I was nervous; defeating a clumsy slave was one thing, but how would I do against trained warriors?

47

"The padded end is where the point would be on a spear, Balam said. If you are touched with it we will consider you dead or disabled. Can Pec! Come here and test this man."

Can Pec turned out to be a tough and wiry looking individual who looked at me the way a wolf might look at a rabbit. He opened with a vicious sweep of the pole intended to knock my legs out from under me. Awkwardly, I jumped up, avoiding the pole by inches. I cursed myself for being surprised and counterthrust. He twisted, avoiding the move and drew back to strike, giving me the opening I needed to thrust the padded end to his stomach. He looked startled.

"Again," said Balam. Can Pec, more wary this time, squared off again. He was quick, aggressive, and fought like a man possessed. He landed several smart blows on my arms and one on my leg, but I kept on, probing for an opening. We fought for several minutes, until I was soaked with sweat inside the padded jacket. As we fought, the other warriors stopped what they were doing to watch, and soon we were surrounded by onlookers. Can Pec's speed and skill had surprised me, but soon the tide started to change, as the long hours of practice and the tutoring by both Hectore and my uncle started to tell. Finally seeing an opening, I thrust the padded end and caught him squarely in the middle of the chest. Exhausted, we both stood there gasping for breath.

"Well done," said Balam with obvious satisfaction. "Can Pec is our most skilled warrior with the spear. You must work with all our warriors to raise the level of their skill."

So by virtue of giving one slave a well-deserved beating, I had gone from being a slave with a name nobody knew to fencing master to a Mayan army.

I was feeling rather pleased with myself when an older warrior appeared. He was built like the trunk of a very large tree and showed numerous scars and tattoos as he folded his arms over his massive chest. "Who is this man?" he demanded, and Balam told him.

"He is a slave and a dzul," the warrior grumbled. "He cannot be a warrior of Ixil."

Balam explained that I was not a warrior, merely a teacher to help with training. The older warrior looked at me suspiciously, grunted contemptuously, and walked away.

"That is Cuac Caan," said Balam. "He is the older Nacom of our warriors. He trusts no one, especially dzulob. You would do well to avoid him, Gonz-lo."

I looked at the menacing figure walking across the dusty courtyard. "I will certainly try," I said.

That night there was a feast in the main plaza by the pyramid. Cimi had tried to tell me about it, but I wasn't paying close attention at the time. Anyway, a raid into a neighboring town had been successful and brought back three prisoners. Rows of torches lit the plaza, their flames looking soft and hazy in the warm dampness of the tropic night. Low tables were laid out with bowls of corn, tortillas, sweet potatoes, beans, turkey stew, roast boar, and dog. There were some other meats I couldn't identify, but didn't think it wise to inquire, since I had been told that sacrificed captives were sometimes eaten. With my new status as almost a warrior, I was allowed to attend as long as I stayed off to the side. There was a dais at the foot of the pyramid and the ruler, or Batab, whose name was Chan Oc, sat there along with various nobility, including my former master Chac Pacal looking as wise and unconcerned as ever.

I saw Cimi before her mother took her home to bed. She was sitting in the children's area gobbling the food and chattering away at the other half sized Maya around her. I talked briefly with Can Pec and later with Balam, but I felt lonely seeing families and relatives together. Balche was the featured drink. Made from fermented honey, balche is very much like the Mead brewed in Europe. I had noted hundreds of beehives made from hollow logs with the ends stopped with

49

clay. Honey was a trade item as well as being a sweetener and, apparently, a source of intoxication.

I was sipping a cup of balche and feeling sorry for myself when, through the milling throng, I saw the woman from the house of the books again! She was moving with grace and ease through the crowd, and in the light from the torches, she looked more beautiful and elegant than ever. Trying to contain my excitement, I pushed my way through the crush of people until I came up beside her.

"Hello. It is good to see you again," I said, trying to sound both romantic and casual.

She looked at me curiously, and smiled faintly. In my warrior regalia, she apparently didn't recognize me.

"We met this morning," I said, a little too anxiously, "at the house of the memories."

She tilted her head slightly in a way that I found maddeningly erotic. "I would hardly call it meeting," she said with just a hint of amused sarcasm, "But you seem to have changed yourself. Were you in disguise then or are you in disguise now?"

She seemed to have a habit of asking awkward questions. "I am instructing the warriors in the art of weapons," I said, trying to sound important.

She frowned as if she was having trouble understanding, though I had the impression this woman had never had trouble understanding anything in her life.

"I am confused. This morning, you said you wished to learn, but tonight you say you wish to teach." Once again, her eyes seemed to be beckoning me. Their soft brownness sparkled with the reflected light of the torches.

"I wish to do both. I have taught you my name and wish to learn yours." I thought that was clever: Consuelo would have loved it.

"This morning, your name was Gonzalo Guerrero and you were a servant. Do you change titles as you change

50

garments?"

She remembered my name! My heart soared. "Well," I stammered, "I've had some good fortune since then."

"So it would seem," she remarked dryly. "You must have been so disappointed to find the post of Nacom was already filled."

Was she mocking me? I decided to try another tack. "What good fortune I have had started when I first saw you, my lady. May I ask your name?"

"And why do you wish to learn my name?" she said warily.

By now, the crowd had ceased to exist. Spain, too, had disappeared, as had every aspect of my previous life. There was only the night and this extraordinary woman. I had no more clever answers. I looked into those eyes again, then took a deep breath. "Because you are the most beautiful woman I have ever seen," I blurted out, "and from the instant I first saw you, every moment away from you has been empty. I want to be with you, to look in your eyes and to hear your voice calling my name. When I was a slave, they had captured my body, but you have captured my soul."

I braced myself, waiting for a cutting reply, but she just stared for a moment, her mouth slightly open as if in surprise. Then, in a voice almost too soft to hear, she said "I am Zazil Ha, daughter of Chan Oc."

Then she turned and disappeared into the crowd.

Zazil Ha...clear water; something cool and beautiful, but hinting at hidden depths and turbulent currents. A storm of emotions hit me all at once. I was utterly smitten by this exquisite woman. She had beauty, intelligence, wit, and an aura that drew me irresistibly to her. I sensed, too that she was attracted to me. But she was the daughter of Chan Oc, the Batab, or ruler of the city. As far as I could tell, I was still a slave. What chance would I have with royalty? I had traveled thousands of miles, risked death and finally found someone who would have made it all worthwhile, only to find that she was unattainable. That night, my dreams were filled with Zazil Ha and those soft, impossibly brown eyes.

Chapter 7- Captives

In which I get a frightening taste of Mayan warfare

In an effort to forget the unreachable Zazil Ha, I threw myself into the training with all the vigor I could muster. Day after day, I worked with the warriors to hone their skills with the sword-club, the long spear, and the knife. They also used the bow and arrow, and a short, throwing spear. This spear was hurled with great force by the use of a device that extended the arm and therefore the leverage of the thrower. This device, called the atlatl, looked something like a long wooden soup spoon.

Although they were all skilled in the use of these weapons, they hadn't developed the more complex European techniques that I was able to teach them. The army, or holcom as they called it, was made up mostly of peasants called up for military duty, but there was a core of professional warriors organized into two elite military societies; the Jaguars and the Eagles. These would be roughly equivalent to the knights of Europe, and, like the knights, anchored the rest of the army. Both the Jaguars and the Eagles wore fantastic, colorful costumes that made them look like their namesakes. A wood and skin helmet made to resemble a jaguar or eagle head topped off a body-covering garment that was yellow with black spots or covered with feathers. Although to my eyes they looked like children dressing up, the Jaguar and Eagle warriors were tough, fearless, and vicious.

I was attached to the Jaguars, although I worked with everyone. Each day I would demonstrate what I had learned from my brother, my uncle, and Perez, and every day someone would challenge me. Other than Can Pec, however, no one was a serious threat to my reputation. Balam and Cuac Caan watched me closely, one with approval and one with resentment.

Part of the holcom's duty was to patrol the outer reaches of Ixil and its fields, so Balam ordered me along to observe. The warriors were tireless. In the stifling damp heat one afternoon, they ran for almost an hour until they came to the far side of the milpas and the edge of the jungle. I was gasping for breath when we stopped and rested.

Balam was amused at my discomfort. "What's the matter, Gonz-lo? Don't you care for this trip? Perhaps you should run back."

"I don't see why we were in such a hurry to get here," I wheezed, "The corn wasn't going anywhere."

Can Pec decided to join in the fun. "Gonz-lo, if we proceeded at the pace you prefer, the corn would be ready to harvest by the time we got here!"

Our laughter was cut short by the rumbling voice of Cuac Caan. "The survival of a warrior may well depend on his speed. The holcom can only move as fast as its slowest man. If the pace is too great, Gonz-lo, you may return to being a slave, but if you wish to continue here, you will keep up with the others." He turned away contemptuously.

We ate our rations before moving on. They consisted of small sacks of corn meal flavored with peppers and onions. We had also brought skin pouches of water, since there were no streams.

I talked briefly with Balam, and asked him why Cuac Caan disliked me so intensely.

"Cuac Caan has been a warrior for a long time and has served the people of Ixil well. He has stayed alive by skill and experience. Once, long ago, however, he was an Eagle warrior on a raid to a distant town. He was brave, but he was young and not yet wise. The raid went well, and the 30 men in the

54

party started back with 10 prisoners. Soon, they came upon a farmer who offered to be a guide through the unfriendly territory. That night, however, the farmer cut loose the prisoners and gave them weapons. A fight ensued and the farmer, if that is what he really was, was killed as were six of the prisoners. But four of the Eagle warriors were also killed. Since that time, Cuac Caan has had a fear of treachery from anyone not born in Ixil."

I seemed to have a talent for making friends and enemies in almost equal numbers. There was no time to dwell on this, however, because just then, a shrill, eerie sound tore through the humid air. Several scouts that had been sent out into the jungle were sounding their conch shell trumpets in warning. Cuac Caan bellowed the order for battle formation.

Before I realized what was going on, everything started happening at once. The warriors were instantly alert and grouped in ranks, weapons at the ready. There were about 15 of us altogether, not counting the few scouts that had been sent into the jungle. Weaponless, I just stood there awkwardly, looking nervously from side to side wondering what was to happen next. Something unpleasant and possibly fatal, I was afraid. My eye kept searching the forbidding green blackness of the forest in front of us.

"Can Pec," I said in a whisper, "What is happening?"

He motioned me to be still and stood with his eyes fixed on the forest. In a few seconds our scouts came running from the tree line and joined the ranks. There was quiet for a few moments, then the sound of rustling in the undergrowth growing louder and louder until the woods seemed to suddenly burst with armed men.

Like a summer thunderstorm, a swarm of enemy warriors was upon us. They were mostly painted red and were screaming, howling and blowing on conch shells with a fury of sound that was enough to shake the leaves off of the trees. So sudden and tumultuous was the attack that I was

55

momentarily frozen in place. As if in a dream, the two sides crashed together and the battle raged all around me. While I stood stupidly watching, Can Pec was struck from behind with a club. A big, red painted warrior was upon him in an instant, but instead of finishing him off, started to drag him away. Finally, I snapped out of my stupor and grabbed a spear that was lying on the ground. The red painted warrior saw me coming and prepared to smash my skull in with his club. He swung and missed, then I caught him on the side of the head with the blunt end of the spear and he went down. Before I could catch my breath, two more red warriors came at me with clubs swinging. I struck the closest one with an upward blow to the groin. While he was rolling on the ground, I faced the second one with my spear. After a few blows and counterblows, he too went down.

Meanwhile, the warriors of Ixil were driving off the warriors with the red paint. Surprisingly, there were no deaths, only several wounded and a few captives. Balam walked up to me and said, "That was good work, Gonz-lo. Your methods enabled us to defeat a greater number and you saved Can Pec."

"Yes," added Can Pec, "and you have three prisoners!"

"How does this man have three captives when he is not a warrior?" demanded Cuac Caan, and the others fell silent.

"I was just trying to help Can Pec," I said defensively, but he wasn't having it.

"Can Pec is a Jaguar warrior. He drinks the blood of our enemies and has brought back many captives. He needs no help from a slave."

I wanted to point out that he was in need of a great deal of help at the time, but held my tongue.

On the walk back, the six captives were tied together, and marched in silence. They were from a town to the west called Xcalampak, hoping for a quick surprise raid. They had not counted on our level of skill or our coolness under attack.

Now, six of them would pay the price. I had no illusions about what awaited these unfortunates; death by sacrifice, or slavery. This was the basic object of Mayan warfare; a quick ambush or surprise attack aimed at capturing prisoners for sacrifice or slavery. This is why there were no dead. They had not been trying to kill, but to capture.[10]

I couldn't concern myself with them, however, because my own fortunes had risen significantly. Not only had I rescued Can Pec, but I had also taken three captives, a rare and prestigious feat. The fact that I had merely been defending myself and never intended to capture anybody didn't matter in the least. Everyone, with the significant exception of Cuac Caan, was congratulating me and treating me like a hero. Balam was beaming with pride at my performance, because he had been my sponsor.

When we arrived back in Ixil, we turned the captives over to a cage similar to the one in which I had been kept. Then Balam took me straight to Chac Pacal, the elder. Cuac Caan, however, had arrived first.

"Chac Pacal," said Balam with a bow, "this man was assigned as an instructor. He has distinguished himself in battle and has captured three prisoners. Our holcom is in great need of such a man. I request that he be allowed to become a full Jaguar warrior as his feats have entitled him to be."

Chac Pacal looked wary. Cuac Caan had obviously tried to sway him before we arrived. "A dzul as a warrior of Ixil is one thing, but one who cannot follow commands is another. Would he follow sometimes and not others?" Chac Pacal stroked his chin in thought, and finally said; "Permission for a dzul to become a warrior involves the security of all of Ixil. Such a question can only be decided by the Batab, Chan Oc."

So, a meeting with Chan Oc was arranged the next day, and I was taken to the sweat bath to prepare. This was a small stone building heated almost to the point of combustion by hot stones. Bowls of water were used for rinsing off the sweat that resulted. I emerged feeling cleaner than....well, cleaner than ever. Next Balam gave me the finest warrior regalia I had seen. I had a richly woven garment that wrapped around my waist and came down almost to my knees, somewhat like a skirt. To this were added sandals, and heavy bracelets and necklaces. Around my shoulders was a heavy mantle, and on my head was a massive crest of green Quetzal feathers. I wondered briefly what my brother Hectore would say if he could see me like this.

We were about to depart when I saw Cimi and Ix Chan watching us critically. Cimi nodded her small head with approval.

"Dzul, you don't look so funny anymore. You look like a warrior."

"Thank you, Cimi," I said, and I meant it.

"Sometimes I help my mother make headpieces out of the Quetzal feathers. We trade for the feathers in the market. I got a broken feather and gave it to Ix Chan, but she lost it. Yesterday, I saw a cloud that looked like my cousin, but it blew away. Can you touch a cloud from the top of the pyramid? I think you could if you jumped."

"Goodbye, Cimi," I said, "I have to go."

The palace was something of a disappointment; although it had more rooms than Chac Pacal's house, the rooms were still small and cramped. I was beginning to notice that all Mayan buildings were like this on the inside, no matter how grand they were on the outside. The massive, thick walls left little space for large interior spaces. Like the other buildings I had seen, even this one looked in need of repairs and maintenance. Large pieces of the plaster coating had fallen off of the walls leaving exposed stone to show through. Some of the stones were loose or had weeds growing between them. Once again, I had the impression of a civilization whose best days were behind it.

The Batab was in a ceremonial chamber along with about a dozen attendants, guards, and retainers. Chan Oc was a slender man with a thin scraggly beard and a calm, regal bearing. He was seated on a raised dais covered by a spotted jaguar skin. On either side stood guards holding long spears festooned with feathers and streamers of multicolored cloth. Except for the skin color and the clothing, it could have been a European king flanked by men at arms. When we arrived, the Batab was finishing a meeting with an emissary of the Batab of our ally, Dzilpan. The emissary was speaking for his Batab, Pom Tzec, who I assumed was no relation to Tzec the slave. Then I realized Pom Tzec was the terrifying figure I had seen emerging from the morning mist while I was in the cage. Dzilpan must have been where I was first captured before escaping.

"Lord Chan Oc," the envoy was saying, "Twice in the last uinal, our traders have been attacked on the road north of Ixil. (The Mayan year is made up of 18 months called uinals that are 20 days long) Your warriors are supposed to have these areas secured. My lord Pom Tzec is concerned that Ixil is not honoring its duties to the alliance."

Chan Oc nodded sympathetically. "You may tell lord Pom Tzec that I share his concerns, but our holcom hasn't enough warriors to cover every road at all times. We are presently increasing our forces, however, and believe the problem will soon be solved."

"I will convey your message to my lord Pom Tzec." The emissary bowed and left the chamber. Now it was our turn.

After some preliminaries, Balam stated the case for making me a warrior and Cuac Caan argued against it. Chan Oc grasped the issues quickly, and asked me to come forward. He peered at me intensely, causing wrinkles to form around his eyes.

"Tell me of the land of your birth."

I wasn't expecting that question, but answered as best I could. I spoke of the distance to Castile and of the land, people and history. I left out any reference to the Inquisition or to the rapacious search for gold and souls that was taking place as I didn't think it would help my case.

"And how do you come to be here?"

"My people have settled on some islands far to the east of here. A storm blew us to this land."

Chan Oc considered this a moment, then responded dryly. "And may we expect more uninvited visitors from your land in the future?"

"I cannot say, lord Chan Oc, but for the present, they do not know of this land's existence."

He was silent for a moment then said "Wait outside, I would confer with Balam, Cuac Caan, and my advisors."

I was relieved to be outside again, away from the Batab and his apparent suspicions. I sat on a carved stone in a courtyard and watched the people come and go. There were warriors in their paint and mantles, priests in white robes, merchants carrying goods to sell, peasant farmers wearing loincloths and women wearing brilliant white dresses and carrying pots or bundles of firewood. The sun was hot and the air was humming with the sound of insects. Finally, after perhaps half an hour, Balam and Cuac Caan emerged from the chamber.

"The Batab has decided that you are to be made a Jaguar warrior," said Balam, smiling.

Cuac Caan was smiling also, but it was a sly smile. "...providing you follow all Mayan traditions," he added. This did not seem to be a problem, I thought.

"You will not be disappointed," I said. "But I would like to express my thanks to Chan Oc as well. I will be brief."

With that, I walked back into the audience chamber to express my gratitude to Chan Oc. As I entered the room, I saw Chan Oc once more, and there at his side in earnest

60

conversation with him was Zazil Ha! Neither of them had seen me, so I beat a hasty retreat. Was she the reason he had agreed? Had she interceded on my behalf? My heart soared. I was a Jaguar warrior and had found favor with Zazil Ha and Chan Oc. Perhaps there was a chance to win the hand of Zazil Ha after all!

Chapter 8- The Blood of a Warrior

In which I am elevated again, only to face even greater danger

I had expected an elaborate ceremony to mark my induction as a Jaguar warrior, but it was rather modest. As the other warriors stood in a circle around me, I was presented with a helmet made from wood and feathers that resembled a Jaguar head. Then I was given a new war club, bow and arrows, flint knife and two spears, one short and one long. The weapons were placed on the ground at my feet and a priest appeared to say a prayer. I was feeling happy and proud until the end of the prayer when the priest handed me a long thorn, and pointed to the weapons in front of me. With a sick feeling I realized that I was expected to drip some of my blood on the weapons as a sacrifice as the priests and Chan Oc had done, and what's more, I was expected to get it from my male member!

Everyone was looking at me expectantly as I remembered that Cuac Caan had said I would be expected to act according to their customs. My hand was trembling slightly as I pulled back my loincloth. I bit my lip to keep from crying out as I slowly stuck the thorn in my flesh until I saw blood. I'm not sure which was worse, the pain or the embarrassment, but I tried to get a drop on each weapon, and finally did. The encircled warriors then raised their war clubs in salute and said "May the next blood on your weapons be that of our enemies!"

Amen to that, I thought, and the ceremony was over.

I was invited to eat at the house of Balam that night and I gratefully accepted. A heavy rain had started as I arrived and streams of water poured off the overhang of the thatched roof and splashed on the ground. Can Pec was also there along with Balam's wife, Ix Kutz. Cimi was also there (I was right about Balam being her father) and I was surprised to see that she had a brother named 7 Ahau. Cimi and Ahau greeted the guests and Cimi jumped into every conversation she could for a while, but soon she and Ahau were put in two small hammocks off to one side of the hut and promptly fell asleep. Ix Kutz was a typical Maya wife in some ways; she kept the household, cooked, cared for the children and wove most of the cloth. She and Balam had been married since they were both 14, which was typical. Although it was an arranged marriage, they had become very compatible and seemed to act as a team, with each one complementing the other.

We dined on the usual tortillas with chilies, beans, turkey meat, roasted dog, and, of course, corn. There was also an amazing drink called chocolate, which was thick with foam, richly flavorful, and like nothing I had ever tasted before. The beans from which this drink is made are so valued that they are used as money.

We sat cross-legged on the floor and ate from bowls in our laps, a procedure I had to do cautiously because of a certain tenderness I still had from the ceremony. This was the first real conversation I had had with anyone over the age of six since I had been here. A great deal of it I didn't understand, either because they talked too fast for my still developing language skills to grasp, or because I still wasn't familiar with many areas of Mayan life.

"Chac has been good to us this year," said Balam, indicating the rain that was falling outside in torrents. "The crops in the milpas will be abundant." (Chac was the god of rain. He was depicted on many of the buildings and always had a grotesque curled nose, like that of an elephant.)

"Yes," agreed Can Pec, "if we can keep the warriors of Xcalampak from raiding them."

"Warriors raid crops?" I asked.

"Yes," said Balam. "Sometimes they burn crops to create a diversion, or to take them for themselves, or simply to weaken us. The cities of our land are independent and are constantly fighting among themselves. There are alliances, such as the alliance of Ixil and Dzilpan, and a loose federation of cities from Ecab in the north to Chetumal in the south for purposes of trade and mutual defense, but each city goes its own way most of the time. For this reason, we must always be prepared to deal with raids and border fights with our neighbors."

"Are there wars of conquest?" I asked.

Balam shrugged. "Sometimes an alliance will overrun a smaller place, but usually, the forces are too close to being in balance to permit a complete victory by one side. And so we continue to struggle to protect our homes, our food supply, our territory and our trade routes. In fact, we will soon be leaving for a raid into Xcalampak, a city to the north."

As I was leaving, Balam said "Get a good rest, for tomorrow you will participate in the sacrifice."

I couldn't believe it. "Not another thorn?" I asked with a groan.

Balam and Can Pec laughed uproariously. I didn't know why, but I didn't like the sound of the whole thing.

"A thorn? Oh no, Gonz-lo! How can you cut out a man's heart with a thorn?"

My stomach went numb when I heard these words, for I knew I was trapped. It was no surprise to learn that Cuac Caan himself had suggested that I be given this rare honor; usually only a priest performed the ritual. As a result, I was now obligated to perform a task I could not do. Killing someone in the heat of battle was one thing; this was murder. Of course, any one of the three I had captured would have done the same to me, but that didn't make it any easier. The plan was both simple and foolproof. Because of my culture and background, I could never perform the sacrifice; but if I refused, Chan Oc's condition that I obey all the customs of the

64

Maya would be broken and I could be made a slave again, if not a sacrifice myself. Checkmate. I tried to think of a way out. I still wasn't ready to escape, and with my desire for Zazil Ha, I wasn't even sure I wanted to. When dawn broke, I was no closer to an answer.

The air was damp and relatively cool when I was escorted to the pyramid the next morning through the crowded plaza. On the temple platform, I could see Chan Oc and several nobles on one side, and Cuac Caan and Balam on the other as I reached the top. In the gloomy temple behind the sacrifice stone was a hideous idol that represented Chac. In front of Chac was a bowl that would receive the heart. Dried blood coated the idol, the inner walls, and even stained the paving stones underfoot. Flies and the stench of death both hovered, and to my fear was now added nausea. The chief priest, Ah Kin Mu, stood there with his black face and tangled, blood stiffened hair.

"Gonz-lo," he began solemnly, "today, a great and rare honor has been given to you. Because you have brought three captives, you will make the first sacrifice." With that, he held out an ugly looking knife with a blade of glass-like volcanic stone. The handle was shaped like a skull and was still stained from the last bit of infernal work it had performed. One glance at the knife and you knew exactly what it was used for.

As Ah Kin Mu stood there holding out that obscene knife, I looked down the steps and saw two of the captives, now painted blue, being marched up to the block. Neither of them were ones I had captured because it's considered sacrilege for anyone to sacrifice his own captive. I suppose even executioners must have some standards.

I still didn't know what to do, and started to reach for the knife. The victims were only a few steps from the top now and the five sub priests were coming forward to help hold them down. The crowd had gone silent, all of them watching me.

Now the victim was standing by the stone.....

I stepped back without taking the knife. There was a gasp from the crowd and I turned to address them.

"People of Ixil!" I shouted, "You and the great Chan Oc have given me a home and the great honor of being a warrior. But I am a dzul and am not worthy to participate in a sacrifice until I have proven myself a true son of Ixil. This is now my home, and I must not risk the anger of the gods on the people who have given me so much. All my efforts will be to make myself worthy in the eyes of the gods and the people of Ixil."

I stood holding my breath. The crowd was still. From the corner of my eye, I could see that Cuac Caan and Ah Kin Mu were furious. Ah Kin Mu opened his mouth to speak when suddenly there was a roar of approval from the crowd.

"Sacrilege!" hissed Ah Kin Mu. "You have risked the wrath of the gods! You will pay with your own life."

But Chan Oc, who had been standing quietly, spoke up. "Ah Kin Mu, there is truth in the words of Gonz-lo. What if Chac is offended by a sacrifice performed by a dzul? Let us wait until this man has given longer service before we entrust so great a task to him."

"But the very act of changing the ceremony may offend Chac!" said Ah Kin Mu. He was wide-eyed in disbelief.

"Chac will understand our motives," said Chan Oc. "We will give Gonz-lo one year in which to prove himself worthy by his deeds and by his following of our ways. At the end of that time, he will do as the gods see fit."

"And if he has not proven himself by then?" said Cuac Caan.

"Then we will be certain we were correct in not letting him participate in the sacrifices today," said Chan Oc coolly.

Ah Kin Mu started to speak, but changed his mind. He gave a command to the sub priests who grabbed the victim and threw him on his back over the stone. Ah Kin Mu then plunged in the knife and drew it across the captive's chest, twisted it to force the ribs apart, and thrust in his hand. With a violent twist, he yanked out the glistening red heart, still throbbing. A hot stream of blood splashed across my face and I thought I would faint from the sheer horror of it. The dripping heart was handed to a sub priest who held it up in the air before taking it into the temple. A rivulet of blood ran down his arm and dripped from his elbow, adding to the stains and splatters already underfoot. Blood was everywhere, and I thought if I didn't get away from that terrible place, I would go mad. The victim had been drugged somewhat, not for mercy, but to lessen any struggle or screaming. He gasped in pain and cried out incoherently as a man having a nightmare sometimes does, but from this nightmare he would never awake.

Chapter 9- Zazil Ha

In which I court a beautiful Mayan woman

I was still light headed and nauseous as I descended the steps of the pyramid, but I had escaped the trap that Cuac Caan had laid for me. I didn't know what would happen in a year's time; I only wanted to survive the day.

The crowd parted to allow us through, and everyone seemed to look approvingly at me. How long would that last, I wondered? At the edge of the crowd, off to the side, was a small group of women in the shade of a tree. They were ordinary women in white dresses and sandals, and were plain looking.... except for one. There standing among them, standing out like a swan among a group of hens, was Zazil Ha! She didn't speak, but as our eyes met, she smiled and nodded approval. I wanted to shout for joy. If I had her blessing, what else mattered?

Cuac Caan was about to remind me of what else mattered.

"You may have fooled the Batab, Gonz-lo," Cuac Caan rumbled when we were past the crowd, "but I am not deceived, and neither are the gods. You have said you will prove yourself? We will see how well you prove yourself against those who will not be swayed by your words."

Then he turned away and I was alone. I would worry about him later. First, I had to find Zazil Ha.

The next day, dressed in my finest warrior clothes, I went to the residence of the Batab. There was no sign of Zazil Ha, so I went to the shade tree and questioned the women nearby. Several of them said that Zazil Ha came and spoke with them often, but no one had seen her since the ceremony. I was distraught. In two days, I would leave for a raid from which I might not return. I had to see her again, but where could I find her? In desperation, I went once more to the house of the memories where the books were kept and where I had first seen her, but it was empty. Defeated, I sat on the steps with my head hanging. Was it all a dream? Would I ever see her again? Maybe I had only deceived myself. Maybe I should reconsider my earlier plan to escape; I might get back to Spain yet.

Then a shadow fell across my line of vision. I looked up, hardly daring to hope, and there she was! She was standing directly in front of me, her long black hair gently rustling in the warm breeze.

"My lady Zazil Ha!" I said leaping to my feet, "I was hoping I'd see you. May I speak with you?"

She looked at me for a moment, then spoke softly in a voice like that of an angel. "Let us walk awhile."

So we walked together through the streets of the town. Her presence beside me was almost intoxicating. I had to force myself to keep from staring at her constantly.

"I was hoping you would come again to the house of the memories," I said at last.

"Yes, I go there often," she said matter-of-factly. "There is much wisdom in the books."

"But I thought women couldn't read the books." I said.

"That is true. But when I was a little girl, my teacher was Chac Pacal. He is a wise man, but he could deny me nothing. I made him teach me to read the signs as well as any priest or elder."

I could sympathize with old Chac Pacal. I didn't believe I could deny her anything either.

"But are you not breaking a tradition by reading?"

She frowned slightly. "It is true my people live by traditions. Traditions give us a purpose and strength to guide us through the cycles of time. But we must always balance those traditions with the need to grow and to gain wisdom. Sometimes we must choose between what is expected and what is right."

Her tone was self-assured and confident, but I thought I detected a slight hesitation and wariness. After all, a woman in her position usually would not speak to a dzul, and never alone.

We walked on and she became thoughtful. "That was a brave and dangerous thing you did yesterday," she said, finally.

"As much as I wish to appear brave in your eyes, I have to admit I was terrified," I said. "I only wanted to run away."

"I know," she replied. "That is why it was brave. My people have been sacrificing captives for many years. But it is an alien idea brought by the Toltecs many katuns ago. If only everyone had the courage to refuse as you did. That's what it was, of course, a refusal. I never believed that speech about being worthy ....neither did Chan Oc."

I was astonished. "What? Chan Oc knew that I was merely trying to avoid the sacrifice?"

She laughed. "Chan Oc is wise in the ways of men. He is not deceived so easily."

"But if he knew I was not sincere, why did he support me?"

"There were two reasons. With Ixil surrounded by enemies, your skills will prove useful as a warrior."

"And the other reason?" I asked.

"He was advised by one he trusts."

"By you?"

She didn't answer, but seemed somewhat embarrassed. Finally, she asked me to tell her about my home.

"I am from a land called Spain, though many in my part of it call it Castile. We have fought an invader for almost 700 years and have finally won. We drove them out, along with their false religion."

She nodded. "Tell me about your Gods."

"We have only the one god."

"Only one?" she was surprised.

"Yes, only the one true god, and his son."

"His son? But you said there was only one god. I suppose there is a mother as well?"

Theology was clearly not going to be easy to explain.

"Well, no. The mother was a mortal woman who lived long ago," I said.

"Ah, so she is now dead?"

"Well, yes, but we pray to her."

"You pray to her? But how can a dead woman hear you?" She was beginning to lose patience.

"She is in heaven-the sky. There is earth, and there is heaven where those who are good go when they die and there is hell, where those who are bad go. God lives in heaven and Satan lives in hell."

"Satan? Now there are three gods? Soon you will find as many gods as we have!" She was laughing. "And do you build temples to all these gods?"

"We call them cathedrals," I replied, gesturing enthusiastically. "They are like prayers made of stone. You should see them. In Seville, our cathedral soars upward to the sky and shines in the sunlight. And the towers! The towers are like graceful sculptures that seem to reach the clouds. Inside, the cathedral is cool and rich with gold and polished wood and fine cloth. The sun shines through the colored windows scattering jewels of light everywhere. Standing in such a place, you can almost hear the voice of God speaking to you alone."

I stopped suddenly, aware that Zazil Ha was looking at me curiously. "Colored windows? What a strange idea," she said.

"Well," I stammered, "I suppose it's all hard to understand since it's so different from the Mayan religion."

She shrugged. "Perhaps not so different. We too have a

71

supreme god, and he has a son, Itzamna. With his wife, Ixchel, Itzamna is the father of the other gods. There are worlds in the sky like your heaven, and Xibalba under the earth, like your hell. You pray to your gods and we pray to ours. Do you have priests to intercede with your gods?"

"Yes, and they also seek out"...I paused, since there is no Maya word for heretics.."those who do not believe, and punish them." I preferred not to tell her of the Inquisition.

"But if people do not believe, why punish them? Is not an afterlife in your Xibalba punishment enough?"

I had to admit she had a point. "Zazil Ha, someday, I would like to take you to meet the Pope. He is our chief priest."

"Yes, I will have a great many questions for him."[11]

The day was hot, but the sky had become overcast with gray clouds, sparing us the direct rays of the sun. We had been walking down straight, well-tended streets with a mixture of buildings, some stone and some wood, along them. The town was laid out similar to Dzilpan. The main ceremonial plaza was at the center and the stone houses of the Batab and the nobles were also in this area. The more important a person was, the closer he would live to the center. As you got away from the center, the houses became more humble until the stick and thatch homes of the peasant farmers were reached among the milpas. Most of the men were either in the milpas tending the crops, or tending small gardens. The women were grinding corn or making pottery, or weaving with a simple loom that was tied to a tree or building on one end and the woman on the other.

"Tell me of the canoe that you traveled in for 40 days. How big was it?" she asked.

"It was as tall as that tree over there," I said, "and as long as that house over there. There were 60 people on board."

She cocked her head with suspicion. "No! How can there be a tree so big? Or paddles so long?"

"It was made from many trees fastened together," I replied laughing, "and we had no paddles. We used large pieces of cloth to catch the wind and push us." To my surprise, she instantly grasped the concept.

"Yes, I see. A clever idea."

"But tell me about yourself," I said. "Do you have tasks to perform as the daughter of the Batab?

"Oh, yes. I am expected to appear at each public ceremony, I teach the women of Ixil, and I must travel to other cities sometimes. Last year, I accompanied my father to Ecab."

"Where is that?" I asked, anxious to learn more of the geography of the land.

"Ecab is a city seven days journey to the north. It is the seat of the Halac Uinic of the Ecab Maya."

"The Hala...what was it?"

"The cities in this part of the land are in an alliance for mutual protection and trade. The Halac Uinic is the ruler and each Batab owes allegiance to him. They are all related in one way or another."

"But I thought we were allied with Dzilpan?" I said, confused.

"Within the Ecab alliance are many alliances and disputes among the members. Sometimes, there is open warfare over a boundary or trade rights, but we are still part of the Ecab Maya, just as children can fight and still be in the same family. To the Maya, fighting and arguing are a way of life."

I nodded; it sounded too familiar. "In Spain, there were similar small kingdoms such as Castile, Aragon, and Andalusia. Finally, they were united under Ferdinand and Isabella," I said. Then an unsettling thought occurred to me. "As a member of the ruling family, will your marriage be arranged?"

"My mother, Box Naab, wants me to be contented in marriage, and my father wishes to strengthen the people of

73

Ixil with my marriage. There have been suitors, but either they had nothing to offer the people, or nothing to offer me."

I wondered if I had anything to offer.

We were soon at the market, which was near the main square with the pyramid. There were probably a hundred people haggling over food, pottery, cloth, green feathers, bows and arrows, copper axes, obsidian bladed knives, necklaces, bracelets, and freshly killed game. Most of the buyers and sellers were women and some sat cross-legged in the open while others had erected cloth or thatch canopies as protection from the merciless sun. Turkeys, dogs, and half-naked children scampered here and there. As we walked amid the swirling chaos of colors, smells and voices, many of the people seemed to know Zazil Ha and greeted her. She responded in a warm, natural way that others seemed to find as charming as I did. We passed the pyramid, and I repressed a shudder as I stole a glance upwards remembering my shipmates. At first, I thought she hadn't noticed, but I had underestimated her as usual.

"Do not judge my people by the sacrifices," she said after we had walked awhile. "The Mayan people are far more than that. We have those who follow the course of the stars, and those who keep the count of time from the beginning of the world until thousands of thousand years to come. We have those who know the arts of healing, and those who know the arts of building. And we have those who know the art of writing to record it all. Our astronomers reach out to the heavens themselves and our timekeepers reach across the ages to the end of the world. Yes, there is death here, too much; but there is also life, and the greatest gift of the gods: knowledge." Her voice had changed as she spoke these words. Now it was filled with passion and the earnestness of deeply held beliefs.

We spent another hour together and talked earnestly of the different worlds we had come from. My mind was still having trouble accepting the idea that this woman came from the savages who practiced human sacrifice. I was continually surprised by the extent of her knowledge, her curiosity, and her quick wit. But she also had warmth and a charm that would have melted the heart of a stone idol. Returning to Spain now seemed much less important, or, at least less urgent, and I began to consider the idea of marriage to this woman. Finally, she turned to me and said she must return to the house of the Batab.

"Zazil Ha," I said, gazing into her eyes, "tomorrow, I leave for the land of Xcalampak, but wherever I go, I will carry your memory with me."

She returned my gaze, and said nothing. She only smiled.

"In my country, when a man says farewell to a lady who has captured his heart," I said, "this is what he does to show her." With that, I took her hand and slowly raised it until I could kiss it gently. She gasped faintly, then looked at her hand, then looked at me.

"Perhaps there is much we could learn from each other," she said softly, "Farewell, Gonzalo. May the gods protect you, and bring you back."

Chapter 10- A Raid on Xcalampak

In which I face war and a poisonous slander

The next morning, I left with Can Pec, Balam, and 50 others for our raid into Xcalampak. The sun was just rising over the city as we reached the milpas. I looked back and saw Ixil looking blurred in the low morning mist. Already, smoke from copal incense was rising from the still indistinct bulk of the pyramid. Soon, we reached the edge of the farthest milpa and entered the jungle. We followed a path through the forest, and everyone seemed to know the way but me. From the position of the rising sun peeking through occasional breaks in the trees overhead, I could tell we were heading North West. All that day we marched until nightfall, when we camped.

As we ate our corn meal paste and chilies that night, I sat on a log next to Can Pec, who seemed to be eager with anticipation. Can Pec, whose name means Snake Dog, lived for being a warrior. He had never married, saying he was married to the holcom, but was a pleasant companion who accepted me without reservation. He didn't have much of a sense of politics, the way Balam had, but he knew the life of a soldier as well as anyone.

"We are now in the land of the Cupul Maya," he said. "Xcalampak is a city somewhat bigger than Ixil. Tonight, we rest. In the morning, we attack their outposts and take captives."

"What is our plan?" I asked.

Can Pec shrugged. "Our usual plan, Gonz-lo. We set an ambush for an isolated group, then attack while they are surprised."

It seemed like a simple plan, but very predictable and not very effective. But I said nothing and my mind wandered. I thought again of Zazil Ha and wondered if I was not being foolish to pursue her. For all her beauty and charm, she was still a member of a violent and unpredictable race. I might very well become unfit to be either a Maya or a Spaniard. What would happen if I were to marry her? Would I be able to take her back to Spain, or would I be trapped into spending the rest of my life in this heathen land among these bloodthirsty people? With all these thoughts pursuing each other in my head, I fell into a troubled sleep.

We arose before dawn and were at the outskirts of Xcalampak at first light. The city loomed silently out of the morning haze like an abode of the dead. Xcalampak looked similar to Ixil, but it was bigger and had a taller pyramid surrounded by plazas at various levels. The stone buildings at the center seemed to extend further outward than those in Ixil, but otherwise, the town looked the same. The plan was to lay in wait for the first group of warriors to leave the holcom area and head out to patrol the borders. We would ambush them, taking captives as we could. This is similar to what happened to us several days earlier. It seemed to be almost a tradition. It also seemed to be much too predictable, especially since the warriors of Xcalampak would be expecting retaliation. I approached Balam and Can Pec.

"How many will be out on patrol?" I asked.

"Probably 20 men. They have to send patrols over a wide area." replied Can Pec.

"So, if all goes well, we will capture 20 men?" I asked.

Can Pec laughed. "No, of course not. Most of them will be alert for trouble and will run for reinforcements as soon as we strike. If all goes well, we may get three or four. Even if we captured more, we would not be able to get them back to Ixil before the bulk of the warriors caught up with us. The extra captives would slow us down too much."

"Do raiding parties only attack warriors?" I asked.

"No," said Can Pec. "Sometimes a small raiding party of 10 or 12 will not be big enough to attack a patrol. They will simply take a few peasants for slaves and try to avoid the patrols."

I thought for a moment, then remembered a story my uncle had once told me of a trick the Moors had played.

"Suppose we were able to capture the entire patrol?" I asked. "And to do it in such a way that the others will not be alerted, and will not pursue?"

"And who will help us do that?" Can Pec snorted.

"They will," I said.

About an hour later, the first peasants started coming into the fields. We were in a wooded area at the edge of the milpas. Soon, a patrol of 20 Xcalampak warriors could be seen heading in our direction. They couldn't see us yet, but, because of the way a clearing was situated, would see us in a few minutes. They looked alert, as if they were expecting trouble. They would not be disappointed.

As the Xcalampak warriors neared the edge of the milpa, they heard cries for help coming from the woods. They ran toward the sound, still alert for an ambush. Suddenly, the source of the sound came in view; 10 Ixil warriors had captured two peasants and were trying to carry them off. The peasants were struggling and screaming for help. The Ixil warriors, seeing they were discovered and outnumbered, fled into the woods in a desperate attempt to escape. The leader of the Xcalampak warriors shouted. "Ha! The cowards are trying to run away! Get them!"

The Ixil warriors were only about 200 yards away when they were first pursued, but the Xcalampak warriors were surprised how fast they moved considering they had two reluctant peasants in tow. Deeper and deeper into the forest the chase continued, the gap steadily closing. Finally, when they had gone about a mile, the Ixil warriors suddenly turned

78

to face their pursuers. The Xcalampak warriors, sensing an easy victory, smiled in triumph....until they saw the other 40 Ixil warriors surrounding them. A quick fight and the 52 Ixil warriors subdued the 20 Xcalampak warriors with only minor injuries to both sides. Only then did Balam and I reclothe ourselves in the warrior garb we had cast off to impersonate captured peasants.

"May the gods be thanked!" said Balam. "Gonz-lo, your plan worked to perfection. They sensed an easy kill, so they did not alert the others. By the time they realized what was happening, we had lured them too far from Xcalampak for them to send for reinforcements, or to escape. We will be halfway back to Ixil before Xcalampak realizes these men are missing. Even when they do, they won't know where to look. Never have we brought back so many captives at so little a price."

I was a hero. Once again, my presence had led to a rich haul of captives. Of course, I had the Moors to thank. Retreat to lure the enemy into an ambush was a trick the Moors used on more than one occasion. To the warriors of Ixil, however, it was a brilliant idea on my part. My good luck had been phenomenal, and I was determined to make it continue. I tried to recall all I had learned from my uncle and from Perez that would be new to the Maya and would be advantageous to them. I had to admit that as religious as we were in Castile, there was little that anyone could teach us about killing. I would use my knowledge to advance my fortunes. As we made our way back to Ixil, with no one in pursuit, I began to feel that my troubles were over.

Once again, I was wrong.

Everyone was excited at the prospect of returning to Ixil with so many captives, and looked on me as an informal leader. Only Balam was restrained.

"Gonz-lo," he said when we stopped to rest that afternoon, "you have done well. Ixil will sing your praises, but you must be careful of danger."

I was shocked. "What danger?"

"You have powerful enemies in Cuac Caan and the priest Ah Kin Mu. Cuac Caan is a great Nacom, but he will never accept a dzul as a warrior. Ah Kin Mu is anxious to gain influence over the holcom's warriors to enhance his own power. He sees alliance with Cuac Caan and opposition to you as a means to accomplish this. There is also Pom Tzec to consider."

"Pom Tzec?" I had heard the name before; the frightening figure in the mist. "Isn't he the Batab of Dzilpan?"

"Yes. Currently, we are allied with him, but he is a ruthless and ambitious man and the alliance is weak. He seeks a pretext for either breaking the alliance or bending it to his favor. He could well claim that the rising influence of a dzul warrior will undermine the protection Ixil has agreed to give the merchants of Dzilpan, and demand other concessions."

I thought of the emissary I had seen and his complaint to Chan Oc of merchants being attacked.

"But, I am well thought of by the people. Cuac Caan and Ah Kin Mu had to give way. Surely, they are no further threat to me now."

Balam picked up a short spear. "If I thrust this spear at you, what would you do?"

"I would step to one side to avoid the blow."

"And then?"

"Then I would counterthrust."

He nodded. "Exactly. Cuac Caan and Ah Kin Mu are not defeated; they have merely sidestepped a thrust. Soon, they will counterthrust. A single blow does not decide a battle. Now is the time you must be cautious, or the counterthrust will bring you down."

With that sobering thought, we resumed our march.

When we returned to Ixil, the people lined the streets to see the amazing sight of 20 captives being marched through the town. Soon, the story spread, and I was being hailed as a great warrior by passers-by. Just a few months before, no one would even notice me; now everyone wanted to be my friend. Such are the fortunes of war, I suppose.

The next night, there was another feast. This time, I was invited to sit near the front with Balam and Cuac Caan. The symbolism was not lost on the other guests; I was being placed as an equal with the two Nacoms. And my sister Maria had always said I would never amount to anything.

One problem with my new position was that I was not free to wander around as I had been at the last banquet, and, as a result, was not able to talk to Zazil Ha all night. Cuac Caan was civil to me and smiled at the other guests, but I could tell he was seething inside.

At one point, Balam's wife, Ix Kutz came by to see him with Ahau and Cimi in tow. Cimi held up her doll when she saw me.

"Hello, Dzul. I brought Ix Chan to see you. Her head fell off again, but my mother fixed it. She said it was an accident, but I think Ahau did it."

"I did not! You stepped on her," said her brother indignantly.

"You better be good, Ahau, or your head will come off, too. If it does, I won't even ask mother to fix it."

Ix Kutz shook her head. "If the holcom finds itself in need of warriors, perhaps we could turn these two against our enemies."

The next day, I tried to see Zazil Ha, but was disappointed to find that she was teaching at a special school for women and would not be free for five more days. The education of men and women was quite different, as it was in Castile. In fact, education seemed to be highly specialized. The highest level was for the priests and the astronomers and the timekeepers. These were all taught by others of their group

81

and they learned to read the sacred books and learned all the knowledge of time, space, and the heavens that the Maya possessed. This was not merely an intellectual exercise, because this knowledge was the basis of the agricultural cycle. The precise times to plant, and to harvest the crops, especially the corn, was the responsibility of these men. It is not an exaggeration to say that the very survival of the community depended on this knowledge.

Next was the nobility who learned a limited amount of reading and a basic knowledge of history and warfare. Next were the warriors who learned the arts of war and some medicine. Somewhere in this area were the more specialized people such as scribes and healers and builders. Women were taught basic homekeeping, weaving, and child rearing along with the social arts. At the bottom were the peasants who received no formal education at all. I had a feeling that if Zazil Ha was teaching the women, they would learn far more than cooking and weaving.

I spent the next five days wandering around the city admiring the buildings and the industriousness of the people. I was still amazed to think that while we in Castile talked of primitive, naked savages, these people were living in cities of stone and charting the heavens. At one point, I came upon two workmen repairing a crumbling wall. Instead of replacing the stones, they were covering the crumbling area with a thick coating of plaster. It seemed a haphazard way of fixing anything and I asked them about it.

"Ixil had many more people when these buildings were built," one said as he spread6 the plaster with loud scraping noises. "Now there are not enough skilled people to rebuild such structures."

"I see. And what is that you are doing?"

"This is a plaster made from heating the soft stones until they crumble. The powder is mixed with water, and hardens like stone."

The soft rock was probably limestone. When heated, it crumbles into a type of mortar we had sometimes used on the farm. Producing mortar would require large amounts of wood to heat the stone. They must have had to cut down whole forests to build on such a scale.

One afternoon. I went back to the milpas and observed with my trained farmer's eye. The corn was well along, but seemed to be very dry. Farmers were carrying water in jars and watering individual stalks; a tedious job. The soil seemed to be very poor and dusty, and I could see why water was a constant concern. The soil was so coarse that the rain must quickly soak into the ground, leaving it dry again within a day or two. This, coupled with the hot sun must make crop failures a constant threat. I asked one farmer when it had rained last, and he said it had been 11 days, which was uncomfortably long. If rain didn't come soon, there would be danger to the crops.

I remembered the last rain. It had been the night before the sacrifice on the pyramid.

Back in the town, I passed by a small area of rocks and trees where a number of children were playing. I had just passed when I heard the familiar voice of Cimi calling me.

"Dzul! Dzul!"

"Well, hello, Cimi," I replied.

"and?......"

"Oh, yes. And Ix Chan, too."

"Everyone says that you captured 100 warriors," she said, excitedly, "Is that a lot? I don't think I have 100 toes, but I might if you count my fingers. Why are fingers longer than toes when feet are longer than hands? My mother took me to the market this morning. I got a new feather."

I laughed at the numbers. "No, it was only 20 warriors, and I had a lot of help."

"Help doing what?"

"Never mind. How is Ix Chan's head? Is it still attached?"

"Of course. My mother fixed it. I got mad at Ahau yesterday and threw a corncob at him. It didn't even hit him and I was punished anyway."

Another thought popped into her head and she suddenly frowned and looked worried. I had never seen her express anything but curiosity and enthusiasm before, so I asked her what was wrong.

"Dzul," she said, "did you really make the rain stop?"

"Did I what?" I was astonished.

"At the market this morning, I heard someone say that the rain had stopped because a dzul had offended the gods. What did they mean?"

I felt tightness in my stomach. So this was the counterblow. A timely drought had given Cuac Caan and Ah Kin Mu their opportunity to discredit me and make the people resent me. If all went their way, I could wind up a slave again, or maybe even a sacrifice myself, and it all depended on the rain. I looked up at the sky. There was not a cloud in sight.

Chapter 11- The Drought

In which I seem doomed to a horrible death

I rushed back to the Jaguar compound to try to find Balam, but he wasn't there. A slave stood by the door waiting for me to arrive.

"I bear a message from the lady Zazil Ha, daughter of Chan Oc."

Zazil Ha! "What is the message? Hurry!" I said, anxiously.

"You are to come to the house of the memories before the sun sets," he said. I was on my way in a second.

I ran to the house of the memories and was relieved to see Zazil Ha calmly seated on a carved stone reading one of the folding books.

"Zazil Ha; I have been waiting to see you again," I said, breathlessly.

"Do not talk, Gonzalo." She was holding up a hand, palm outward. "You have little time. The servants of my father are looking for you to summon you to the house of the Batab for a council of the elders at the setting of the sun. They will hear the complaint of Cuac Caan and Ah Kin Mu that you have offended the gods and caused Chac to withhold his rain. The life of my people depends on the rain to grow the corn. There is no greater crime than stopping it. You are in grave danger. Even Chan Oc must put his people first if they are facing the loss of the corn."

"What about you?" I asked. "Do you think the gods are angry because of me?"

"What matters is that the people are angry. They must be convinced that the drought is not an act of vengeance by Chac. Now listen carefully. You will be questioned by Chan Oc and the elders. You must ask that a man called Akbal Dzib be called to present certain information. He will be in the chamber already."

"And he will help me?" I asked.

She held up the book she had been reading. "*This* will help you. Now, here is what you must say..........."

An hour later, I appeared at the house of the Batab. Inside was the chamber I had seen before. There was a long raised platform at one end covered with a mat, the symbol of authority, and several jaguar skins. On this mat, seated cross-legged, were Chan Oc and on each side, two elders, including old Chac Pacal. They were fitted out in intricate feathered headbands, jewelry, ear-plugs, and brilliantly colored capes. Chan Oc also wore a cape of Jaguar skin. On the wall behind them was a brightly painted mural showing an assortment of fantastically arrayed rulers, gods, and warriors. The whole scene was lit by torches that flickered, giving off eerie, dancing shadows. Outside, hundreds of townspeople had gathered to hear the proceedings. Cuac Caan and Ah Kin Mu stood off to the side waiting to make their accusations.

One of the guards blew a blast on a trumpet made from a seashell and the trial was underway. Since the offense was religious in nature, Ah Kin Mu spoke first. In his white priest's robe, he paced back and forth waving his spindly, blackened arms, like some spider from the pit.

"This man has scorned to make a sacrifice to Chac and has, by so doing, brought disaster on the people of Ixil. Chac has withheld the rain ever since the offensive act of Gonz-lo. The corn will soon die in the fields. Soon after, the people of Ixil will also die, for corn is life. We have accepted this dzul as one of us and now we pay the price for our generosity, for he has betrayed our customs and endangered us all. It is true that he has brought us many captives, but without rain, they are merely more to feed. Hear me, Ixil! We could have cast this man out, but now, that is not enough. The only way that the gods will be appeased is by the sacrifice of Gonz-lo!"

At that, the crowd outside grumbled its approval. Were these the same people who had thought I was a hero just a few days ago? Once again, I had managed to add more names to the ever-growing list of people who wanted to kill me.

Cuac Caan spoke next. He really had nothing to add, but had great respect from the elders and that alone helped move me a little closer to the knife. He said that I was a good warrior, but had brought the wrath of the gods to Ixil. He ended on a rousing line.

"If you ask 'Where is the proof?' my answer is, 'Where is the rain?'"

There was another ripple of approval from the crowd. I had no doubt that any one of them would have volunteered to hold the knife. I had a sudden vision of the bloody sacrifice I had witnessed, only this time, the victim had my face.

Finally, it was my turn to answer. I tried to put the terrible specter of the sacrifice out of my mind and proceed as Zazil Ha had told me.

"It is true that I was a dzul, and it is true that Ixil was kind to me," I began, my voice trembling slightly. "But I am no longer a dzul. I have fought for Ixil and I have learned the language and the ways of the Maya. If I believed that the rain has stopped because of me, I would go to the stone of sacrifice this very night, so great is my love for Ixil."

I paused to let that sink in, and was about to begin again, when an elder spoke up.

"Nevertheless, Cuac Caan's question remains unanswered; where is the rain?"

"If the council will permit, I would ask Akbal Dzib to provide some information I will ask of him." I said, and held my breath.

The council members conferred with each other,

obviously confused. "Akbal Dzib the scribe and keeper of the past?"

"Yes"

The council members conferred again. Finally, Chac Pacal spoke. "Akbal Dzib, you will provide information to the council."

"Thank you," I said, with some relief. "Akbal Dzib, do you not keep the records of the count of days and the deeds of the people of Ixil?"

"That is so," he replied.

"Would you have your servant bring the books that have the records of the past in them?" Akbal Dzib gave the order, and the servant was back in a few minutes.

I addressed the elders. "The withholding of the rain is something that would have happened even if I had never come here. The books show that such droughts happen in cycles and have happened many times before." I turned back to Akbal Dzib. "Will you see if any such droughts happened in the past?"

There was silence in the chamber except for the slow turning of the stiff pages. When the tension had become unbearable, Akbal Dzib spoke at last.

"Two years ago, at this time, the rain stopped for 20 days. Two years before that, the rain stopped for 22 days, and two years before that, the rain stopped for 18 days."

Several of the elders looked at each other and nodded. I breathed a sigh of relief. Thank God Zazil Ha knew how to read; she knew what the books said all along.

"As you see, a drought for 11 days or more happens at this time every two years, even without a dzul. So I ask the council to be patient. The rain will return....just as it always has."

The hot, airless chamber buzzed with voices. Everyone seemed to be talking at once for a while, but when the babble settled down, Chan Oc spoke.

"There is truth in what you have said, Gonz-lo, but the

rain is the very blood of our people. It must resume. We will withhold our decision for seven more days. If the rain has not returned by then....," he paused, "we will decide what steps to take."

I decided to throw caution to the winds. After all, what did I have to lose now?

"And if the rain has returned," I said, "it will be a sign that the gods are pleased with the service I have given as a warrior of Ixil, and a loyal subject of Chan Oc, will it not?"

They agreed that it would.

"Then, at that time, I would ask the great Chan Oc for permission to marry Zazil Ha."

It is hard to describe the sound of several hundred people gasping at the same time, but that is exactly what happened.

Chan Oc's scowling brown face regarded me from beneath the cascade of green feathers of his headdress, like an evil spirit peering out of a thick forest. Then in a voice of barely contained rage, said, "First, pray for the favor of the gods before you seek the favor of Zazil Ha. You will return here in seven days. The council will make their decision then. You may go."

As I bowed and walked out of the chamber, everyone frowned at me silently. I thought that this is what the people must look like at a hanging. When I was away from the crowd, at the edge of the plaza, I had another surprise. Zazil Ha stepped out of the shadows.

"Zazil Ha! I am so glad......."

"Do not speak to me, Gonzalo," she said hotly. Her face was flushed with rage and her fists were clenched. "I gave you the means to save yourself and you show your gratitude by embarrassing my father and treating me with contempt!"

"But, I...."

"No man will marry me unless I consent first. Did you think I would be so agreeable to marry you that you need not even ask? Did you think that Chan Oc would commit to my marriage without due private consideration? I have given you your life and you ask for mine as well! Do all your countrymen think they can gain by force or by trickery that which they cannot earn?"

"Zazil Ha, please forgive me. I was blinded by my love for you......" I saw my whole world slipping away.

"Enough! You will not see me or speak to me again unless I send for you."

Before I could reply, she was gone, and I stood alone in the hostile crowd. I didn't know what would happen when the seven days were up, but I felt as if my heart had already been cut out.

For the next two days, I was in the blackest of moods. My world was crumbling beneath me. I had won great honors in battle as an elite Jaguar warrior, and was regarded as a leader by the others. I was pursuing a woman who embodied everything I had ever dreamed of, and she had been responding. Now suddenly, Zazil Ha was gone and I could be dead in five more days. Each day, I looked for rain. Sometimes a few small clouds would form, but they soon scattered, leaving the sky empty except for the burning sun.

When I first came to Ixil, people ignored me; then they praised me; now they were hostile to me. People would glare at me as I walked by, then grumble about the drought, and the anger of Chac. Balam and Can Pec remained friendly, but even they were wary of associating too closely with someone who might have brought disaster on Ixil by offending the gods. The worst part was that there was nothing I could do. Everything depended on the rain.

Days passed, and still the drought continued. According to the records, a drought of more than 18 days was common, in fact, the last one had been 22 days. So it was likely that this one would last beyond the next seven days, long enough to see me dead.

During the next two days, I spent my time in long walks around the milpas, and in the forest. Each day, both the corn and my chances for survival looked weaker than the day before. As I walked, I stirred up small clouds of dust that followed me as if to remind me of my impending doom. I couldn't help think of the bitter irony of the situation. Of course it would rain again, but probably not until after the deadline, if past records were any indication. They would sacrifice me, and, when the rains resumed soon afterwards, would assume that it was my death that made it happen. Thus, I, who came with a group of men who wanted to spread Christianity, would help perpetuate a pagan religion of human sacrifice. Perhaps I had been foolish to think I could be part of this world; I had danced too close to the fire, and now it was about to consume me.

There was a lot of time to think during those days, and mostly I thought of Spain and of my family. My parents, my sister Maria, my brother Hectore, and my uncle Fernando appeared in my thoughts and beckoned me home. Most of all, I thought of Hectore and relived the golden days of our childhood together.

On the morning of the sixth day, I resolved to escape and head east toward the coast. There were only a few wisps of clouds in the blazing sky, and my time had almost run out. It would mean never seeing Zazil Ha again, but that seemed likely no matter what happened. Even if, by some miracle, I survived, Zazil Ha wanted nothing more to do with me. So I made plans to escape that night. I would take my walk to the forest, and keep on going. All that day, I anxiously waited for the afternoon sun to weaken so I could start. Finally, it seemed dark enough to begin. Trying to look unconcerned, I walked down the street by the plaza and turned toward the road that went east.

"Gonz-lo, you are to come with us."

I stopped dead when I heard the command. Two guards

had appeared in front of me and two behind. There was no chance of escape.

The morning of the final day, I found myself in the wooden cage in which the guards had placed me the previous night. It was similar to the one in Dzilpan, but this time, I would not escape to another town. They hadn't known about my plan to escape; this was just a precaution to be sure I appeared at the meeting that night. All through the long day, I watched the sun move through a cloudless sky like the hand of a clock measuring the hours until my doom. By the afternoon, I was resigned to my fate. I had no cards left to play. By this time tomorrow, I would be dead. If it had not been for the prospect of a horrible death, I would have appreciated the irony. I left Spain to escape being unjustly condemned by religious fanatics of the Inquisition only to end up unjustly condemned by religious fanatics of the Mayan priesthood.

I sat half praying and half dozing in the sticky heat of the late afternoon, thinking of the home and family half a world away I would never see again. I wondered if Hectore would be sleeping when they cut my heart out, and if he would somehow sense the brother he loved had been murdered. Then, in the midst of all this gloom, I thought I heard someone say my name.

"Gonzalo." I thought I heard it again.....

"Gonzalo!"

I awoke with a start and turned to find the source of the voice. There, in the shadows on the other side of the wooden bars stood Zazil Ha.

The surprise so stunned me, I couldn't speak, but just stood up and stared stupidly.

"Gonzalo," she said softly, "tonight you will face the council and there is still no rain. There is nothing more I can do to save you. The gods have turned away. This night, you must die."

That much I already knew. Had she come to gloat?

"I was angry with you for what you did," she continued, her voice slightly unsteady, "but I know you did it out of love for me. I couldn't bear the thought of you dying without knowing that I share that love. Each of us has a spirit that needs the other. My soul seeks yours as a tree seeks the sunlight. We could have been two halves of the same being, but now, that will never be."

"Zazil Ha," I said, finally finding my voice, "if I had to die to hear you say these words, I will die a happy man, for I will die knowing that I have your love."

She reached through the bars and stroked my cheek. I grasped her hand and kissed it.

She smiled faintly. "I like that custom," she said quietly.

"We have another," I said. "Come closer to the bars."

And there, in that wooden cage on my last day on earth, I tenderly kissed Zazil Ha for what I knew would be the first and last time. Her lips were soft and warm and her hair smelled of flowers.

"Farewell, Gonzalo," she said finally. "Take my love with you when you go to your heaven in the sky."

Darkness covered Ixil when the guards took me to the council meeting. The scene was the same as before; if anything, there were even more people gathered. Another difference, I noted with a chill, was that a fire was burning at the top of the pyramid. My sacrifice would take place the same night. I stood before the council looking for Zazil Ha. Finally, I saw her standing in the background. Her face was without expression, and her wonderful brown eyes looked dull and lifeless.

"Gonz-lo," began Chan Oc, "the rain has not fallen for 18 days, and soon the corn will be lost. We can wait no longer. Do you have anything final to say?"

I had nothing to lose now, so I thought I might as well end

on a positive note for Zazil Ha's sake.

"My lord Chan Oc, I say again that the gods have not withheld the rain because of me, but if my life would bring the rain back, I would gladly give it for the people of Ixil and, most of all for Zazil Ha, the woman I love."

The last time I had made a remark about Zazil Ha, everyone had gasped, but this time, the reaction was completely different. The crowd outside started talking among themselves, their voices growing louder and more excited.

"Guard!" said Chan Oc, "Go outside and tell the people to be silent."

"Yes, my lord Chan Oc."

The guard left the chamber and Chan Oc began to speak again.

"Gonz-lo, it is the decision of this council...."

"My lords!" The guard was running back into the chamber.

He was soaking wet.

"My lords," he shouted, "the rain has returned!"

And it had. Outside, it was raining; raining in torrents. Rain soaked the happy crowd; streams ran from rooftops and splashed on the ground; children played in puddles that were forming on the plaza; and far out in the darkened milpas, the corn began to grow once more. On the pyramid, the pounding rain caused the flame of sacrifice to sputter and die. There would be no hearts cut out this night. The chamber erupted with celebration, and then I saw the most welcome rain of all: tears of joy running down the cheeks of Zazil Ha.

Chapter 12- Alliances

In which local politics and intrigue complicate my life

The next few weeks almost made up for the hopeless despair of the past seven days. The rain continued for most of the night, then, two days later, it rained again. The corn seemed to be almost growing as I watched it. Now that the danger was past, I was a hero once again. Everyone congratulated me on the haul of captives from the Xcalampak raid, and I was the pride of Ixil once more.

My publicly stated love for Zazil Ha, which had been seen as insolence before the rain returned, was now seen as a bold, romantic act. I saw Zazil Ha often now and many people accepted our eventual union as decided. Of course, there were still a few staunch traditionalists, such as Cuac Caan and the priest Ah Kin Mu, who viewed the match with disfavor. The possibility of the daughter of the Batab wedding an outsider was too much of a break with tradition for some, but the great popularity of Zazil Ha made them hold their tongues for the most part. Even so, I was always aware of that these resentments might burst forth if circumstances changed.

The more I saw of Zazil Ha, the more I found that we were, as she had said, two halves of the same being. Although we were from worlds as different as any two on earth, we had a common spirit, and complemented each other. She had had many suitors, but her restless intellect had found them insufferably dull and narrow-minded. In me, she found the fresh perspective, and mutual respect she had been seeking. For my part, I was entranced by her beauty, poise, and spirit. She had a cosmopolitan outlook in a provincial land, and filled an emptiness in me that I didn't even know I had.

Consuelo might have been my first love, but Zazil Ha was the love of my heart.

Among the Maya, the notion of romantic love in the European sense is unknown. Parents arrange most marriages, and mutual love comes later, if it comes at all. Many couples, like Balam and Ix Kutz, find that the match was a good one and the partners develop a mutual respect that deepens into love. Others find that their parents have tried to match two people who can't stand each other, and live lives of unhappiness and resentment. Overall, the success rate seems to be about the same under either system. Generally, unmarried Mayan women were not permitted to associate with men, but Zazil Ha, I was not surprised to learn, had always been a free spirit and usually got her way. She seemed to have enchanted everyone in Ixil, so that she could do almost anything and it would be tolerated, or even applauded. This had much to do with the fact that, although she was beautiful and highborn, she was not self centered or conceited. She was friendly, supportive, and genuinely interested in even the most humble of her fellow citizens.

So the golden days passed by as we strolled the streets, visited the market, or watched one of the entertainments that were often staged on a stone platform on the plaza. These were skits, dancing, or singing, and were greeted with great enthusiasm by the people. We also visited the house of the memories and she tried to teach me to read the books. To me, the writing was tremendously difficult. It was partially phonetic, like Spanish, where a symbol stood for a sound and words were constructed of these sounds. At the same time, though, the system was also partially pictographic, where a symbol means a whole word. In addition, the symbols all looked the same to me, but slight differences had great meaning. The symbols were mostly square with rounded corners. Sometimes they depicted a face, or an animal, or a part of the body. Other times, they had a complex, abstract design. Along with the symbols were vivid, grotesque illustrations of gods, monsters, or people. When I told Zazil Ha of the writing I was familiar with, she was amazed that we could know the meaning without colors or pictures.

All the while, the subject of marriage was never far away. Finally, I decided it was time.

"Zazil Ha," I said finally, "I have no wish to offend anyone, least of all you, but I love you and want to marry you. Your love gave me the courage to face death; now I must have it to face life."

She smiled. "My marriage is a matter of concern to the people of Ixil. I also wish to marry you, but you must go to Chan Oc."

I was afraid she was going to say that.

"Chan Oc knows what is in my heart. He knows our marriage would benefit me, but you must convince him that the marriage will benefit the people of Ixil as well."

The next day, I stood before Chan Oc in my finest warrior dress. I had thought about what Zazil Ha had said about showing how the marriage would benefit Ixil, but had to realize that I had little to offer.

"My lord Chan Oc," I began, "I have come before you to ask for permission to marry Zazil Ha."

There was no reaction. I could not tell if this was a good sign or not, so I continued.

"In the time I have been among you, I have rendered service to the people of Ixil. It is true that I was a dzul, but I believe that is a great advantage to Ixil."

Now I had his interest. "What advantage, Gonz-lo?" he asked.

"I have come from a land far away; a land that has learned new ways of war and of peace. Ixil can profit from that knowledge, as you have seen at Xcalampak. The warriors of Ixil are brave and strong, but they are few in number, so they

97

must win by their wits."

"What you say is true," said Chan Oc, leaning back comfortably on a stone platform draped with jaguar skins, "but you do not have to marry Zazil Ha to use that knowledge. Her marriage should provide an alliance with another city or federation for the protection of Ixil."

He was right, of course. I had to use a risky strategy to satisfy this objection.

"I can offer no formal alliance, my lord, but, consider this; the land from which I come is a land of conquerors. Even now, they are reaching farther and farther in our direction. Many lands have already fallen to them. The day may come when they arrive to invade the lands of the Ecab Maya. If that day comes, only Ixil will have a daughter of a Batab married to a nobleman of that land. I speak their language and I know their ways. No one else in Ixil would be able to deal with the Castilians as I could as husband of Zazil Ha."

Of course, I wasn't a nobleman, but the rest of it was plausible enough. He seemed interested in the argument.

"I will consider your request and answer in two weeks' time." he said. "You may go."

So I would have to wait some more. I returned to the warrior compound and helped with some of the training. The day was hot and overcast and the warriors went through a series of sparring exercises in pairs around the area. As always, there were small groups of children watching, and in some cases, imitating. A group of sweating warriors gathered around some jars of water and drank deeply, while another group on the other side laughed good naturedly with some peasants who had stopped to chat on their way to market. It was a sleepy and peaceful scene and was actually restful to watch. But I knew we had two more raids scheduled in the next two weeks, so I reluctantly resumed the training drills.

The two raids went smoothly and netted the usual haul of

loot and captives. Thanks to my training and to new tactics I introduced, we were beginning to have a power far greater than our numbers would indicate, and I was beginning to feel invincible. On our way back from the last raid, however, all that changed.

We were in dense woods near the outer edge of the milpas, almost in sight if Ixil. Everyone was weary, but glad to be almost home.

"It will be good to be back in Ixil," Balam was saying. "Cimi is learning to weave and I promised her I would select a design for a new mantle."

Just then, the forest all around us exploded with noise and confusion as a mass of screaming bodies seemed to drop from the trees and leap from the surrounding foliage in a surprise attack. Xcalampak had come for revenge. We lashed out blindly in all directions at the enemy warriors who seemed to be everywhere at once. We were outnumbered almost three to one; now we would see how good my training had made us. In the swirling chaos and confusion of the fight, men were falling all around, and I knew the bitter taste of fear in my mouth as I stabbed, parried and thrust until my hands were sticky with blood. Out of the corner of my eye, I was horrified to see Balam fall, but was too busy with three screaming warriors to come to his aid. The biggest of the three charged me, but was a little too slow. I parried his spear and plunged my own into him so hard it jammed between his ribs and I was almost killed by the others as I tried to retrieve the weapon from my now dead opponent. In that little corner of hell, we fought fiercely with the living while stumbling over the bodies of the dead.

The fight seemed to go on for hours, and I have no idea how many of the enemy I dispatched, but finally the tide turned and we drove them off. Wearily, we dragged our wounded back to Ixil, leaving a trail of blood and bodies through the green forest.

At the edge of the milpas, we saw reinforcements and a delegation from Ixil coming to meet us. A patrol had seen us and brought back word of our condition.

I was pleased to see that Zazil Ha was with the people who came to the fields with Chan Oc to inspect the scene. When she saw me, she threw her arms around me in front of everyone. Afterwards, her white dress was stained with patches of blood as we walked back toward Ixil.

"Thank the gods you are safe," she said with relief. She was genuinely concerned, bless her.

"Yes, but Balam is badly wounded. He had an arrow in the back. The arrow was pulled out, but he needs to be attended."

She nodded. "Today and tomorrow, I must go to the families of the fallen to console them. You and I should go to the house of Balam first."

"Yes, I owe him a great debt," I said.

"As do I."

The house of Balam was surrounded by a low wall enclosing a courtyard. As we approached, Ix Kutz stood at the gate with her arms around Ahau and Cimi. Her eyes searched the ranks of the returning warriors for Balam and did not find him.

"Ix Kutz," I said, "Balam has been wounded, but he will live. You must tend him so that he can regain his strength."

Ix Kutz trembled slightly and Zazil Ha comforted her. Ahau was crying softly, but Cimi looked up at me with a steady gaze.

"But Dzul," she said, "how could you let them hurt my father?"

I felt as if the arrow had struck me instead. In fact, the way Cimi looked at me, I almost wished it had. I got down on one knee and put my hand on her shoulder.

"Cimi, your father is a warrior and sometimes a warrior gets hurt. You must be a brave warrior too, and help your mother make him well again."

She bit her trembling lip, holding back the tears. "I will be brave."

Balam was brought to the house and placed on a low platform where Ix Kutz could tend to him. He was conscious now, but very weak. The family gathered round and began the healing. I looked at Zazil Ha. She was having the same thought; Balam would recover quickly with such support. I reached over and squeezed her hand. She looked at me and smiled a smile of understanding.

The next week, I was summoned to the house of the Batab, where Chan Oc congratulated me on our victory and talked about the importance of the warriors. Then, almost as an afterthought, he said, "Gonz-lo, you have permission to wed my daughter, Zazil Ha."

I stammered some sort of thanks and almost ran from the chamber. At the door, Zazil Ha waited with a smile on that lovely face.

We embraced, but she turned away when I tried to kiss her.

"Please, we must be discreet. The people will tolerate much from me, but I do not wish to test the limits of their indulgence. There will be time for that later, in private."

"All right," I said, reluctantly. "What happens now?"

"My father has already conferred with the elders and will make our marriage known to the people. We are to be wed in one month."

I went straight to Balam's house to see how he was doing and to tell them the news. As usual, Cimi was there to greet me.

"Dzul, do you know what? My father is better. He can't walk yet, but he can sit up and talk. He still sleeps a lot, though. Why does he do that? Is he still tired from the battle?"

"No, Cimi," I said, "Sleep lets your body rest so it can get

101

well. The more he sleeps the better he will feel. You have to help him."

"I know," she said, nodding vigorously. "Mother says I have to be quiet while my father is sleeping. Today I said 'I'll be quiet, mother. I'll be so quiet, you won't even know I'm here. I won't make a sound. Everyone will wonder where Cimi went because it will be so quiet. My lips will be so tight together, it will look like I'm frowning at something. You will be so proud of me for being so quiet. I'll be the quietest child you ever saw.' "

"And what did she say to that?" I asked.

"She said to be quiet, only she said it so loud she woke my father up. Sometimes I just don't understand big people," she sighed.

Balam was awake and Ix Kutz was with him. They were both happy to see me.

"I'm glad to see you looking better," I said "It will take more than an arrow to keep you down."

He smiled. "My recovery is because of Ix Kutz, not because of any great strength on my part."

"Yes," I replied, "and the fact that Cimi is being so quiet."

Ix Kutz laughed. "That child could talk a monkey out of a tree."

We talked for a few more minutes, then I told them of my appointment and my upcoming marriage to Zazil Ha. To my surprise, Balam looked worried.

"What is troubling you?" I asked.

"My concern is with the marriage," he said thoughtfully.

"What?" I couldn't believe what I was hearing. Balam, of all people should appreciate the desirability of a marriage based on love.

"Your marriage to Zazil Ha will be affected by more than simply you and Zazil Ha. There could be....consequences."

"What do you mean?" I said, still not following him.

"Ever since our alliance with Dzilpan three years ago, Pom

Tzec, the Batab of that city, has sought to wed Zazil Ha. Some say it is the real reason he sought the alliance in the first place. Chan Oc has been skillfully avoiding either accepting or refusing outright."

"But why?"

"Chan Oc does not want to lose the security the alliance brings, but he will not promise Zazil Ha to one such as Pom Tzec either," he said, sitting up slightly. "Pom Tzec is an evil man. He and his nobles rule the people of Dzilpan by terror and blood sacrifices."

"But we also sacrifice," I reminded him.

"In Ixil, we sacrifice prisoners when there is some special event or time of troubles. There are perhaps five or ten captives sacrificed each year. In Dzilpan, Pom Tzec sacrifices any captive unfortunate enough to fall into his hands, and he often sacrifices his own people, using the practice as a way to remove those who might oppose him. He is a man of great appetites for food, drink and women. He met Zazil Ha three years ago and vowed to have her for his own. Zazil Ha was repulsed by him, and swore she would die rather than submit to him. And so Chan Oc has neither refused nor accepted, until now. Now Pom Tzec will know that Zazil Ha has not only married someone else, but a dzul as well. It could mean war with Dzilpan."

Nothing in this land was simple, it seemed. Everything had unforeseen consequences, and the consequences were often deadly.

Chapter 13- Marriage

In which I marry the love of my heart, but cause more danger

For people who love large, elaborate ceremonies, the Maya have a surprisingly simple marriage ritual. Once, when I was about 15, a cousin got married and I remember how long and complex the planning, the ceremony, the reception dinner, and the entire ritual was. Knowing the Maya, I would have thought that they would make a week long affair out of it, at least. Instead, I was not allowed to see Zazil Ha for two weeks prior, but the ritual itself consisted mostly of a banquet at the house of the Batab followed by speeches from Chan Oc and a few of the elders, and finally, a short ceremony. An outdoor area had been enclosed, covered with a thatched roof, and heavily decorated with flowers and hanging banners made of multicolored feathers. A small house had been built next to the house of the Batab and Zazil Ha and I would be expected to live there.

Zazil Ha, as always, was completely poised and regal looking, appearing almost to float rather than walk. She was wearing a long white dress trimmed in a rich pattern of red, yellow, and black. Her normally straight hair was braided and coiled with flowers giving her the appearance of a goddess. Never have I seen a woman, however beautiful she might be, give out such an aura of charm and intelligence. I wished that my parents and Hectore and Maria and Uncle Fernando could have been there. They would never have approved of the religious aspects of the ceremony, of course, but I think they would have been proud to have Zazil Ha in the Guerrero family.

The actual ceremony consisted of Zazil Ha and I tying the

ends of our mantles together to symbolize our union, then reciting a short prayer at four points around the room representing the four cardinal directions. The points were marked by four poles painted with the colors of the directions: white for north, yellow for south, red for east, and black for west. When we finished our prayers at the final pole, we were husband and wife.

So Zazil Ha, who I had once thought unattainable, was now my wife. From the instant I had first seen her standing in the doorway of the house of the memories, I had been enchanted by her. My goal had changed from escaping to winning her favor. When I had found that she loved me, even the specter of impending death couldn't dampen my happiness. Now she was my wife, and I felt myself among the very few people in this world who can say they have all they want. I had come to the new world seeking treasure, and I had found it beyond all expectations.

There was more feasting and a few impromptu speeches, as well as the interesting sight of Chac Pacal tripping over a pot of flowers after he had too much balche. Finally, well after midnight, we went to our new home. We talked of the wedding for a while, comparing notes, then, as if by signal, we embraced.

"Zazil Ha, I have loved you since I saw you in the house of the memories. You have filled my thoughts and my dreams. I once told you that every moment away from you was empty. Every word I said was true. I will love you and care for you until the day I die."

"Gonzalo," she said softly, "I too felt a stirring at the house of the memories." Her breath felt warm on my neck as she spoke. "You were a slave, but had a spirit that drew me to you. I was troubled by my feelings until we met at the banquet, and you were a warrior. Still, I resisted any feeling toward you, until you spoke to me words of endearment. No one had ever spoken to me that way before. I have been sought by princes and Batabs, but until I saw you, I did not know love."

There was a silence, then we began to get undressed. The house was dark, the only light being the faint glow from the moon outside. The hum of the crickets softly serenaded us. Otherwise, there was no sound. She untied the sash from her waist and removed her jade necklace and bracelets, carefully placing then on a niche in the corner. She began to fumble with her dress, then stopped.

"Gonzalo," she said, almost too faintly to hear, "I don't know what women in Castile are like, but ..." Her voice trailed off, then she tried again. "You will...that is..."

"Yes?" I reached out and stroked her cheek. I had never seen Zazil Ha at a loss for words. What could be troubling her? Suddenly, I realized she was nervous. For all her poise and sophistication, Zazil Ha must have led a somewhat sheltered life, at least where men were concerned. Besides, most Indian women were taught to be passive in the bedroom, regarding lovemaking as a duty rather than a pleasure. The prospect of sex, especially with a foreigner must have been daunting.

"Never mind," I said, kissing her cheek. "There's nothing to fear."

I gently slipped her dress over her head and Zazil Ha stood naked in front of me. The smooth contours of her body seemed to glow faintly in the moonlight. She was beauty, grace, and desire all in one. I kissed her lips, then her neck, as I gently placed her on the bed platform. She was still somewhat stiff and apprehensive, but her body was smooth and soft to the touch as I embraced her and whispered endearments. As gently as I could, I coupled with her and she tensed, then sighed softly as our bodies locked together and we slowly made love. She didn't say a word, or react in any way; she just laid there with her eyes wide and I was afraid she was in pain.

Finally, I lay next to her without speaking, wondering if

she was all right but she continued her silence. Finally, she turned to me.

"Gonzalo?" she said softly.

"Yes?"

"Could we do that again?"

The next day, I was back at the warrior compound again. There was some good natured jesting at my expense by Can Pec and Balam, but otherwise, it was the same as any other day.....almost.

Cuac Caan summoned me into the house of the jaguars. I sensed that he was somewhat disappointed to find that my wedding night had not killed me, for his eyes narrowed as he regarded me with malevolence.

"So now you have married the daughter of Chan Oc." He almost spat the words. "The gods have favored you so far, but the favors of the gods shift with the winds. When that happens, where will you turn? To your real homeland?" His deep, croaking voice was almost shaking with rage. "In the great cycle of time, all things return to their source. Hear me, Gonz-lo. The day will come when you will betray the Mayan people and run to your own. When that day comes, I will be there, and by the gods, I will kill you with my own hands."

With that startling statement. Cuac Caan turned and stalked out of the jaguar house and away toward the pyramid. I was so stunned, I was speechless for once. My heart raced with both anger and fear as I tried to decide if my position was strong enough to challenge him. Sooner or later, I knew I would have to.

Cuac Caan did not appear again that day or for several days after, and I tried to put the incident out of my mind and concentrate on my upcoming dinner with my new in-laws.

My new father-in-law proved to be a most interesting person, as was his wife, Box Naab. Zazil Ha and I dined with them that night, as was traditional. Chan Oc was seated on a mat that was covered with a jaguar skin. He wore his usual jaguar skin mantle and heavy green feathered headdress, along with layers of heavy jade jewelry. Zazil Ha's mother, Box Naab was seated to his right. This was unusual in Mayan society, because women usually ate apart from the men. If Zazil Ha was any indication, however, the women in the Batab's household were of an independent turn of mind. Box Naab wore a white dress with heavy embroidered trim along with only slightly less jewelry than Chan Oc. Her hair and her headdress had been woven together to create a spectacular effect that seemed to float around her head. Zazil Ha, of course, looked radiant as always in what looked like the same white dress with red trim that she had worn the day we had met.

We sat cross legged on black spotted yellow jaguar furs and faced each other across a low plank table. Cups of balche were brought and Chan Oc started the proceedings.

"Gonz-lo, you have wed the daughter of my flesh. It has pleased the gods that you do so and it has pleased us as well."

I didn't have any idea what the protocol was, so I responded as best I could. "Lord Chan Oc, Zazil Ha is the love of my heart and I will cherish her and protect her and serve the house of Chan Oc."

He nodded, and Box Naab spoke up. She was as poised and elegant as her daughter, and spoke with the same cool intelligence.

"Tell us of Castile and the land called Spain," she said.

I told them about Castile as I had done before, but this time, they asked numerous questions and seemed to be absorbing everything. Chan Oc asked about military matters and politics and Box Naab asked about religion, education, and the role of women. Zazil Ha jumped into the discussion and soon the conversation was flying off in all directions, covering the comparative religions, diets, clothing, technology and philosophies of Castilians and the Maya. Box Naab seemed to have an intellectual outlook and was interested in fine points of religion and philosophy. Chan Oc was more absorbed in practical matters such as military tactics, crop yields, tools, and weapons. Zazil Ha seemed to combine both these outlooks with a mind that could grasp philosophy or farming with equal dexterity.

Finally, the food was served; tortillas, corn, turkey, monkey meat, dog, squash cooked with chilies, and bowls of the foamy rich drink made from cocoa beans called chocolate.

We ate with our fingers from common bowls placed between us. Small helpings of meat and corn were placed in a tortilla and wrapped up into a tube that was then eaten. I had cooked tortillas myself, as a slave. Corn flour was made into a batter that was cooked on a flat stone spanning over a small fire. The result was an unleavened fried bread in flat round pieces about as big as your hand.

During the meal, I asked about the Maya and their history.

"We are an ancient people," said Box Naab. "We have borne the burden of time through the ages from the birth of the gods. Our priests have charted the heavens, and our builders have raised temples to the gods. Many Katuns ago, our land was invaded by the Toltecs, a warrior people from the west. They brought new gods, gods who demanded blood. They built their temples at Chichen Itza and many other places. But the building took too many from the milpas and could not be sustained. In some places, there were bloody revolts. Today, the Toltecs have been absorbed by the Maya, but the land has never regained its former glory. The temples are mostly abandoned, or, as in Ixil, used by descendants of the builders. Throughout the lands of the Maya, people live among the remains of a civilization they cannot regain. But in the cycles of time, the age of glory will return."

"What is meant by the 'burden of time'?"

109

"Our people have been commanded by the gods to be the timekeepers and to keep the sacred calendar. Each day is the day of a different god and the fortunes of men depend on that god's favor. There are rituals and ceremonies to please each of the gods on each of the days, so careful records must be kept of the cycle of time. The calendar repeats the sequence of days every 52 years. But there is also a sacred calendar that keeps the time from the beginning of the world and can predict the cycles for thousands and millions of years to come."

This devilishly complex timekeeping system was giving me a headache, so I asked about something else.

"Why there is so much fighting among the cities?"

Chan Oc laughed. "That is our way. People of the Mayab are not united, but are broken up into smaller lands under individual Batabs. We are independent and resent being ruled from afar. That is why our alliances are always shifting and the present federations such as the Ecab, the Cocom, the Ah Canul, and the Cupul Maya are so loose. To be a Maya means to serve the gods, to struggle to grow corn and to fight against your neighbor. It has always been so."

"Lord Chan Oc," I said, "we fight among ourselves in Castile, also, but we band together against a common foe."

"Let us hope the Maya could do the same," said Chan Oc, "but there is no common foe, so we fight among ourselves. You, Gonz-lo, will help us be strong in the face of our enemies. We must always be on guard against Pom Tzec and Dzilpan."

"Is an attack likely?"

Chan Oc shrugged. "That is for the gods to decide. Pom Tzec is treacherous and unpredictable, but he is seldom foolish. He is aware of our growing strength because of the tactics you have devised, so he realizes we will not be as anxious to preserve the alliance with Dzilpan, so we will have no need to agree to his constant demands for concessions."

"Such as marriage to Zazil Ha," said Box Naab.

110

Now we had gotten to the heart of the matter. My marriage to Zazil Ha had served several purposes for the wily Chan Oc. The advantages I had pointed out were only part of the picture. He had wanted to avoid a union with Pom Tzec, both for Zazil Ha's sake and because he didn't trust him. But the threat from Xcalampak made a military alliance necessary for defense, so Pom Tzec was put off but not actually refused. Since Dzilpan was the closest city of any size, Zazil Ha's betrothal to a nobleman from another city would have caused an alliance by marriage with another Batab who would be too far away to be a useful ally. But when Zazil Ha married me, the pressure to marry Pom Tzec was eliminated without the provocation of alignment with another city. At the same time, our growing military strength made our dependence on Dzilpan's favor lessen. Pom Tzec had lost his advantages. But, would my marriage to Zazil Ha provoke an attack on Ixil?

"Pom Tzec is as crafty as he is untrustworthy," said Chan Oc. "If he attacks, it will only be after careful deliberation. He may be enraged by Zazil Ha's marriage, but he won't act in undue haste. He prepares well and will be hard to surprise."

"The holcom will be ready," I said.

"Good," said Chan Oc nodding his head. "In two months time, if no attack comes, you will travel to Coba and then to Cozumel with Zazil Ha and a party of warriors. The purpose of the trip, you will make known, is to seek the favor of the goddess Ixchel, whose shrine is on Cozumel.

"Ixchel..." I said, "Oh, yes. The goddess of the moon."

"She is also the goddess of childbirth."

"Oh."

"It is our custom for young brides to travel to the temple of Ixchel on Cozumel to ask for children and easy childbirth," said Box Naab.

"But there is another reason for the trip," said Chan Oc. "You will stop at Coba on the way. It is a city to the north. There you will meet with a merchant named Tolatl to discuss

111

opening new trade routes for Ixil. You will be my personal representative. If I send anyone else, word could get back to Pom Tzec and he would act to undermine any separate arrangement we might make. Ixil produces honey, cloth, jewelry, knives and other tools. Until recently, Xcalampak could cut off the northern trade routes at will, making it impossible to establish ourselves there, but now, we have a chance to open up a new market."

"Who is this Tolatl?" I asked. "Tolatl is not a Mayan name."

"Tolatl is a potecha, a traveling merchant from the land of the Mexica, far to the west. The Mexica, who some call the Aztecs, are a warrior nation, much like the Toltecs of long ago. They rule a vast empire of vassal states from their capital, Tenochtitlan. They are a bloodthirsty race, who sacrifice thousands to offer hearts to their war god; but they are also a rich nation that seeks trade."

So now I was to be a diplomat as well as a warrior. It was not what I expected when I left Castile, but it certainly was better than farming.

"Gonz-lo," Box Naab said, "you came to us as a dzul, but you are the one man Zazil Ha has found who makes her heart glad. You are part of our world now. You must be a part of the struggle to preserve that world. For if our world dies, so dies Zazil Ha and all who depend on you."

After more balche, Zazil Ha and I said goodbye and returned to our house. The sun had set and a soft evening rain had begun.

"Zazil Ha, Chan Oc has given me great power and responsibility, but will I be accepted into your world by your people?" I said.

She put her arms around my neck and pressed her lips on mine long and passionately. "What matters," she whispered directly in my ear, "is that you have been accepted into my heart."

I looked in her eyes and held her close, and we each glanced at the bed platform. Zazil Ha was always quick to learn new things, and lovemaking was no exception. Once she got over her initial apprehension on our wedding night, she found it enjoyable, so I looked forward to our nights together.

The rain was falling harder now. The sound beat a steady drumbeat on the ground and ran in silver streams from the thatch of the roof. We shed our clothes as we stood embracing, our ardor rising. The air was cool from the steady rain and we sank to the bed in each other's arms. Then, we could wait no more. When we finally coupled, the intensity was like the raging thunder and lightning that was now crossing the stormy sky.

Chapter 14- A Journey to Cozumel

In which I see more of the Mayan world and its customs

In the jaguar house the next day, I asked Balam if Cuac Caan had arrived yet.

"No," he replied. "Cuac Caan is gone."

"Gone? Gone where?"

Balam's fist was clenched around the handle of his war club. He looked both angry and concerned. "He has not been seen for five days. This morning a spy has reported him in Dzilpan with Pom Tzec. Cuac Caan has gone over to our enemy."

We had spies watching Dzilpan, but there was no reaction or sign of preparations for an attack. Pom Tzec's emissary expressed his congratulations on Zazil Ha's marriage and even sent a jade necklace as a present. No mention was made of Cuac Caan's defection, but he must have been advising Pom Tzec. Balam took over as senior Nacom and I was elected in his place.

"Cuac Caan will be a dangerous foe in the service of Pom Tzec." said Balam as we discussed the situation. It was a hot day and especially steamy due to a morning rainfall.

"We will have to change our tactics," I said. "If we ever fight Dzilpan and Cuac Caan has taught them our strategies, we are finished. I think we could use our bows to better advantage if they were longer and the arrows carried further."

Balam nodded. "Good. You and Can Pec see what can be done. I will increase the patrols just in case."

In spite of this uncertainty, our domestic life settled down somewhat. Zazil Ha saw me as not only a husband, but as a source for new information. Soon, she knew as much about Spain as I did. She even insisted that I teach her Spanish, which she picked up a lot faster than I had been able to learn Mayan. Like Chac Pacal, so many years before, I could deny her nothing.

We spent much of our time in long walks among the houses and milpas and forest. The more we wandered, the more evidence I saw of the vanished greatness Box Naab had spoken of. Large sections of what I had assumed to be forest were actually the overgrown remnants of a much larger city. There were hundreds of ruins of stone buildings with intricate carvings, all overgrown by vegetation. Trees had grown through stone walls and foundations, the roots prying apart the work of long dead masons. Ixil must have been at least five times as big as it was now. What I had taken to be a complete, if somewhat shabby city was only a better maintained section of the original. I had learned to look on the present Maya with respect, but I now regarded the previous inhabitants with awe.

One day, I determined to use my newly found power and influence to help my old friend de Aguiller, who, as far as I knew, was still a slave. If I could persuade him to be a little more flexible, perhaps he too could rise to a more comfortable position. After a few inquiries, I found that he was now in the service of a nobleman named Tax Matz who lived to the east. One day, I went to see him. It was cloudy and overcast and the walk took several hours. Tax Matz lived in an outlying area of Ixil. I approached the stone house I had been directed to and paid my respects to Tax Matz, a fat, affable man with a mischievous smile.

"Aguiller?" he said. "Oh, yes. One of my best servants; and loyal, too. He's in the back."

When I saw de Aguiller, he was wearing only a loincloth

115

and cutting firewood with a copper axe. Seeing us together, few would have suspected we were both shipmates from Spain not that long ago. At first, he did not recognize me, but when he did, he was delighted and his weary face lit up.

"Gonzalo! May God be praised! You are alive and well. I have prayed for you for all these past months."

"It is good to see you, my old friend," I said, grasping his hand. "God has preserved us both."

"I didn't recognize you at first, Gonzalo. You look like a Maya," he said with astonishment, and a questioning look.

"Jeronimo, I am a Maya," I said. Then I told him of my present station and how I had gotten there. He looked troubled.

"Gonzalo, we are in a heathen land and we must make the best of it, but we must not forsake our God and our people. The church teaches us to resist temptation and to trust in God for our deliverance. We must not become like the Indians," he said.

"Jeronimo," I replied. "We are in a land our countrymen do not even know exists. The closest Spanish settlement is probably 400 miles away. We can never leave, so we must adapt. If a Maya were stranded in Castile, would he be well advised to dress and act like a Maya or like a Spaniard? If you remain a Spaniard, then you will also remain a slave!"

"But Gonzalo," he sputtered, his indignation rising, "these people worship idols and cut the hearts out of strangers. You cannot wallow in the mud and expect to stay clean!"

"I don't agree with everything they do," I answered, "but I don't agree with the Inquisition either. Both the Maya and the Spaniards have their share of atrocity and stupidity. That doesn't mean I am a part of it."

"But Gonzalo," he said with an embarrassed look on his face, "The Church has not sanctioned your marriage. You.....you are living in sin with that woman."

I stiffened and choked back my anger. When I answered,

it was between clenched teeth. "Jeronimo, you are my friend and I owe you my life, but do not ever speak of Zazil Ha and sin in the same breath. The world is full of death, violence and hatred. Where two people share love such as ours, no god can call it sin."

He looked at me silently for a moment, then his disapproving gaze softened and he put his hand on my shoulder. "I'm sorry for my words, Gonzalo. You must answer to your conscience, not to me. I spoke out of turn. This Zazil Ha sounds like a fine woman. I will pray for her soul as well as yours."

We talked for another hour about the voyage, our old companions and the Maya. We spoke no more of our differences, but they were just below the surface. De Aguiller believed in fighting to retain your former habits, outlook and values. I had accommodated to my surroundings, and tried to understand, if not agree with the Maya and their world. I viewed de Aguiller as hopelessly impractical, while he viewed me as abandoning my values. As we talked, I was saddened to realize that we had chosen different paths, and as time went on, those divergent paths would take us farther and farther apart. As I went to leave, we said good bye for what might be the last time.

"Jeronimo," I said, "my uncle once told me that if I couldn't make the world a better place, I should at least try to keep it from getting worse. That is what I have done, and my conscience is clear. You and I once talked of saving these people for God. I am saving them from death and destruction at the hands of their enemies, and I have helped keep their world from getting worse."

He considered this for a moment, then he smiled his good natured smile of true Christian charity I remembered. "We must all serve Our Lord as best we are able. Our ways are different, but who can say where they will lead? God works in mysterious ways, and he could be working through you as well, Gonzalo. You will remain in my prayers. Goodbye, my friend. *Vaya con Dios*. Go with God."

I was overcome by a strange emptiness and sadness I couldn't quite explain. As I walked away down the path back toward the pyramid, I stopped once and looked back. De Aguiller was still standing by the wood pile watching me go, and making the sign of the cross.

One of the shortcomings of life among the Maya was their lack of horses or draft animals. I was already aware of how this lack of suitable animals made plowing impossible, but when we started out on the journey to Coba and Cozumel one hot morning, I would have given much for a few horses. Since the nearest horse was at least 400 miles away, however, the entire journey would have to be made on foot. As royalty, Zazil Ha could have been carried on a litter, but insisted on walking like everyone else.

The traveling party consisted of Zazil Ha and myself, five other women bound for Cozumel and their husbands, the scribe Akbal Dzib, an escort of 20 warriors, and another 20 slaves to carry our baggage, food, and trade goods. It was a colorful procession, with the ever-present feathered headdresses, mantles and feathered banners of the warriors and similar finery for the others. As pilgrims to the temple of Ixchel, we should be given safe passage, but with the Maya, you could never be sure, so the warriors stayed alert.

We traveled on the remains of a sacbe, or ceremonial road, linking Ixil and Coba. The road was mostly overgrown now, but was clear enough that we could see where it was and follow it. The name sacbe means white road because the road had been made with white stone, giving it a striking appearance. Since the land is mostly flat and featureless, the road had been built in a perfectly straight line.

We started passing ruined stone buildings when we were still half a day's journey from Coba. Many were no more than mounds, and others were still standing in various states of decay. On and on we walked and still the ruined buildings were all around us. Coba, in the time when it was fully inhabited must have been larger than Seville. Zazil Ha confirmed it.

"Yes, Coba was a mighty city. Its holcom was powerful and its trade reached the ends of our world. Today, only a small part is still inhabited, but it is still a trade center. That is why the merchants come here from far away," she said.

"With all these buildings," I said with a smile, "surely there is one in which we can be alone."

She smiled slyly and tilted her head in a way that almost made me forget our mission, and said "Perhaps.... We will see." As we got closer to the center, we passed a large lake. This was the first body of water I had seen since the shipwreck. I was even more surprised when Zazil Ha said that the lake had been constructed by the builders of the city. Soon, we passed another lake and saw a pyramid that was at least twice the size of the one in Ixil. I tried to imagine what this city of shimmering lakes, soaring pyramids and thousands of inhabitants must have been like at one time, and shook my head in amazement.

As we approached the center of the city, the buildings became more numerous and in better repair, though still shabby and overgrown. There were stone buildings and many houses of wood with thatched roofs. I saw no evidence of any new building of stone, and once again, I had the impression of squatters living in the remains of someone else's buildings. There were smaller houses of sticks and thatch for the use of travelers, since Coba was a center for traveling merchants and pilgrims to Cozumel alike. For a few cocoa beans, we obtained lodgings for the married men and women and larger roofed over places for the warriors and for the slaves.

"We must bathe after our journey," Zazil Ha said as we settled in. "We are dirty and wet with sweat. Let us go to the

119

lake."

This sounded like a good idea to me, so I went with her to the lake which was not far away. I was surprised to see that the rest of our party had the same thought and were already at the lake shore.

I should note here that the Maya have a very different view of bathing than Europeans. In Spain, bathing was thought to be unhealthy and was done infrequently. Some even thought the smell of sweat to be erotic, though I never shared that view. The Maya, however, bathed daily, and sometimes even more often. They bathed in cenotes and ponds and whatever water they could find. In addition, they also took a sweat bath in a small stone building heated with steam generated by dripping water on hot stones. Although the men and women seldom bathed together, they didn't hesitate to bathe naked in a public place.

This is what they were doing when we arrived. A group of naked men was bathing only about 100 feet from the naked women. No one seemed the least bit embarrassed by this display, and went about the business of washing completely unconcerned. I stood amazed at what I was seeing.

"By the saints," I said to Zazil Ha as I watched, "this would never be allowed in Castile. What are people thinking of?"

"What do you mean?" she said.

I turned to her to reply and was stunned to see that she had slipped off her dress and was standing there naked. My jaw quivered trying to form words. I had never seen her naked in full daylight before, and, had we been alone would have made passionate love to her right there. Her body was a honey brown in color and perfectly formed. Her long black hair tumbled over, but only partly concealed her breasts and nothing else. She was absolutely magnificent, but she was standing there for all to see!

"Zazil Ha," I finally stammered, "what are you doing?"

"Bathing, of course," she said laughing, and turned and

walked into the water.

That evening, we had our first argument as man and wife.

"How could you walk around naked in front of other men when you are my wife?" I demanded.

"Should I bathe fully clothed, then? I will not get very clean."

"You know what I mean," I said angrily. "Your body should not be for the pleasure of other men."

"What? Do you accuse me of lying with another?" She was outraged.

"Of course not! But other men have seen your body, even the parts that are for me alone," I said indignantly.

"For you alone? You have surely come far, Gonzalo. You were a slave owned by others and now, it seems, you own me!" She was raising her voice.

"I didn't say that," I protested, "I just don't think it is right to go naked in front of other men. In Castile, no proper lady would think of it."

"In Castile, you would not be married to the daughter of a Batab! Let your proper lady of Castile come to Coba and see how SHE bathes!"

"If she had to undress before men she would not bathe at all!" I said, and was immediately aware of how stupid it sounded.

Having found an opening, Zazil Ha then thrust her verbal sword in to the hilt. "Perhaps that is why you traveled so far away from Castile," she said sarcastically, "for some clean air to breathe!"

I tried to think of a retort, but, after a few seconds of silence, broke out in laughter. "All right; you win the contest. I know it is the way of the Maya, but it makes me uncomfortable."

She laughed too, and the tension was broken. "Perhaps I can make you comfortable," she whispered seductively.

And she did. That night, we joined together in a slow

121

sensual coupling that brought us to new heights of excitement and pleasure as I remembered how she had looked glowing in the afternoon sun.

Chapter 15- The Wind from the West

In which I encounter the Mexica and an old problem reappears

The marketplace of Coba was several times as big as the one in Ixil and served as a center for trade between the inland areas and the great trading canoes that plied the coast from ports at Tulum and Xelha. Throngs of people from all over the Maya world bartered and haggled over a staggering variety of goods. There were weapons, cloth, fresh killed game and foodstuffs and crops of all sorts, feathers, pottery, large jars of salt, jewelry, and even small gold ornaments. This was the first gold I had seen in the new world and the amount was small, but at least it existed. I had an uneasy feeling that it was fortunate that the existence of this gold was not known in Castile, or the land would be overrun.

The market was almost in the shadow of the pyramid that seemed to tower to the sky. No one had built anything of this magnitude here for a very long time, to judge by the weeds and disrepair of this mountain of stone. Zazil Ha, Balam, Akbal Dzib the scribe and I were looking for the Mexica traders and Tolatl under the awnings and canopies of cloth and thatch that lined the sprawling marketplace. As we rounded a corner by a broken stone column, we saw the Mexica merchants.

There were five of them and were seated under a red cloth canopy with yellow trim. They had a rich array of goods such as gold ornaments, tools and pieces of obsidian, the glass-like volcanic stone that was used to make knife blades, arrow heads, and the edges of war clubs. The merchants, or potechas as they were called, were dressed in clothing that was modest, but of good quality. One appeared to be the leader, and I asked if he was Tolatl.

"That is my name. I am a humble potecha of the Mexica. May I be of service?" he said, in an accent that I had not heard before. He was a tall, slight man with a thin moustache that drooped at the corners of his mouth. He wore a red mantle with black trim that was similar to those of the Maya except that, instead of being tied, the ends were held at the neck by a gold clasp. His hair was cut short with a part in the middle and a wide head band with several green feathers.

"I am Gonzalo of Ixil. This is Akbal Dzib and Balam. (Zazil Ha had faded into the crowd, since women were not allowed to negotiate trade agreements.)

He smiled and nodded. "Oh yes, I have heard of this place. You have recently become stronger, have you not?"

I was surprised that he knew this, and noted that his sources of information must be excellent.

"That is true. So we now have cleared the trade routes and have begun to consider several new arrangements regarding where to direct our merchants, and which merchants to invite to trade in return."

He nodded, still smiling. "And you would do well to trade with the Mexica." This seemed somewhat presumptuous, but I let him continue. "The riches of our empire are limitless and we too seek suitable outlets. What you see here is only a small sample of what we can trade. As for the bounty of Ixil, I understand your weaving is superb."

This negotiation continued for over an hour before we agreed on the terms of the trade. The first visit would be in six months. I was disappointed in the long wait.

"It is regrettable, I agree," said Tolatl shaking his head. "But I am due to return to the capitol of the Mexica, Tenochtitlan, and the journey is a long one."

"Tell us of this Tenol..."

"Tenochtitlan," he laughed. "Many find our tongue difficult, but Tenochtitlan is a wondrous place. Imagine a city the size of Coba, but with every building in good repair and in use. The city is built on a series of islands in Lake Texcoco in the central highlands many days journey from here. The only access is by boat or by one of several causeways. From the heights around the lake, Tenochtitlan shines white in the sunlight. The city is crossed by a series of canals that allow us to move people and goods with ease. Along the canals are wondrous gardens of trees and flowers. The climate is temperate and the land to the farthest horizon is under our control and pays tribute to the ruler, the great Moctezuma."

"I have heard there is a great pyramid at the center big enough to support two temples," said Akbal Dzib.

"Yes, there is a pyramid dedicated to the rain god Tlaloc, and the war god Huitzilopochtli. This is where the sacrifices are made several times a day to ensure the favor of the gods."

"Several times a day?" I said, appalled.

"Of course," he replied matter-of-factly. "The gods have given us much and demand much in return. Without the nourishment of human hearts, the gods could destroy us, but so long as we do the will of the gods, we are invincible. No power on earth can defeat the Mexica."

From what I had heard of the Mexica, or Aztecs as some called them, he was probably right. They had vast armies, an inaccessible fortress capitol and were utterly bloodthirsty and ruthless. I shivered to think of what would happen to the first Castilians who tried to invade their domain. The Maya were hundreds of small states forever squabbling among themselves, but the Aztecs were a solid, centrally ruled empire as powerful as Rome in its day.

When we again met Zazil Ha and started back to our quarters, she was disgusted to hear of the sacrifices practiced by the Aztecs.

"These people are nothing but bloodthirsty upstarts," she said, contemptuously. "They were wandering naked in the deserts when our people were charting the heavens and building temples that reached for the sun. Now they agree to trade with us some of the riches they have stolen from more worthy peoples. Are we supposed to be grateful?"

"Naked in the deserts?" I asked.

"The Aztecs are newcomers." answered Akbal Dzib. "They came from a place called Azatlan only a few hundred years ago and became servants and mercenary warriors for the established peoples around Lake Texcoco. But they grew and through warfare, alliances and treachery became the rulers of the vast empire they now control. They may be upstarts, but they are very successful upstarts; and their wealth, no matter how they obtained it, makes them valuable trading partners."

"Their trade will enrich Ixil," said Zazil Ha. "But it sickens me to deal with these bloodthirsty demons."

I thought this attitude was somewhat self-righteous coming from the people who had cut the heart out of Ortega, but I saw her point; embracing the Mexica while keeping them at arms length could become a problem.

With our trade arrangements with Tolatl and the Mexica finalized, we departed the next day for Cozumel. The route took us through the forest to the seacoast town of Xcaret, from which pilgrims departed by boat to the island. Although we passed several swamps, other sections looked barren, and the forest was thin, as if struggling to survive. As we approached Xcaret, we started to pass travelers who were returning from Cozumel.

The town of Xcaret, itself, was a handful of stone buildings nestled among a few dozen small huts made of sticks and thatch, but at the edge of town was a small inlet and a white sand beach lined with palms and giving onto a sea of brilliant blue-green. Along the beach were lines of long canoes and many more either on their way to Cozumel, or returning. There seemed to be an almost constant flow of people going to and from Cozumel, and this trade seemed to be the base of the economy of Xcaret. In a way, it was almost a smaller, Mayan version of Seville, with Cozumel as the traveler's destination rather than the new world.

Cozumel means Island of the Swallows, and we arrived at the beach in the late afternoon. We had crossed over in a large canoe that Akbal Dzib had arranged. It was very much like the one the drunken sailor had described to me in the tavern in Seville. The blue-green waters sparkled under a brilliant blue sky. As I paddled, I could see features of the sea bottom through the clear waters. Below us we saw a great forest of plants, as well as fish and sea life of bright colors and great size.

We beached the canoe and made our way to the first shrine before stopping for the night. This shrine was small and primarily for a safe journey to and from the island. Zazil Ha and the women placed small pieces of jade and grains of corn on a small altar already crowded with such items. They then said a few prayers, and we set off to find a place to stay.

The next morning, Zazil Ha led the other women to the principal shrine of Ixchel. The shrine was a temple with one large room and numerous smaller ones that were barely big enough for one person. The shrine was oriented to catch the sun and consequently was bright and almost cheerful, especially compared to the dark gloomy temples on top of the pyramids. There was a statue of Ixchel and a long carved stone alter that was piled high with offerings of corn, jade, jewelry, small statues, gold ornaments, or cocoa beans. Many women offered blood from their earlobes or tongues as well, a practice that was usually not allowed in other temples. There were bowls on either side of the statue to receive blood, but some would smear it directly on the statue, as the priests do with the blood of sacrifice victims in the temples.

The name Ixchel means "lady of the rainbow", though the statue depicted a figure far less attractive than that name would imply. Ixchel was the wife of Itzamna and the mother of the other gods. For this reason, I suppose, she was also the goddess of childbirth, so every Maya woman who was able came to her shrine to pray for children and for a safe and easy delivery. I remembered what Zazil Ha had said about Ixchel being the Mayan counterpart of the Virgin Mary, and had to admit there were parallels. Late in the afternoon, Zazil Ha and I slipped away together to a shady beach to watch the sun go down.

"The sun is born in the east." she said as we sat waiting for the sun to set. "That is why the Maya color for east is red. But the sun dies each night in the west, so the color for the west is black."

"No more Maya religion today," I said, drawing her close to me. "The day is ending and there is only you and me. Nothing else matters."

"Do you know what I prayed at the shrine today?" she said, looking out to sea, "I prayed for strong children who had the best of each of us. I also prayed for Ixchel to watch over you."

I nodded. "In Spain there is a river called the Guadalquivir that leads from Seville to the sea. At the place where the river meets the great sea there is a place very much like this one. Some days I would sit on that beach much as we are sitting here now, and I would watch the great ships setting out for the new world with sails set and banners flying in the sea winds. I always thought there was some great treasure awaiting me at the end of that journey, and I was right."

We sat in silence for a few moments, her head on my shoulder, then with mischief in her voice, she said "Do you still forbid your poor wife to bathe in the open?"

"Well," I said, taking the hint, "perhaps not if I am present to escort her."

"Good," she replied, pulling her dress over her head, "Then you may escort her now."

So, laughing and playing, we both bathed naked in the

waves on the deserted white beach as the sun went down. We splashed each other, then washed each other, then caressed each other. Her body glistened in the fading light and tasted cool and salty from the sea water. Then, as the sun began to sink from sight, we made love on a grassy area beneath a palm. Finally, our passion spent, we lay coiled together as the soft sea breezes rustled the palm branches overhead. The horizon glowed red and we thought that this was as close to heaven as two people were ever likely to get on this earth.

The next day, we departed for home by way of a city called Tulum to the south. Late in the afternoon, we got our first glimpse of the place. The setting was dramatic; square stone buildings painted blue with red trim stood on a rocky bluff overlooking the sea. There was no pyramid, or any building that was of impressive size, but Tulum seemed better maintained than other cities. Unlike Coba, where people inhabited a small part of a once great city, Tulum seemed to be fully inhabited. A stone wall surrounded the place and a white sand beach between two temples provided a landing place for canoes. Tulum looked like a vision from another world. The temples perched on rock cliffs on either side of the landing beach seemed much bigger than they actually were as we beached the canoe. We climbed the slope up from the beach and found ourselves in the middle of the city. Although Tulum was in good repair, it was small in scale. The biggest temple was only about the size of a parish church and the other buildings seemed to be of poor quality. The stonework, instead of being carved, was decorated with thick layers of plaster, indicating that though the Maya could still build, they had lost much of their artistry and craftsmanship. We didn't linger in Tulum, however, and were soon on our way back to Ixil.

In two days, we arrived back at Ixil. There was still no trouble from Pom Tzec and Cuac Caan, but the city was on edge. As I grappled with this problem, other events were occurring in Ixil.

Almost a year had passed since my refusal to sacrifice my captive at the top of the pyramid. The condition of my escape was that I would have one year to prove myself a true son of Ixil. There was little doubt that I had proven myself; even rumors spread by Cuac Caan and Ah Kin Mu couldn't succeed in tarnishing my standing. Of course, my marriage to Zazil Ha hadn't harmed my popularity either. But now I faced the same problem as before; how to avoid the sacrifice. Not only was I personally repelled by the idea, but I couldn't do it simply because of Zazil Ha's opposition to sacrifices. So I searched for a way out.

"You can't do it, you know," said Zazil Ha one night. We had just finished a particularly strenuous and delightful session of frenzied lovemaking, and we were lying on the sleeping platform with our arms loosely wrapped around each other's naked bodies. She was lightly stroking my back as I lay idly nuzzling her ear and neck.

"Mmmmmm....." I replied. I was not at my most eloquent at such moments.

"You can't sacrifice a captive," she continued. "You would be betraying everything we believe in."

"What?" I muttered, somewhat indistinctly because I was still chewing on her earlobe.

"I'm serious, Gonzalo," she said, slipping into Spanish. We often spoke in Spanish when we were saying something that we didn't want anyone to overhear.

"Yes, I know you are," I said. "But how can I refuse a second time?"

"There must be a way," she said, "My father is sympathetic, but even he must follow tradition, lest the gods be angered."

We were both sitting up now, earnestly discussing our dilemma.

"Tradition!" I said in disgust. "Must something be done over and over simply because it was done before?"

"Of course," she said, "that is what tradition means. And tradition is strong among the Maya. You know that."

"Wait," I said suddenly, "maybe that is the answer. The council meets with Ah Kin Mu the priest in three weeks time to discuss religious matters. I will attend that meeting."

Chapter 16- Traditions

In which Ah Kin Mu strikes, and I become a father

One day at the warrior compound, Ix Kutz came by to see Balam. She had brought along Cimi who was sitting on a low wall with her legs dangling and Ix Chan in her lap. If anything, Cimi had grown even more curious and inquisitive in the year and a half since I had come to Ixil. And she was the only person in Ixil who still called me dzul.

"Hello, Dzul," she said enthusiastically, "Mother brought me here while she talks to my father. I like coming to the warrior place. There are so many people trying to hit each other. Do they get hurt when they get hit? My father got hurt, but he got all better and I helped. Did you know that?"

"Yes, Cimi, I knew that," I replied as she took a breath.

"That man over there is trying to hit three men, and they are all trying to hit him. I don't think that is fair," she said

"Well, Cimi," I replied, "they are just practicing that way so they will be able to fight three people if they have to." The three man attack was a drill I had started to help give our perpetually outnumbered warriors some hope of survival.

"One person fighting three people?" she said, wrinkling her nose, "That isn't fair. If the other warriors want to attack you like that, you shouldn't let them." she said in a tone that indicated that this was the final word on the matter.

I laughed to myself. "Well, Cimi, you always seem to know more than anybody. I'll remember your advice."

"That man has water coming out of his stomach," she said, indicating a warrior who was urinating against a tree on the far side of the compound, "Did he get stuck with a spear?"

A few weeks later, Zazil Ha announced she was going to have our first child, and for once, I was speechless. Zazil Ha became the focus of attention in Ixil when her pregnancy became known. Strangers stopped me on the streets to offer congratulations and advice, and Can Pec kept talking about "another warrior". Balam said he hoped the baby would be born on a Cimi day so there would be two of them. That way, they could talk to each other, and the rest of us would get a chance to say something. As for Cimi, herself, she was so excited, I thought she would burst, although she didn't fully understand just what was going to happen. It was the only time I have ever seen her not know what to say.

Chan Oc and Box Naab acted like expectant grandparents everywhere, and waited eagerly for the arrival, bragging to the elders whenever they got the chance. Box Naab visited her daughter more frequently, usually accompanied by an old woman who was the Maya equivalent of a midwife, much to the dismay of Zazil Ha.

"I appreciate my mother's concern," she said one day, "but why does she have to tell me stories of women who died giving birth or who were in childbirth for days before delivering? If she is trying to change my mind, she is too late."

"Well, I'm sure she is only..."

"And the midwife! " Zazil Ha continued, throwing up her arms, "All she does is ask about your private parts. She keeps asking if they are the same as those of a Maya. She must think the baby will have two heads."

"And are they?" I asked.

"What?"

"Are they the same as those of a Maya?"

"The next time we are all bathing in Coba, you can see for yourself," she replied dryly. "I will invite the midwife along. She might find it instructional."

The next day was the meeting of the council with the chief

133

priest, Ah Kin Mu to discuss religious issues that had arisen in the last month or so. With Cuac Caan in Dzilpan, Ah Kin Mu was the only one still determined to undermine me in Ixil, and I was wary of facing him on what was essentially a religious issue.

The council of the elders along with Chan Oc sat on a raised dais under a thatched canopy in the courtyard of the Batab's house. They sat cross legged on a long mat and all wore their most elaborate and top heavy headdresses, some as much as three feet high. They looked like a flock of peacocks. Ah Kin Mu stood to the side with his blackened face, tangled hair, and long white robe, looking like a walking nightmare. Usually, these meetings were formal, dull affairs, since few religious problems arose. But I knew that Ah Kin Mu would be reminding them that my year was up, and it was time for me to make at least one sacrifice of a captive. I had asked to speak to the council and had a counterargument prepared. A great deal had changed since the previous year, including my marriage to Zazil Ha and impending parenthood. My position was far more secure, and I felt they would be well disposed to listen to me.

"One year ago, the gods were affronted when a sacrifice was not carried out as dictated by tradition," Ah Kin Mu began. I noticed he was being careful not to mention me by name, but was trying to make it purely a religious issue. "The gods have seen fit to grant us continued good fortune in the year that has elapsed, but we can tempt fate no longer. We must take steps to reestablish the tradition dictated by the gods for the good of Ixil."

"And how do we do that?" asked Chac Pacal

"We must require that the one who refused to sacrifice become a full participant in the rite," Ah Kin Mu answered smoothly.

There was talking among the elders. Clearly, they would have preferred not to have to deal with this question. Chan Oc

134

glared at Ah Kin Mu, but said nothing.

Now was the time. I rose to my feet.

"My lords," I began, "I would address the council."

"Proceed, Gonz-lo," one of them said.

"My lords, Ah Kin Mu is right," I began, and paused while they recovered. "The gods value tradition, and they show us that they value tradition by bestowing good fortune on us when we follow those traditions. During the long history of Ixil, no one not born in Ixil has ever sacrificed a captive on the pyramid. (Zazil Ha had found this out from Akbal Dzib) One year ago, Ixil almost broke that tradition, risking the wrath of the gods. But, in the end, the tradition was upheld. Since that time, we have had a good harvest, grown in strength, and obtained a trade agreement with the vast markets of the Mexica nation. Surely, the gods have shown us that they approve of continuing the tradition of only those born in Ixil conducting sacrifices. Let us heed the clear message of the gods and continue that tradition."

"No!" shouted Ah Kin Mu, leaping to his feet in a rage, and waving his arms wildly. "Are we to be instructed in the will of the gods by a dzul? Before he came here as a slave, this man had never heard of the gods, now he claims to know their will! If he wishes to know the minds of the gods, let him study to become a priest. He can start by making the sacrifice!"

Ah Kin Mu was lashing out in frustration, afraid that I would slip off the hook once again. He stalked around in a half crouch while he raved, his thin arms and legs making him look like a malevolent spider. When he was finished, the council conferred for a few minutes while I held my breath.

"We have a conflict of traditions, Ah Kin Mu," said Chac Pacal finally, "But the good fortune of the last year is unmistakable. The council has decided that only those born in Ixil should sacrifice."

I thanked the council and bowed. I had won.

135

By now, Zazil Ha was close to the time to give birth. She was as competent at pregnancy as she was at everything else, and carried the life within her with ease and grace. Finally, one day she was grinding corn meal and stopped suddenly. She was still, almost holding her breath, as if waiting for some sign. Then, a few minutes later, she told me to get the midwives.

That afternoon, our first son was born, and named 3 Chuen, for the day of his birth. The midwife was relieved to find that he only had one head. He had thin black hair and somewhat Spanish features. When I first saw my child peering out of the blanket, all tiny, wrinkled and red, I was in awe of miracle of birth, and I had an overwhelming feeling of the sacredness and continuity of life. Seeing this baby I had helped bring into this world, I was more certain than ever that in spite of the differences in our cultures, Zazil Ha and I would endure.

According to Maya custom, Chuen was washed twice after birth, and wrapped in a red cloth. I said a few silent prayers to the Virgin Mary as well, just to be on the safe side. Zazil Ha looked tired and there were drops of perspiration on her forehead as she held Chuen.

"Do you know who this is?" she asked me. I thought it was a strange question.

"Of course. Our son," I said.

She smiled. "He is more than that. This baby is the very first to be born of mixed blood between the Maya and the Castilians. The day will come when many more from your land will be here. There will be much hardship, and many will be born of mixed blood, but Chuen is the first."

"Certainly he is the first," I replied, "but the others may never come."

"They will come," she said. "They will come."

The addition of a child had a strange effect on our life. We were both conscious of his presence and of his mixed

136

heritage. We both sensed that something historic had happened, but neither of us was sure where it would lead. In deference to my beliefs, and because Zazil Ha didn't approve of the practice either, we didn't strap boards to Chuen's head to try to develop the sloped forehead that was the Maya fashion. We also didn't suspend a bead on a string in front of his face to make him cross-eyed. These practices were fading out anyway, so no one thought it unusual.

Of course, we lost some of the freedom we had enjoyed, but still found plenty of time for each other.

As months passed, life settled down again. There was no attack from anyone, our trade with both the Mexica and Tulum increased, and the rains were plentiful. Pom Tzec sent emissaries again and our alliance with Dzilpan remained uneasy, but intact. The long range bows and arrows we had developed were put in a storehouse in case they were ever needed. The crops were at record levels and even the production of honey was high enough to trade.

In the first month of the next year, Zazil Ha announced she was going to have another baby. By the spring of that year, Chuen had started to walk on his own. His hair was now long and black in the Maya style, but his eyes were green. Since this was the color of Jade, everyone agreed it was a good omen.

On a sweltering hot summer day, our second son was born. He was small and had dark brown hair and green eyes. Another good omen. He was named 7 Imix, and I was happy and contented. Zazil Ha and I were as close as ever, and thanked the gods each day that we had found each other. After all this time, I still couldn't look into those soft brown eyes without feeling the same thrill I had felt that morning at the house of the memories.

We built another room onto our house for Chuen and

137

Imix that month. I seldom thought of my former life now. Spain was a fading mirage, though sometimes, in the still hours before dawn, I longed to see my brother Hectore again. I thought about de Aguiller from time to time, and made inquiries to see that he was well, but I never went to see him. Our worlds were too far apart now, and I wouldn't know what to say to him.

Cimi was now almost nine years old, and several inches taller. She was as lively and talkative as ever, but was seen without Ix Chan more and more frequently. She stopped by to play with Chuen often and to give us the benefit of her company.

Our two sons had very different personalities. Chuen was quiet and studious, while Imix seemed to be impetuous and rebellious. After Chuen began to walk, he used his new skill to explore and to find new things to ask questions about. He loved to have Cimi come visit, because he always found something new in her non-stop talking. He asked her hundreds of questions, to which Cimi responded confidently, whether she knew the answer or not.

When Imix started to walk, he used his new skill to run away and to find things to get into. At the market, merchants would cover their goods when they saw him coming with Zazil Ha, because of his habit of grabbing everything in sight. She finally stopped bringing him to the market after the unfortunate incident when he ate an entire hot pepper before he knew what it was.

We tried to find a way to teach our children both traditional ways and our own philosophy of progress and rational thought. We were careful explaining the troubling tradition of human sacrifice. Even though Zazil Ha opposed human sacrifice as much as I did, she was, at the same time, somewhat defensive about it. Once, when I remarked how barbaric the practice was, she said that at least the Maya did not burn people alive because of religious differences as the Spaniards did. She had a point, of course, although I didn't see how one group's excesses excused another's. It is remarkable just how much killing goes on in the name of theology.

Chapter 17- **The Shadow of Castile**

In which I must make a terrible choice

In spite of their intellectual gifts, I often felt the Maya were slaves to foolish superstition. The blood sacrifices, the bewildering array of gods, and the belief in evil spirits seemed ridiculous to me. But superstition was not always as easy to dismiss as I assumed it was, because during this period of relative tranquility, a curious thing happened that I still cannot explain. The Maya have a strong streak of mysticism and are great believers in magic and in divination. I had always dismissed these traits as baseless, and I still do, but I must admit that I am still mystified by what I learned one day from Chac Pacal.

It was a cloudy, relatively cool day. Black thunderheads were building and slowly moving towards us over the horizon. Thunder rumbled intermittently off in the distance as the storm approached. Zazil Ha had been trying to teach me to read the Mayan writing so that I could read the sacred books as she did, but I was not making much progress. I have already written of the difficulty of Maya writing and was finding it perplexing.

On that day, we were looking through some of the books in a section of the house of the memories that we had not yet explored and I picked up a dusty book and tried to decipher the text. The task was made harder because the pages were badly stained with mold and were mostly unreadable. The only words I could recognize were "east", "stranger(dzul)", and "conquer". Since conquerors had usually come from the west or the south, I was curious as to what the book was talking about. I asked Zazil Ha, and she looked through it and frowned.

"This is the book of the Jaguar Priest," she said. "When I was a girl, I remember Chac Pacal speaking of this book, but I have never seen it."

"Who is the Jaguar Priest?" I said

"A priest and astronomer who has written of the future," she said, slowly turning over the stiff pages. "I can't read much of this, but from what I remember of what Chac Pacal told me, the book says that bearded men will come from where the sun rises and will conquer the land and all who are in it. There will be much suffering and death."

The faint growl of far-off thunder was the only sound for a moment as we thought of the reference to bearded men. As we sat in silence, I noticed that I had been unconsciously stroking my chin.

Chac Pacal sat on a jaguar pelt on a stone ledge along the wall of his house. In the wall next to him was a niche in the stone that held a small statue of Kukulcan, the feathered serpent god of wisdom. We had gone to Chac Pacal to find out more about the prophesies of the Jaguar Priest, and waited patiently as he finished looking through the book. The storm was closer now, and thunder could be heard more frequently. Drops of moisture glistened on the grey stone walls; the humid closeness of the room was oppressive. Finally, Chac Pacal closed the accordion like pages of the book and was silent for a long while before he spoke.

"Yes," he said at last, "this is the book of Chilam Balam, the Jaguar Priest. He was the greatest of our soothsayers, and a master of the stars and of the count of time, from the beginning until the end of the world. To him, the gods gave gifts of divination far above the meager talents of the Ah Kin priests. Chilam Balam lived in Mani, which is near the ancient city of Uxmal. He is dead now, but was still alive when I was a boy. "

141

"In the prophesies," Chac Pacal continued, "Chilam Balam said that, within a few years, a race of bearded, light-skinned conquerors would appear from the east. These conquerors will reject the gods, and worship a single god. They will destroy any who refuse to pay tribute to their god, but spare those who worship him. Chilam Balam also said that these strangers would have a standard that they carried before them, and that all would flee from the standard because it represented the strangers' god. I was told that the Batab of Mani had the standard fashioned in stone and placed in the temples to placate the strangers when they should arrive."

The room was silent for a moment, except for the sounds of the growing storm outside, but there was a question I had to ask.

"Chac Pacal," I said, "did the Jaguar Priest say what this standard looked like?"

Without saying a word, Chac Pacal bent down to the floor, and with two strokes of his finger in the dirt, drew......a cross.

We seldom mentioned the Chilam Balam prophesies after that, probably because neither of us wanted to admit they had a good chance of coming true. So we pushed the Spanish threat to the background of our lives, where it waited patiently for the day it would burst forth and consume us.[4]

By 1517, six years had passed since the shipwreck that brought me here, and my transformation was complete. My black hair was long and tied in the back, my beard had been plucked out hair by hair so I no longer had to shave, my skin was brown from the sun, my ears were pierced for ornaments, and I had scars from battle and from blood sacrificing. Although I was several inches taller than most, it must have been difficult to distinguish me from anyone else. Ixil was as close to being at peace as a Mayan city ever got, so my life as a Maya continued according to a comfortable routine and I felt contented with my lot. But sometimes, in the deadness of the night, with Zazil Ha sleeping softly beside me, I would lay awake and think of Spain. By now, I had reluctantly accepted the idea that I had long ago been given up for dead by my former friends and family. Even my brother Hectore, my truest and closest companion must have forgotten the brother he once duelled with on the farm near Seville.

One morning, Chan Oc told me that he wanted me to go to an upcoming meeting of Batabs in Ecab, the city on the northern coast that was the seat of the Ecab federation. Chan Oc felt that the journey would be too much for him, since he was getting old and didn't have the stamina he once had. Zazil Ha had recently informed me that she was going to have another child so she would not be going. I was uneasy about the prospect of spending time without Zazil Ha, but Ixil had to be represented.

"Go, Gonzalo," she said, "Chuen, Imix and I will be waiting."

"Zazil Ha," I said, "you know how I hate to be apart."

"Our love will cross the miles and hold us together," she said. "Our destiny brought us together over a far greater distance then a trip to Ecab."

I reached out and gently stroked her cheek. "I have loved you since that day at the house of the memories. You were my dream, my hope, and my life. "

"I will miss your touch," she whispered. "Let me feel you close one last time before you leave. Chuen and Imix are with my mother, Box Naab."

I drew her close and kissed her. Her lips were warm and soft as always. Soon we were on the bed together softly fondling and caressing, our passions slowly rising. Afterwards, we lay together for a long time, neither of us wanting to separate.

The city of Ecab sits on the top of a bluff overlooking and

about a half a mile back from the ocean on the northeast tip of the Yucatan. The buildings, including the pyramid, are mostly stuccoed and painted white. I had several days of talks with Batabs from the other cities of the federation. I met Nachan Can, the Batab of Chetumal, and Chan Oc's cousin. The talks involved trade routes, relations with each other, and relations with other federations. Not that it really made much difference; I had no doubt the cities represented would be fighting each other again within a week.

In addition to its dramatic location, Ecab seemed to be a rich city. There were numerous temples, and there were small gold offerings and ornaments in many of them, the first gold I had seen since Coba.

Late one afternoon, I climbed the steep steps of the highest pyramid to get a better view of the surrounding country. From the top, the green forest rolled to the misty horizon on one side of the city, and on the other was the vast sparkling blue expanse of the ocean. I had never seen the sea from this height before and it was breathtaking. On a brilliant white pyramid rising from a white city, I could see the splendor of God's creation perfectly complementing the splendor of man's. This was the world of the Maya; my world. Here I would live out my life with my friends, my children, and the woman I loved. In a euphoria of perfect contentment, I paused for one last look before descending. As I gazed out over the waters, I suddenly stopped in shock. Something else was out there; something I had not noticed before.

There, far away towards the horizon against the blue of the water, were the white sails of three Spanish ships heading directly towards Ecab.

There was a heart stopping moment, a fraction of a second, when I had lost my balance at the top of the yardarm of the *Sangre de Cristo*, and knew that I was about to plunge to my death. At that moment, I had felt an all-encompassing

144

realization of impending doom that I thought I would never feel again. At the instant I saw the sails in the distance, the same feeling came flooding back. The Spaniards had finally reached the Yucatan. My comfortable life, and the world of the Maya were about to be shattered forever.

I sat on the top step with my head in my hands. There was no one else on the top of the pyramid, and no other place in the city high enough that anyone else could have seen what I was seeing at that moment. The ships must have spotted the white buildings rising from the forest in the distance and were coming to investigate.[5] They would probably arrive after dark and wait until daylight to come ashore. By this time tomorrow, I could be face to face with my former countrymen again. Somehow, I had always known that this day would come, and I had wondered what I would do when it did. If I had had this opportunity six years ago, before I met Zazil Ha, I would have been elated at the chance to escape and return to Spain. But what would I do now?

I sat on the top step looking out to sea. At last I had the opportunity to resume my former life with people of my own race, people who believed in the true god, people who spoke Spanish and knew the things I knew. I could go to greet the ships and return to my home. I would be hailed as a returning hero. I could see my parents again, my brother Hectore, my sister Maria, My Uncle Fernando, Spain.....

But what of Zazil Ha? Would she be willing to leave the land of her birth and go with me? If she did, how would she be treated in Castile? How would Chuen and Imix fare in a faraway land of strangers? Even if Zazil Ha had been willing to go, she would not be able to travel for months. How could I tell Chan Oc and Box Naab that they would never see their only daughter or their grandchildren again? What would I say to Balam, who had supported me and protected me? Or to Chac Pacal who gave me his wisdom and taught me of the greatness of his people? Or to Can Pec, confirmed bachelor

145

and head of the Jaguar warriors? Or to Cimi; irrepressible, curious, happy Cimi. What would I say to her?

My mind was in turmoil as I descended from the pyramid into Ecab. The more I thought, the more I realized I could not go back. I couldn't betray these people. For better or for worse, they were my world now. And I could never leave Zazil Ha. She was right; the bonds of our love were too strong. Nor could I tear her from the land of her birth to travel to a strange land where she would be a curiosity at best. Only a few years ago, Spain had expelled the Jews, even those who had lived there for generations, and the Moriscos, Moors that had chosen to remain under Spanish rule after the *Reconquista*. How would they treat an Indian woman and her mixed blood children? No, there was no way of going back unless I went alone, and that I could never do.

But simply not returning was no answer. What would happen tomorrow when a landing party came ashore? Would the Maya resist? Would the Castilians have guns and horses? What part should I play in the drama that was about to unfold? I thought of Perez, who wanted to kill every Indian he saw; of Cortes, who spoke of defeating vast armies by shifting alliances; of the planters, who viewed the native population as simply a resource to be used as necessary. So many images filled my mind as I walked through the twilight in the streets of Ecab. I saw a burned village on Hispaniola; an armored Spaniard reading a royal decree of conquest to the bewildered Arawaks; and, most of all, the face of the ravished woman in the village in Jamaica, a face filled with hurt and rage so intense I had to look away.

As I walked through the darkening streets, I saw people going about their business under the fading twilight, as they had for centuries, completely unaware of the calamity that was about to befall them. Men gathered in groups to gossip, laugh, and gamble. In the failing light, cooking fires flickered here and there as women prepared the evening meals, single

146

women talked and laughed in their own groups, and mothers cared for their children.

I suppose it was the mothers who made up my mind as to what I must do. God knows the Maya were not perfect; they were quarrelsome, superstitious, tradition bound, and violent. They had murdered my friends and made me a slave. But when I saw the mothers with their children, my mind went back to Zazil Ha and Chuen and Imix. Until today, they were respected citizens, but if the Spaniards take over, they will be simply three more Indians to be dealt with as some Castilian adventurer sees fit. Their entire world will end if the Castilians gain a foothold, and all of the Yucatan will become like Hispaniola; peopled only by ghosts and fading memories of what once was.

I remembered again the words of my Uncle Fernando that if I couldn't make the world better, I should at least try to keep it from getting worse. The world was about to get infinitely worse for these unsuspecting people cooking meals, gossiping and tending babies. I was the only person in the Yucatan who knew, first hand, what was about to happen. More importantly, I was the only one who knew enough of Spanish ways and tactics to defeat them. If the warriors attacked in their usual way, they would be massacred by the guns, crossbows and horses. Arrows would bounce harmlessly off Toledo plate armor, and the Spaniards would appear as gods. But if, through my knowledge, other methods were used, the conquest could be delayed if not actually defeated. I remembered what Zazil Ha had once said about choosing between what was expected and what was right.

So it was that I decided to take up arms against my former countrymen. I prayed I would not have to kill Spaniards, but I knew of the terrible consequences to the Maya if I did not. I had been forced to choose between the country of my birth and the woman of my heart. I made my choice and have never doubted I made the right one.

147

Chapter 18- A Clash of Civilizations

In which I must face my former countrymen in battle

I went directly to the palace of the Halach Uinic, or supreme ruler of the federation, Akbal Ek, who called an emergency meeting of the Batabs. They assembled in the courtyard under a series of thatched canopies that protected from the sun during the day. Distorted shadows from the crackling torches danced on the walls of the nearby pyramid as I stood up in the flickering yellow light and began to speak.

"I have seen three war canoes of Castile approaching the city; they will be here tomorrow. Castile is a warrior nation that has already defeated many smaller nations of the great sea. They may profess friendship, but I have seen them before. They mean to enslave us and destroy the gods."

At this, there was an excited uproar among the Batabs, and one of them spoke up.

"How many are they?" he said

I calculated quickly; three ships carrying perhaps 40-50 men would mean between 120 and 150 men.

"What?" roared the Batab of Muyil, "There are at least 1200 warriors here, and you quake at 150?"

"The numbers are not important," I replied, "The Castilians have weapons that speak like thunder and can cut down many men. They have great beasts to ride that can trample men, and they have clothing of metal that arrows or spears cannot penetrate. They can defeat a holcom many times their number. They can be defeated, but not in the old ways. We must strike and drive them from our lands before they devour us all."

148

The debate raged on for hours. Some were in agreement with me, saying that the threat must be wiped out immediately; others said we should welcome the Castilians until we find out their intentions. Still others talked of possible trade advantages. Nahan Pat, the scheming Batab of Cozumel, said that I was exaggerating the threat and that we should welcome the Spaniards as allies and trading partners.

"The Ecab Maya are not like the Maya to the west at Champoton, who blindly attack all who enter their domain," he said in an oily fashion, "We are wise enough to welcome visitors from far away. Their friendship could be an asset to us all."

I told of what I had seen in Hispaniola and Jamaica when people welcomed or declined to resist the Castilians (omitting to mention my own part in it, of course). These people may have sought friendship, but what they got was the *Repartimiento* system, and all the death and slavery that went with it.

In the end, it was decided that we would resist. We had one big advantage; there was no gold or treasures to be found. Conquest of the Yucatan would yield little the Castilians sought. If we could make the cost of conquest high enough, they might decide it was not worth it, and move on to more promising areas.

The plan was to lure a landing party ashore, isolate them from the ships, then ambush them. If the Castilians expected a hostile reception every time they stepped ashore, they might be reluctant to do so in the future.

The next day, the three ships arrived off of the cape and two of them approached the shore while the other stood further out. I stood watching with Balam as the ships got closer.

"By the gods," he exclaimed in astonishment, "never have I seen a canoe so large. It is a floating house!"

149

The ships were actually somewhat small, but bigger than any canoe. Closer in, their sails looked gray and stained and their hulls were streaked with tar and salt. A bearded crewman in a blue stocking cap appeared at the rail and threw over a pail of slops. The ships seemed to be an unclean and defiling presence on the clear blue waters as an anchor splashed and a chain rattled in the still air. The red and gold flag of Aragon and Castile flapped lazily from the mast of each ship, and I noted that on the mainsail of one of the ships was a cross.

By now, a sizable crowd had gathered on the shore to watch the show. Ten canoes were sent out to the ships to greet the Spaniards and invite them ashore. The Castilians were cautious and remained on their ships that day, even though several of the Maya in the canoes actually boarded the ships and made friendly gestures in sign language. I stayed on the beach that night watching the dark forms of the ships with their faint lanterns reflecting off of the gentle ripples of the water. It was a peaceful sight, but it represented two mighty civilizations on the brink of collision, and a torrent of fire, blood, and death about to be released.

The next morning the canoes again went out, and again acted friendly and gestured for the Castilians to come ashore. Finally, I saw boats being lowered. The crowd on the shore cheered excitedly and prepared to welcome their guests. The Spaniards, I noted, had maneuvered their boats so that they all beached at the same time. Very wise, I thought. That way a small group wouldn't be cut off before the others arrived. They were still cautious as they disembarked on the beach and formed up two abreast to start inland towards the city with Maya on all sides of them. There looked to be about 50 of the Castilians and they were heavily armed with firelocks, pikes and crossbows. The stocky, bearded adventurers were almost a foot taller than the surrounding Maya, and as they walked their armor clattered and gleamed in the sun. Metal clad man looking suspiciously from side to side were led towards the city by one of the Nacoms of Ecab. I don't remember his name, but the Halach Uinic had insisted that he be given the job.

The path from the beach leads through dense forest just before opening up to an outlying plaza that contains several small temples. The ambush point was in this dense patch and the Spaniards were to be cut off before they got to the plaza. If they entered the plaza, they might find shelter in one of the buildings, and be hard to dislodge. Tensely, I watched from a distance as the party got closer to the ambush point and I said a silent prayer for the souls of those who were about to die.

As the party entered the dense area, I waited for the signal from the Nacom to attack, but it didn't come. The Spaniards were almost to the plaza and still no signal came. I had urged that Balam be allowed to lead the attack. He knew his business, and would have ordered the attack at precisely the right moment. This Nacom was waiting too long!

Finally, as the first Spaniard was only yards from the plaza, the Nacom gave the signal, and hundreds of warriors rose from the foliage. With an explosion of ear splitting war cries and blasts from conch shell trumpets, they loosed a hail of arrows, spears and stones at the Castilians. I had instructed them not to aim for any shiny surfaces, because the armor was too strong, but I could clearly hear the rattle of missiles bouncing off Toledo plate. Even so, the first attack wounded 15 of the Spaniards and gained the advantage of surprise. A hand to hand struggle ensued in which warriors fell by the score. Though greatly outnumbered and surrounded, the Spaniards kept their heads and brought their firelocks to bear with a crashing explosion of light and smoke. The first volley of the guns almost caused the Maya to break, but I had warned them of the noise and destruction and they held.

During the battle, the Spaniards had moved into the plaza as I had feared. With the more open space, the guns and crossbows were more effective and the warriors retreated. After regrouping and entering several of the buildings, the Spaniards finally retreated back to the ships, taking their wounded with them. We organized a pursuit, but they had gone. Within the hour, the ships hoisted sail and headed west along the shore.

As we surveyed the losses, I was horrified. The effect of firearms and steel edged weapons on flesh was sickening. The Maya casualties had missing arms and legs, or holes blown in their chests. Brownish red splashes of blood were everywhere, forming puddles in some places. And this is only the beginning, I thought. We had lost 18 killed and 65 wounded. The Spaniards had at least 35 wounded, some seriously. Their percentage losses were far greater than ours. Now, at least, they might be reluctant to invade such a hostile land for no gain.

The Nacom who had led the attack came back to report. I was critical of him for waiting too long and allowing the Castilians into the plaza. The Nacom was defensive.

"They were defeated," he said indignantly, "That is what matters. They entered the plaza, but they were driven out. All they were able to do was to steal a few temple offerings."

"What did you say they stole?" I snapped.

"Very little...necklaces, metal discs, wooden chests, and some metal images of ducks and fish...the usual offerings. They only took a few handfuls."

"Offerings?" I shouted, "Can't you see what this means? Some of those objects were made of gold! If they return to their people with gold, every Castillian on earth will be headed here to find more! You have given them the one thing that will make them sure to return!"

I was despondent. We had driven the Spaniards off but given them a reason to come back. Now they were headed west along the coast. Soon, they would go back to Santo

Domingo and tell the others.

When we arrived back in Ixil, Balam and I went straight to Chan Oc with the news of the Spanish appearance in Ecab. He asked some questions and said there would be a meeting of the elders that night.

Zazil Ha was waiting for me outside the Batab's house and we embraced happily. It was good to have her in my arms once more, to feel the brush of her hair against my cheek and to smell the scent of flower pedals on her skin.

"I have missed you," I said.

"And I longed for your touch each moment," she replied.

We compared notes as we walked back.

"How are Chuen and Imix?" I asked.

She laughed. "They wish to drive me insane. Chuen is so curious about everything, I don't know what he'll do next. And Cimi encourages him.

"And Imix?" I asked.

"It was bad enough when he started to walk," she said, "but now he can run, and he is always chasing our neighbor's turkeys. Last week, a turkey turned on him and bit him on the nose. I wiped his tears, but couldn't help thinking that it served him right."

We had reached the low wall that surrounded the courtyard of our house.

"There is Cimi," said Zazil Ha. "She is supposed to be watching Chuen, but what is she up to?"

Cimi was sitting in the middle of the courtyard with her fingers in the corners of her mouth, holding it open as wide as it would go, while Chuen stood on his toes in front of her and seemed to be looking down her throat. She saw us and greeted us, then I asked her what she was doing.

"I was eating some berries," she said, "and Chuen wanted to see where they went."

Later, when we were alone, I told Zazil Ha of the events at Ecab. She listened quietly, then became strangely troubled.

153

"So they have come," she said, almost to herself, "as I have always feared they would. The prophesies of Chilam Balam have come to pass."

"It was only three ships, and we drove them off," I objected, but she seemed not to be listening. She was staring off in the distance, as if mesmerized by a vision only she could see.

"The great storm is building," she said. "Soon it will strike the land with all its fury and carry away all before it. The Spaniards will take away our land, our gods, and our very lives."

"Not yet, they haven't," I said "We will fight them until the end."

"Until the end?" she said, turning to me at last, "And when will that be? When we are all dead, or...."

"Or what?" I said.

"Or when they come for you?" she said quietly.

At their meeting that night, the council decided to prepare not only ourselves, but neighboring states as well. I had told them that a favorite tactic of the Spaniards was to play off one group against another, so the elders decided that I would train a force that would travel to other cities and warn of the threat and offer to help. In this way, we hoped that the Maya would unite in opposition to the invader.

The first order of business was to train the warriors to fight this new foe. The Spaniards greatest weapons were firearms and horses. The effect of the firearms was as much psychological as physical, so training the warriors to rush before the Spaniards could reload, or to attack in the rain when many weapons would misfire would not only diminish the weapons' effectiveness, but boost the warriors' confidence as well. The horses were another matter. I had never seen horses in battle, but I remembered my uncle's description of the Moorish cavalry. The effect of charging horsemen on

154

infantry was devastating, and would be doubly so on the Maya who had never even seen a horse. I tried to deal with the problem in two ways; traps and pitfalls to stop the horses, and massive attacks with arrows and spears to avoid close in fighting. But, in spite of these preparations, I knew that if the Castilians managed to ally themselves with some Maya factions against others, they would be unstoppable.[6] We heard no more of the Castilians, and in a few months Zazil Ha gave birth to our third son. He was born on 7 Etznab, so that became his name. Unlike his brothers, he had the deep brown eyes of his mother. Imix was jealous and cried when he saw Etznab, but Chuen was fascinated and kept asking where Etznab had come from. He had only recently been asking why his mother's stomach was so big, and I wondered if he would connect the two phenomena. He didn't. But just when Chuen stopped asking about where Etznab came from, he saw the new arrival at Zazil Ha's breast and had a whole new series of awkward questions to ask. Later, I overheard Cimi explaining the whole process to him. It seemed to involve the mother eating a baby seed and the baby growing in her stomach until she burped it out. When I thought about it, Cimi's version didn't seem any more far fetched than what really happened.

So there we were, in the year 1518; Gonzalo Guerrero, locally known as Gonz-lo, Zazil Ha, and three sons Chuen, Imix, and Etznab. It had been almost a year since the Spaniards landed at Ecab, and seven years since I had been shipwrecked. There were no reports of Spaniards and our borders were quiet. There was another good harvest and a celebration with a feast. In the evenings, Zazil Ha and I would relax in front of our house with the evening meal while Chuen and Imix took care of Etznab. It was on one of these quiet evenings when the colors of the sky are warm and the air is cool and soft that Balam came to our gate with a troubled look.

His cousin had gotten ill suddenly with a mysterious

sickness none had ever seen before. He had been covered with boils and had been delirious with fever for several days. Though the priests and medicine men had attended him, the cousin had died. I listened and gave him my sympathy, but inside I was terrified. From his description, I felt I knew the identity of the new mystery killer, because in Spain, we have known it for years; Smallpox.

Chapter 18- The Sickness

In which the Mayan lands are ravaged by disease

Smallpox; the name alone was enough to chill the blood of anyone who knew of the disease. There had been periodic outbreaks of smallpox in Europe for years, of course. Wars had been decided by which side resisted epidemics the best. It was rare, in fact, for the death toll from battle to approach the death toll from disease. But here, the scourge of smallpox had been unknown.

Balam said that his cousin had severe chills and pain in the arms and legs. Then he got a high fever accompanied by red spots that soon filled with fluid and festered. In a few days, he was dead. Smallpox wasn't always fatal. People sometimes recovered, but the disease spread rapidly. I had to warn the others, although I didn't know what could be done about it. I wondered if the disease had been spread from the Spaniards at Ecab.

"Zazil Ha," I said, when he was gone, "I know of this sickness. You must stay away from anyone who seems ill, and keep Chuen, Imix, and Etznab away, too."

I rushed to the Batab's house and saw Chan Oc. As I told him of the disease and its symptoms, the color drained from his face.

"Zazil Ha's mother, Box Naab was taken ill this morning," he said, hoarsely.

For the next week, Zazil Ha and I spent long hours by her mother's side. Box Naab, the one woman in Ixil with an intellect to match her daughter's, but with the fair mindedness to accept a dzul as a son-in-law was dying. She shivered uncontrollably, though she was burning up with

157

fever. On the third day, the red spots started to appear and swell. Zazil Ha was brave, and comforted Chan Oc during the day, but at night she cried silently in the dark. Box Naab seemed to recover slightly after a week, and recognized the anxious faces around her bed.

"I am soon to die," she said hoarsely, and while everyone protested, she turned to me. "Gonz-lo, there were those who disapproved of you as a husband for Zazil Ha, but you have proven loyal and strong. I had faith in you then, and my faith remains. You must protect her from the storms to come, so that you and she can grow old together as I have with Chan Oc, with children to remember us when we are with the gods."

She then turned to her daughter.

"Zazil Ha," she said, "you must be your husband's partner and strong right arm. I have tried to help you know the power and wonder of knowledge. Whatever happens, you must tell the story of our people, and preserve the wisdom we have gathered through the ages. Wisdom and love have power denied even to the gods."

"Your memory will live in me, mother," she said, holding back the tears, "and in my children."

Box Naab smiled faintly. "I would be alone with Chan Oc now."

She died that night.

I can't remember very much about the death ceremony, except that Zazil Ha was brave and consoled Chan Oc with her strength. It was only later that she broke down and cried. I consoled her as best I could, but her loss left a hole in her heart. Chan Oc tried to continue as before, but he was distracted easily and, more than once, was seen staring off towards the horizon during some discussion. I thought I had gotten used to sudden death, but this was a depth of pain and loss I had never known. I thought of the times I had called these people savages and thought that life and death meant nothing to them.

The ravages of smallpox spread throughout the neighboring cities, and throughout the Yucatan. Every city seemed to have suffered losses. In Ixil, reports of deaths accumulated, and soon, there was scarcely a family that had not been affected. The holcom was dwindling as losses from disease mounted, and we planned fewer large scale exercises in an effort to slow the spread of the sickness.

For the rest of that year and most of the next, the epidemic raged. For all their virtuosity at mathematics and record keeping, the Maya did not, as far as I could tell, keep track of population. So I can not say just how much the Maya's numbers fell, but the losses must have been considerable. The dwindling of the population could be seen in other, more subtle ways. There were more abandoned houses than before, sitting forlornly among ever growing weeds and foliage. Of the houses that were still occupied, many had a neglected look because the death of some of the occupants spread available labor too thin. What little building there had been stopped altogether, as the supply of buildings exceeded the availability of people to fill them. The forest was reclaiming several of the milpa fields as farmers died, and the harvests were smaller because the plantings were smaller. Trade between cities dwindled and almost stopped as markets shrunk. Warfare diminished overall, but several cities attacked neighbors that they thought were weakened.

The worst part, however, was the uncertainty and the instability. People who were in good health suddenly became ill and died a few days later. If you didn't see someone for a while, you wondered if he had died. The priests and the medicine men responded with renewed prayers and calls for sacrifice.[7]

Chan Oc lost a part of himself when Box Naab died and

never fully recovered. Affairs of state were increasingly in the hands of Chac Pacal and Ah Kin Mu. This was a dangerous development because Chac Pacal's health was in decline. He and Chan Oc were in communication, but Chan Oc was often distant and melancholy. It was a surprise, therefore, when Chan Oc called me to the house of the Batab, and gave me a mission.

"Gonz-lo," he began, "my people are slowly dying. The priests and the medicine men are helpless. Perhaps in Tulum or in Coba there are traders from places that know how to cure the sickness. You must go there and see if there is any help they can provide."

Chan Oc's voice was weak and tremulous. I hoped he would be here when I returned. Chac Pacal took me aside as I was leaving.

"Chan Oc is dying," he said abruptly, "and I will soon follow him to Xibalba. Ixil and the Mayan people depend on you."

"On me? But surely I am only...."

"Gonz-lo," he said, "when you came to me, I could see that you were not an ordinary slave, that you were destined for great things. You are the hope of not only Ixil, but the entire Mayan people. The gods will protect you."

Chac Pacal seemed to have high expectations for me. I hoped he wouldn't be disappointed.

On the road to Tulum, Balam and I passed several small villages that I had remembered from my last trip. This time, however, they were deserted. We looked in several of the empty, weed-choked houses, and saw a skeleton in one. The sickness was here, too.

Tulum seemed less crowded than before, because fewer of the buildings were occupied. The market was noticeably smaller with fewer stalls and a smaller variety of goods. There were, as before, several merchants selling medicines, and we questioned them about their experience with smallpox. They

160

were all familiar with the scourge, which some of them referred to as the "easy death" because it killed so casually.

"The sickness!" exclaimed one, "We have lost many because of it. The gods are not done with us, yet, I fear."

"But do you have medicine that cures the sickness?" Balam asked.

"We have medicine to ease the discomfort," he replied, shaking his head, "Only the gods can cure it."

For the rest of the day, we talked to the merchants in the market. They were well traveled and knew the state of most of the rest of the Yucatan. From them we learned that the sickness had spread widely, and there was no cure. However, the disease seemed to be slackening in its intensity, and fewer were dying from it. Several merchants offered to sell us medicines, but none claimed a cure.

We did learn something truly startling, however; the Spaniards had returned! Several merchants told us that Spanish ships, five this time, had passed within sight of Tulum and had landed on Cozumel. The inhabitants of that island had fled and hid from the Castilians, which was probably wise. In a few days the Spaniards had left and headed north along the coast. That had been several months ago and there had been no report of further landings. One merchant said he had heard that the ships were later seen rounding the northeast cape where Ecab stands, but there was still no landing. Balam and I didn't know where the truth lay.

Near the far end of the market, I was glad to see Tolotl, the Mexica merchant who had agreed to trade several years ago. Ixil's trade with the Mexica had dropped off considerably since the smallpox epidemic began, and I hadn't seen Tolotl since then. He looked as prosperous and confident as ever, wearing a yellow mantle with black trim and a headdress to match. He greeted me warmly.

"It is good to see you again, Gonz-lo," he said, smiling, "I

161

have been concerned for your welfare amidst all of this sickness."

"I am glad to see you also, Tolotl," I said, "Are the Aztec people suffering from the sickness as well?"

"No," he answered, "There have been a few outbreaks on our borders, but Tenochtitlan is far away over the mountains. That is fortunate, for our arts of healing are not as good as yours."

"And ours can do nothing," I said ruefully, "But tell me, have you any word of the five great ships that were seen near Tulum and Cozumel?"

For the first time, Tolotl's smile faded, and he looked worried.

"I have recently traveled from Tabasco on the northern coast." he said, "My people maintain a garrison there as it lies at the outer edge of the empire of the Mexica. While I was there, messengers brought word of five ships moving eastward past Campeche and Champoton. They had fought a battle at Champoton and driven off the inhabitants, leaving over 200 warriors dead or wounded."

"When the ships appeared, there were only four since one had returned to wherever they came from," he continued, "The Mexica warriors beckoned them to come ashore and trade."

"What?" I said, "You welcome an invader?"

"It is not so simple," he replied, "Our legends tell of the struggle of our gods for supremacy. Quetzalcoatl, the feathered serpent, was driven out by Tezcatlipoca, the smoking mirror. Quetzalcoatl escaped on a raft of serpents over the sea towards the east. He vowed to return one day and reign over all of the Mexica. Since then, we have waited for a bearded man to come over the sea from the east. So, to the Aztecs, the men you call Spaniards must be treated with respect, for they could be gods. Quetzalcoatl may have returned at last."

162

"Tolotl," I said, "these are no gods. They are men; men who will destroy your people if you give them the chance. What happened next?"

"They came ashore and traded for several days and then they departed in peace," said Tolotl.

"What did you trade?" I asked.

"We traded many items," he replied, "but they seemed to like the gold the best."

So it had happened again. Two Spanish expeditions had returned with gold. One because of carelessness, and one because of a superstitious legend.[8]

To make matters worse, I found out that the gold that the Mexica had traded was not a mere handful of temple offerings as at Ecab. The Mexica had traded the Spaniards large gold discs, statues and other gold objects weighing several pounds. If the Castilians had their appetites whetted before, they would be ravenous now. I pleaded with Tolotl to go to his rulers and tell them who the Spaniards really were, and why they must be resisted. I spoke of everything I had seen of the Spaniards and their ways. Finally, when I said that the Spaniards were intent on destroying the Aztecs and their empire, Tolotl affected a superior smirk on his face.

"If they can destroy the Mexica," he said, "then they must truly be gods, for no mortals could ever do so."

On the way back, Balam and I were despondent. We had failed in our mission to find medicine to cure the sickness; and we had learned of a new and more deadly threat from the Castilians, a threat that the holcom was in no condition to combat. We dragged through the outskirts of Ixil, past weed choked milpas, past deserted houses, and past newly dug burial mounds. Finally, we came to Balam's house and called for Ix Kutz. She appeared at the door with hollow, darkened eyes that were red around the pupils. She did not smile, and only said four words: "Cimi has the sickness."

There on a mat covered bed laid Cimi. She was covered with sweat, but was shivering rapidly. Hair stuck in wet black streaks to her cheeks and forehead, and she tightly clutched a blanket to her with both hands. When she saw us, she managed a faint smile.

"H..h.hello father; h..h..hello dzul. I don't feel good."

"It's all right, Cimi," said Balam, with more confidence than he really felt. "You rest and mother and Ahau and I will help you feel better."

"All r..r..right," she said, looking up at him. Balam and I started to leave the room when she said, "Mother, could I have Ix Chan?"

In the adjoining room, we kept our vigil, each praying to whatever god he thought to have power. Balam was silently holding the lumpy, tattered red mantle Cimi had woven for him; I sat staring at the floor lost in my thoughts; Ahau was crying softly; and, in the next room, Ix Kutz sat with a cloth in her hand mopping Cimi's sweating forehead, while a frightened, shivering 13 year old girl clutched a worn wooden doll.

During the next week, I visited Cimi often. I had reported the news of our trip to Chan Oc and Chac Pacal, who greeted it with grim resignation. The human mind has the capacity for only so much bad news; after that, numbness sets in.

During my visits to Cimi, I could see the all too familiar progress of smallpox. Soon, the red spots appeared, and festered, looking like small boils. Then the boils broke and began to dry up, leaving marks on the skin, then the victim started to feel better for a few days, then.....well, you know the rest.

Ix Kutz spent days and nights at Cimi's bedside, even when Cimi was sleeping. Balam brought water and scoured the market for fruit and medicine. We had brought back some medicine from Tulum that, though not a cure, was supposed

164

to ease the suffering. Ix Kutz mixed it up and gently gave it to Cimi.

"Aaaaah!" said Cimi, wrinkling her nose and sticking out her tongue in spite of her weakness, "That tastes terrible. Did father make it?"

"No," said Ix Kutz, "It's medicine. It will make you feel better. It's supposed to taste bad. That's how you know it works. Please Cimi, drink it all."

"All right," she said faintly, "but I'm going to hold my nose."

I was standing in the back witnessing this scene, when Cimi noticed me and called me over. Ix Kutz went to get more medicine and we were alone for a moment. She was thin and hollow cheeked, not like the Cimi I had known for these past seven years.

"Dzul," she said in a faint voice, "if I am ...not here, make sure Ix Chan gets a good home. And promise you will remember me and say goodbye to Chuen and Imix and Etznab. And tell Zazil Ha that I...."

For a terrible moment, I thought she was dead, but she had only fallen asleep again. I pulled the covers up and left.

That night, as I sat with Zazil Ha and the children in the courtyard, the mood was somber.

"First your mother and now Cimi," I said shaking my head. "When will it end?"

"Chac Pacal used to say that if the gods never sent us sorrow, we could not ever know joy," said Zazil Ha, "I hope he was right. The joy is due."

She was silent for a moment, watching Imix run after a bird while Chuen dangled a string for Etznab to grab at.

"There are those who say the sickness came from the Spaniards," she said, without expression.

"They are probably right," I said, "The sickness is known in Castile. It is called smallpox, but there is no cure. Some say

165

it is an affliction from God."

"Here some say it is an affliction from your people," she said, bitterly.

"My people? The Maya are my people," I said, "What are you talking about?"

"If you Spaniards had stayed at home where you belong, the sickness would not have come," she retorted, "and my children would not have to face death."

"Your children?" I said indignantly, "If the Spaniards had stayed at home, I would not be here, and you would have no children; not these children, at any rate. As for staying where you belong, women do not belong in the house of the memories, but you go there."

She looked at me with her eyes flashing, then sighed.

"I'm sorry, Gonzalo," she said, wiping her forehead with the back of her hand, "it's just that I am so worried about us and our children. I want them to have a chance at life."

I put my arm around her and drew her close. "So do I, and I am prepared to make war on all of Spain to give it to them."

Two days later, I returned to the house of Balam. It had been two weeks since Cimi had gotten the sickness and she still hovered between life and death. Finally, one day when her mother had fallen asleep at her bedside with exhaustion, Cimi sat up for the first time in two weeks. Two days later, she was standing, and a day after that, she could walk again. We were delirious with joy. Amidst all the death and misery, there was hope; and it came in the form of a slightly wobbly girl walking once again.

Chapter 19- The Return of Cortes

In which both de Aguillar and Cortez entice me to return to Spain

The sickness never really vanished, and was to continue to take a toll of lives throughout the Yucatan for years to come. But it struck more randomly now, and more of its victims recovered. Almost every city and village had felt the effect. In some places, there had been grim resignation, as at Ixil. In other places, there had been an orgy of sacrifices as desperate people sought to regain favor with the wrathful gods that were slowly destroying them. Temple altars were busy again in many places. In Dzilpan, which was noted for the number of its sacrifices even before the sickness, the number of victims increased still further, until the walls in the temple on the top of the pyramid were coated with clotted blood.

Even more deadly than the disease, however, was the belief that the god of the Spaniards was more powerful than the gods of the Maya, and had brought the disease to show us the futility of resistance. I argued against this belief, pointing out that the Spaniards, themselves suffered and died from the sickness. But many were not convinced, and seemed almost fatalistic about the coming of the Spaniards.

In Ixil, those of us who were left tried to put our lives together again. Chan Oc recovered somewhat, but was not as he had been. Chac Pacal grew more feeble and forgetful, although at times, he seemed as alert as ever. Balam and Ix Kutz resumed life as before, but Ix Kutz sometimes arose at night to assure herself that Cimi and Ahau were sleeping peacefully. As for Cimi herself, with her fourteenth birthday came a new found interest in boys and several marriage proposals from other parents. Marriage at fourteen was

167

common, and everyone liked Cimi and her parents. Ix Kutz, however, having almost lost Cimi to smallpox, was not anxious to lose her to a husband. Cimi still came by and played with Chuen on occasion, but mostly as an excuse to talk to Zazil Ha about the mysteries of the opposite sex.

After some months, we heard no more of the Spaniards, and Chan Oc seemed to rally somewhat. Cimi's mother softened her earlier opposition, but still hesitated to arrange a marriage.

With the threat from smallpox diminished, traveling merchants were once again seen in the market of Ixil. I kept in touch with these merchants for word of events around us, especially news of the Spaniards. But a year passed with no further sightings. Though I was disappointed that the Mexica had traded gold with the Castilians, I consoled myself with the thought that the taste of the gold might persuade the Spaniards to strike the Aztecs first and exhaust themselves in a bloody war with the mighty Mexica nation.

Over all this activity loomed the shadow of Spain. There had been no sign of another expedition for almost a year now, and the last one hadn't even come ashore until it was hundreds of miles from here. Still, I was uneasy. Everything I knew of my former countrymen told me that their coming was inevitable. The only question was when and where they would appear and how they could be opposed. I wanted to give my family a chance at life before the curtain of Spanish domination descended over them forever.

In spite of these worries, I found life satisfying. Chuen was now six years old and growing taller every day. He had inherited his mother's intelligence and curiosity. He was always asking questions about the things around him and exploring as far as we would let him go. Sometimes, when I was talking to him about some arcane bit of knowledge, he

168

would tilt his head in an inquisitive way just as Zazil Ha often did. He had already learned to read numbers, and was starting to decipher a few glyphs as well.

Imix was an entirely different person. He had little interest in knowing things; his passion was in doing things. From the time he arose until the time when we finally were able to force him into bed, he was a whirlwind of energy and motion. From chasing the neighbor's turkeys, he had gone on to climbing trees, sliding down the roof, making mudpies, and annoying our pet monkey, all at the top of his lungs. Zazil Ha said he took after me, and I had to admit, she was probably right. If Imix became a warrior, the rest of the holcom could stay at home.

Etznab's personality was more subtle. He was alert, but usually quiet. He had just started to walk and was making his way around the yard in a wobbly fashion. Although he was starting to talk, he was not even as vocal as Chuen, let alone Imix. His interests were more focused. He would sit by the hour concentrating on building something out of a few sticks and pieces of wood.

As for Zazil Ha, herself, she was somehow able to keep each of these boys in line, and still be just as exciting and enticing as the day I met her. I sometimes thought of what she had said about our children being the first of many of mixed blood. If a whole new race were to arise, there could be no finer mother.

Early one evening, as I was sitting contentedly in front of our house after enjoying a meal of roasted dog and chilies, Cimi came by to talk to Zazil Ha. Upon finding that my wife had gone several houses away to visit one of the other women, Cimi decided to get a male point of view. As always, though, she tended to have several trains of thought going at the same time.

"Are you sure Chuen and Imix are brothers?" she said,

169

watching the boys running around the yard, "They seem so different. If they saw a worm, Chuen would try to measure it and Imix would try to eat it. My brother, Ahau is different from me, but that's all right. Ahau is a boy and they are supposed to be different from girls."

"Er...yes," I said, "I have heard that."

"Of course," she continued, "some boys are so different you can't stand them. That boy Manik, for instance, is really stupid. And Muluc thinks of nothing but hunting. His poor mother has to cook the miserable things he spears. Then there's that awful...."

"Cimi, what are you trying to say?" I asked, confused.

She stopped and looked at me. "How do you know if someone you like is...well....you know."

"Uh, Cimi, maybe you should talk to Zazil Ha about this."

"I'm serious, Dzul," she insisted, her voice rising slightly, "How do you know someone you like isn't going to turn out to be someone you don't like?"

I had never really thought about this vital question, but I did my best. "Well, Cimi, I suppose you just have to spend time with them and get to know them better. If they have any bad habits, you'll find out."

"Is that what you did with Zazil Ha?" she asked.

"Well, yes," I said, "I suppose it was, but we liked each other from the start. And you know what, Cimi? You were the one who brought us together. We owe you a lot."

She beamed with that Cimi smile I knew so well. "Thanks, Dzul," she said, getting up to leave, "You've helped a lot."

She waved to the boys and went off happily towards her house. She was at the age when she was not yet a woman, but no longer a girl. Soon, she would probably marry and be given her adult name, but to me, she would always be a little girl named Cimi.

I watched her go and continued gazing in her direction thinking these thoughts long after she was out of sight. I was so preoccupied that I almost didn't see the shadow of someone who had approached on the other side. When I noticed the shadow, I turned around, thinking Zazil Ha had returned. But I was wrong.

There standing before me was Jeronimo de Aguiller.

He was thinner than before, and as dark as any Mayan. He had a smile on his face and was holding in one hand a number of coils of green beads, and in the other, a scroll on which I could make out a seal; the royal arms of Spain. As I sat there open mouthed, he continued smiling and I noticed there were tears in his eyes. He held up the scroll and finally spoke, his voice trembling with emotion.

"Gonzalo, my friend, our ordeal is over! The Castilians have arrived to rescue us. It is time to go home at last!"

I continued to stare at de Aguiller, not comprehending what he was telling me. He was clearly bursting with joy.

"Gonzalo," he repeated, "don't you see? We're free! We can finally return to Spain. Here, read this. It arrived by runner just a few hours ago."

He handed me the scroll. It was authoritative looking and crackled slightly as I unrolled it. It was written in a rich, flourish of black ink, and bore the seal of Spain. I still remember the words I read in astonishment that day.

"Gentlemen, and Brothers;

Here at Cozumel, I have learned that you are held in the power of a chief, and ask that you come immediately to Cozumel, for which purpose I have sent a ship with soldiers if you need them, and ransom to give to the Indians. The ship will remain eight days waiting for you. Come in all haste and you will be well received and attended by me.

I am on this island with five hundred soldiers and eleven ships. In these, I go, if God wills, to Tabasco and beyond."

Hernan Cortes.

"These beads are the ransom they sent," de Aguiller continued when I looked up from reading. "My master agreed to let me go for some of them and for my loyal service."

"Cortes?" I said finally, "The one we met in the tavern in Santo Domingo? He came here just for us?"

"No, no; of course not," de Aguiller answered. "He came to explore, but learned of us on Cozumel...probably from some traveling merchant."

"Gonzalo," de Aguiller said insistently, "the ship will only wait eight days and it has been six days already since the messenger started to look for us. We must make haste. Gather your things and let us be off. In two days we will be with Cortes and our own countrymen. God be praised!"

So here it was at last. The Spaniards knew of us and were anxious to have us return. No doubt our knowledge would be valuable to them. Zazil Ha had not yet returned, so I looked at Chuen, Imix and Etznab in the yard before I answered the anxious De Aguiller. I knew I could never leave the woman and children I loved. As Box Naab had said, I was needed to shelter them from the storms to come, not to help make those storms worse. I also knew something else; De Aguiller must not be allowed to rejoin the Spaniards, lest his knowledge enable them to destroy us all. I chose the words of my reply carefully.

"Brother Aguiller, I am married and have three children. Look at these fine sons of mine. I am looked upon as a warrior and a Nacom in time of war. My face is painted and my ears are pierced. What would those Spaniards say if they saw me this way? You go, and God be with you, but leave some of the green beads so I can give them to my sons as a gift from my countrymen."

"Gonzalo," he said in amazement, "do you know what you are saying? This may be the only chance you will ever have to escape. We have waited eight years for this. Castile is your home, not this heathen place. We are among murderers and idol worshippers; it is a miracle we have lived this long. God is giving our chance to escape at last. Take your wife and children with you if you must, but come with me now, before it is too late."

"My friend," I said sadly, "it is already too late."

Just then Zazil Ha returned and overheard some of the conversation. She stood next to me glaring at de Aguiller.

"Why does this slave come here to talk to my husband?" she said, angrily, "Go, and leave us in peace!"

"It is all right," I said to her soothingly, "He is my friend, and I owe him my life. If not for him, I would not be here. Come, Jeronimo, I will walk with you a while."

We walked toward the road to the coast. He made another attempt to persuade me to join him, but I cut him short.

"Jeronimo," I said, "you wanted to save souls and bring the word of God to the Indians. Do you think Cortes will share these goals? In Santo Domingo; he spoke of conquering, not saving. Do you wish to be part of that? You saw what happened to the Arawaks when the Castilians came. Can your Christian conscience allow you to participate?"

He looked at me. My appeal to Christian conscience no doubt sounded strange coming from one who looked as much like a savage as I did, but I meant every word. "I know there are abuses," he said finally, "but perhaps I can be a moderating influence on Cortes. I must go."

We were in an isolated place now. I could see that de Aguiller was determined to go, and I knew that he must not be allowed to use his knowledge to speed any conquest. I reached into my mantle and grasped my father's dagger. You may think it shocking and reprehensible that I was considering the murder of a man who had once saved my life, and I suppose it was. At the time, however, I saw him as a threat to my family's safety, and to the safety of all the Mayan people.

I drew the knife and stood in front of him with the point

173

at his throat. He drew back in surprise.

"I am sorry, my old friend," I said, "I have no wish to harm you, but I must protect my family. Your knowledge of the language and of the interior would be invaluable to those who would turn the Yucatan into another Hispaniola. You must not leave."

He stared at me in disbelief for a moment, then reached into a small bundle he had hanging from a belt and drew out a small battered book. It was stained and dog-eared, with several pages torn or falling out.

"Do you know what this is, Gonzalo?" he said quietly, "This is the Book of Hours. I have had it with me for my daily devotions since before we left Seville. I have smuggled it past guards, other slaves and masters. It has been my strength and my solace for all these years. I begin and end each day with this book and with prayer, and the prayer is always the same. I call upon almighty God to deliver us from our captivity at the hands of the heathen. Not me, Gonzalo, but both of us. I pray for you each night, that you will be rescued before your soul is condemned for being seduced by these people. I believe their world is doomed; but not because of anything I could say or do, because of its iniquities. You have adapted to this heathen world, Gonzalo, but I cannot. Each day of slave labor in a land of idolatry has been a torment to me. Each morning, I think I will not be able to face another day, and each night, I fear going to sleep because another day awaits me when I awake. Gonzalo, if my choice is between remaining here and death, than I shall choose death. Good bye, my old friend. If you wish to prevent me, you will have to kill me, and may God have mercy on your immortal soul."

With that, he walked past me with a slow, but deliberate step. I stood holding the knife as he passed, but could make no move to stop him. Then, he turned around and smiled. "Praise, God, Gonzalo," he exclaimed "There is still hope for your soul. Take care, old friend."

"*Vaya con Dios*, Jeronimo," I said, then we embraced.

As he started away, I stopped him once again.

"Jeronimo," I said, "tell Cortes that there is no gold and no riches in this land. Tell him he must seek what he wants elsewhere."

He nodded. "I will tell Cortes. There is nothing for him here."[9]

And so my last link with my former life was gone. Years ago, I had known that we were heading down divergent paths. I suppose that day had been inevitable.

I sent spies to follow de Aguiller and to report back any invasion attempt. They reported back in a week or so that de Aguiller had gone to Cozumel and had later left with the 11 ships on a course northeast along the coast. Once again, there was no invasion, and I was relieved. I remembered that the letter had said that Cortes intended to go to Tabasco upon leaving Cozumel. I had long ago constructed a map of the Yucatan, based on information I had obtained from traveling merchants. Tabasco was on the other side of the peninsula and marked the edge of the Aztec empire. If Cortes went there, would he turn back on us or attack the mighty Mexica?

No one seemed to share my concern. Balam and Can Pec said that the gods had steered them too far away to be a threat. Only Zazil Ha appreciated the danger. We discussed it one evening as we walked by the market just as the daylight was dying and torches were being lit.

"Perhaps the Mexica will destroy Cortes," she said, "In the end, it will make no difference. There will be more of them. Have you noticed, Gonzalo, that each group is larger and better equipped than the one before?"

"Yes," I said, "more ships, and more men. Not only that, but each group is equipped with the knowledge gained by the previous ones. As each expedition is completed, more blank spaces on the map are filled in. Soon, our isolation will be no protection."

175

We stood in silent gloom for a while, watching the fading of the last light of the sun.

"The Mayan people may well fade and die like the light of the sun;" she said, "flooding the sky with red before being lost in darkness."

"But the sun is reborn each morning," I replied. "Remember that."

She was silent for a moment. "Why did you let de Aguiller go?" she said finally, "He will only hasten their conquest."

"He saved my life and gave me comfort when I needed it most," I said, "If I had kept him here, it would have killed him. I don't think it will make any difference. The Spaniards had no de Aguiller in Hispaniola or Jamaica, and prevailed all the same. When they come, we will fight them."

As I said this, the last blood red rays of the sun were extinguished, leaving us in darkness.

Once again, a relative quiet descended and we heard no more of the Spaniards, except for a fragment of information from another merchant who reported that the Spaniards had abandoned Tabasco and sailed onward. He didn't know where.

By the end of that year, the ability of Chan Oc to rule steadily diminished. He was over 50 years old by this time, which was elderly for a Maya. His age, combined with the deflation of his spirit caused by the death of Box Naab had taken a toll. One night, he called us to his side. He lay on his bed in the house of the Batab. His cheeks, normally round, were hollow and sunken. His eyes were dim and his breathing was labored. Zazil Ha sat by his side and held his hand as he spoke.

"My time under the sun is almost finished. I cannot rule Ixil or the Mayan people any longer. Zazil Ha, you have been a joy in my life. You have made me proud and given me fine grandchildren. Box Naab lives in you as you live in your children."

"Father," she said, "you must rest now. Your strength has served Ixil in the past. It must serve you now."

We kept the vigil through the night and into the next day. Ah Kin Mu and several sub priests burned copal incense and chanted prayers while one of them poured small bags of corn kernels and beans into piles and tried to divine the future from them. Chan Oc drifted in and out of consciousness, and spoke with us off and on. The next morning, however, Zazil Ha came out of his chamber and looked at me with sadness in her eyes.

"My father is gone. The gods have received his spirit."

Then she threw herself in my arms, sobbing.

One of the sub priests placed a jade bead in Chan Oc's mouth to receive his spirit, and another brought the burial cloak and decorations that had been prepared before.

Once again a death ceremony was held, but the ceremony for a Batab was more elaborate than any I had seen. The body was dressed in the finest mantle and jewelry. Jade bracelets and ear plugs were put in place, shell necklaces, and copper ornaments were added. New sandals were put on his feet and leg bands with small copper bells were placed around his calves. A breastplate made of a mosaic of pieces of copper was added, and finally, a face mask made of fitted pieces of jade.

Runners had been sent to neighboring cities to announce the death of Chan Oc, and soon, other Batabs began to arrive. Pom Tzec arrived along with Cuac Caan on a litter borne by slaves. He was as ugly and brutal looking as I remembered him, and looked at Zazil Ha and Ixil with equal rapaciousness. Cuac Caan stayed in the background, biding his time. I caught his eye once or twice, but he ignored me and looked away. No doubt he would give me his full attention when the time was ripe.

Pom Tzec was seen in conference with the other Batabs

discussing the succession. Chan Oc had no male offspring and few male relatives of proper age. Chan Oc's cousin, Nachan Can, the Batab of Chetumal would not hear the news until several days after the burial due to the distances involved. This was unfortunate, since Nachan Can was Chan Oc's closest male relative, and as such, was supposed to designate a successor from the family. I had a feeling the question would be settled long before he arrived.

After three days, the body of Chan Oc was taken by a procession to a burial chamber at the foot of the pyramid. The body was placed in a square wooden box and placed in the center of the chamber along with weapons and other implements to help Chan Oc in the afterlife. Then a dog was killed and placed in the chamber to lead Chan Oc in his journey and four slaves were killed and placed there as well so they could serve him. After the burial, the Batabs had a dinner to commemorate the dead. I was disgusted to learn that Zazil Ha would not be allowed to sit with the Batabs in spite of the fact that she was the only offspring of the deceased. The Batabs were to return home the next morning, but the successor must be named within a month or they would no doubt be back.

Zazil Ha and I were deep in a discussion of our limited options as we returned to our house. We had left Cimi in charge of Chuen, Imix and Etznab, and she was entertaining them by holding a contest to see who could spit a mouthful of water the farthest. Puddles of water stood all around the courtyard, and each of the contestants was so wet it looked as if they had spent most of the contest spitting at each other. Zazil Ha sighed.

"Come on Cimi," she said, "let's get them cleaned up."

Later, as Zazil Ha was putting the three boys to bed, Cimi came out and sat down next to me.

"What are you thinking about, Dzul?" she said. Now that Cimi was 16, she had become much better at the habit of interactive conversation instead of her previous monologues in which she asked a question, answered it, commented on it, then moved on to a related topic. At least to her it was a related topic; I often had trouble seeing the connection.

"Oh, I was just thinking about making choices," I said, vaguely.

"Life has too many choices," she said, "It's really not fair. You have to choose when you are not ready, or don't want to. And do you know what the worst part is?"

"Well, I suppose...."

"The worst part is that you have to make a choice when you don't even know what the outcome will be," she said indignantly.

"How true," I said under my breath.

"Caban has been trying to get me to get my mother to agree to a marriage. I really like him, but I don't know if I even want to be married, or what it would be like. My mother is much better about it now. She is really understanding, but I can't decide. I mean, it's not like choosing something you know is good instead of something you know is bad. You don't know for sure until it's too late."

"That's right, Cimi," I said, "and the biggest choices are the ones where you know the least."

The next day Zazil Ha, the boys and I set out for Tulum. We reasoned that Nachan Can would be arriving in Tulum by canoe from Chetumal to make the journey to Ixil. If we were lucky, we could intercept him and warn him of the secession problem in Ixil so we could put up a united front against Pom Tzec.

Tulum was the same as it had been on our last visit several years before. We strolled around the city and watched the great trade canoes arrive and depart from the beach below the temple which also served as a lighthouse. After a few days, we finally saw his canoe arrive. We met him at the beach and he greeted us warmly.

"Gonz-lo!" he said cheerfully, "It is good to see you again. And can this be Zazil Ha? When I saw you last, you were this high." He held his hand up to the level of his chest.

We told him of the secession problem in Ixil. He listened, and said he would discuss it further, but protocol demanded that he pay a call on the Batab of Tulum. He went straight to the Batab's house while Zazil Ha and I waited anxiously outside. Nachan Can appeared worried when he left.

"Let us have food and drink before we decide what must be done," he said. We went to a handsome stone house that was used for visiting dignitaries and servants brought us chocolate drink, tamales made of turkey, beans, squash and chilies. When we had been served, Nachan Can dismissed the servants so we could talk.

"The problem," he began, "is that there is no one from Ixil eligible to become the Batab. You, Zazil Ha, have all of the traits that would make a successful Batab except for your sex. No female can serve as Batab."

"But if no one is able," I asked in exasperation, "what can we do?"

"I can propose someone of high birth from another city," said Nachan Can. "But there is a difficulty. At my meeting just now, I was read a declaration from the Batabs of Tulum and Cozumel. They say that if no one of Chan Oc's family, or no one from Ixil can be found, the next Batab of Ixil should be Can Xoc, son of the Batab of Tulum."

"Never!" shouted Zazil Ha, leaping to her feet, "I know of this Can Xoc. He is a drunken fool. I will not have my father succeeded by him! Ixil would rot and die!"

Nachan Can held up his hand. "I quite agree. Can Xoc would be a disaster for Ixil. He has enough trouble keeping himself upright. Unfortunately, such a request can not be ignored. Tulum and Cozumel control the trade routes and the duties that are charged on goods moving through the area.

The other Batabs will be reluctant to oppose them on such a matter."

"If he is weak," I said, "perhaps he can be influenced."

Zazil Ha looked at me thoughtfully. "Easier than Pom Tzec or Cuac Caan, at least." She was warming to the idea. "Yes, that could be our best chance to save Ixil. We would have a Batab we could control, and alliance with Tulum as well."

Nachan Can frowned doubtfully. "Depending on influence is like trying to climb a rotten tree. It could collapse at any time and take you with it."

But Zazil Ha and I were grasping at the idea like a drowning man at a floating spar. We had convinced ourselves that supporting Can Xoc of Tulum was the best strategy for protecting Ixil, and were optimistic when we left the next morning. We were about halfway back home, when a runner intercepted us.

"I have come from Ixil;" he said, breathlessly, "the city is under attack!"

Chapter 20- Treachery

In which Pom Tzec and Cuac Cann take a bloody revenge

One constant of my life has been how rapidly and completely things can change. In an instant we had gone from being concerned about our impact on events in Ixil to being worried about Ixil's very survival.

Zazil Ha was momentarily stunned by the news. She stared off into the distance, thinking of all the friends and memories that might be gone. But she recovered quickly and turned to me.

"We must get back quickly, Gonzalo; they may need our help!"

I knew that there would be very little our small party could do, but did not say so.

We were still several miles from the outskirts of Ixil when we saw the smoke. The dirty grey clouds drifted lazily above the trees like some obscene, living thing. When we were close enough to see the city, there was smoke rising from a hundred places. We were accustomed to seeing thin plumes of smoke from the copal incense being burned on the pyramid, or wood smoke from the cooking fires, but these fires were different. The smoke rose in the air in fat billowing clouds of black and grey like a thief escaping a place he had looted. And with the smoke were hundreds of scavenger birds circling lazily in the dirty sky.

As we entered the city, we were met with a scene of destruction. Buildings were either burned out or still burning. Bodies of men, women, children and animals lay scattered everywhere. Our own house had burned to the ground, and the nearby house of the Batab was a burned out shell of stone. Turkeys, dogs and a few monkeys scurried aimlessly about the ruins. As we entered each area, clouds of scavenger birds flew upward in a noisy burst of beating wings. For all the bodies, however, most of the population was missing, either escaped or carried off. Etznab was asleep, but I started to order the servants to cover the eyes of Chuen, and Imix from the terrible sights.

"No," snapped Zazil Ha, her eyes dark with anger, "let them see, and let them remember."

I sent the three warriors off in different directions to scout while Zazil Ha and the servants searched the center of Ixil. As we went, I noticed the bodies of warriors of Ixil and warriors of Dzilpan, lying where they had fallen. The bodies were thickest at the north and west edges of the city. The bodies of the warriors made it clear the attack was from Dzilpan. Pom Tzec and Cuac Caan had decided to take matters into their own hands, apparently to make Cuac Caan the new Batab of Ixil, and possibly make Zazil Ha available to Pom Tzec in the bargain.

"But if they have defeated us, where are they?" I asked.

"It is almost dusk," she said. "They probably have withdrawn to their camp until morning. Then they will return to clear away the wreckage and set up Cuac Caan as the new Batab. We must be gone quickly." she said. She stood holding Chuen and Imix by the hand, looking at the ruins of the Batab's house and the mound of ash where our house used to be as ragged swirls of smoke drifted across the plaza. "There is nothing left here for us now. I will always remember this place where I was born and where we first found our love, and where our children were born."

"As will I," I said, placing my hand on her shoulder, "for as long as I live."

Just then the warriors returned with five weary looking people. I was excited to see Can Pec among them. His

183

headdress was missing and he was splattered with blood, though whether his or someone else's I couldn't tell.

"We found him under a pile of bodies, unconscious," one of the warriors said. "He was injured by several spear thrusts, but he can walk now."

"Gonz-lo," said Can Pec, "thank the gods you have returned. Pom Tzec attacked without warning. We were overwhelmed."

He coughed and looked about to faint.

"Rest yourself, Can Pec," I said, "We can talk later."

But he was already unconscious again.

Akbal Dzib, the chief scribe and keeper of the records, was among the people to survive. He had taken a war club and gone to the house of the memories to defend the archives of Ixil from the invaders, but the house had not been harmed. He had remained at his post and watched the townspeople flee to the forest in all directions. Our warriors found him sorting which books to remove to prevent their being destroyed tomorrow. Zazil Ha readily agreed with his request to take the more important books with us as a record of Ixil and its knowledge. We sent him off with three servants and a warrior to gather them. I turned to Zazil Ha.

"Now I must go to the house of Balam," I said. "Wait here. I don't want you to see what I might find."

The house of Balam was several blocks from the Batab's house and I went there with apprehension. Would I find anyone alive? Would I find Cimi? My stomach was churning as I approached the familiar house and courtyard. The house had been spared the destruction and was still intact, but deserted. Had they all been slain, or had some escaped? The house was silent and empty. The only sign of the terrible events of the day was a single overturned table; the table where I had sat with Balam, Can Pec, and Ix Kutz so many times. Reverently, I set it back up and turned to leave. It was then I noticed a small object that had been lying in the corner hidden by the overturned table:

Ix Chan.

I picked up the doll and examined it. I hadn't seen it since Cimi had the sickness several years ago. It was worn and stained from a thousand childhood adventures; the neck still showed the scars of the repairs that Ix Kutz had made to reattach the head. I thought of the first time I had seen Ix Chan, clutched in the arm of a little girl who asked me what was wrong with my face. As wetness was starting in the corner of my eye, I put the doll in my pouch and walked out the door without looking back.

As I made my way from the house of Balam with my head hanging down in sadness, a voice spoke to me from the shadows.

"Gonz-lo the dzul," it said. "I thought you would return here."

A numbing sense of danger ran down my spine and I was instantly alert. "Who is it?" I demanded with more courage than I actually felt.

A heavy set figure stepped out of the shadows and I was face to face with Cuac Caan. I grasped my spear and took a fighting position. In the darkness, he looked like a fiend from the pit of hell. The spear he was holding reinforced the impression.

"Cuac Caan," I said. "You have helped destroy the city that once trusted you. Who is the betrayer now?"

"You are to blame, Gonz-lo," he sneered. "You undermined the holcom and finally the Batab himself. The city I devoted my life to rejected my council and accepted you into their homes like a bird of prey into another's nest. You started the rot which almost destroyed Ixil. Soon I will be the Batab of Ixil and I will ally with Dzilpan out of necessity to preserve what is left of the city."

"Yes," I replied. "I've seen the bodies of those you preserved. I'm sure they are very grateful. You wanted to kill

185

me as well, didn't you? Well, here's your chance."

The words were hardly out of my mouth when Cuac Caan lunged at me with the spear. By the saints, he was quick for a big man! No wonder he was senior Nacom. I jerked backward to avoid the deadly thrust so fast I fell to the ground and rolled upright again. I counterthrust, but he parried.

Cuac Caan was not only fast, but strong as well. He had apparently been hoping for this chance since the beginning and fought like a demon to put me in my grave once and for all. Like something out of a nightmare, our deadly duel rang out in those darkened ruined streets and for the first time in all the times I had faced another in combat, I was truly afraid for my life. Everything was shades of black and grey, lit only by moonlight or the faint glow of the flickering fires. Occasionally, a reflected shaft of light would reveal the twisted malevolence of Cuac Caan's face as he fought. Back and forth our battle raged, until he slashed at me with such force that my spear tip was broken off when I blocked it. He grunted in triumph and pressed me harder. I was getting increasingly desperate as I fought off his thrusts with my broken spear.

I knew I had to do something different, or he would have me, so when he paused for a moment, I reached into my pouch and grabbed Ix Chan. With a quick motion, I threw the hard wooden doll directly at Cuac Caan's face. By reflex, he raised his spear to block it and as he did, I thrust my spear hard into his stomach.

If my spearhead had still been attached, Cuac Caan would have been a dead man, but as it was, the blunted end merely punched the wind out of him and sent him doubling over in pain. I gave him a quick kick in the ribs and wrenched his spear away, but he recovered enough to trip me and then scramble away into the dark shadows.

"The gods have turned on you, Gonz-lo," His voice, still wheezing from the spear thrust, called out from the darkness.

"We will meet again, and when we do you will have no more tricks to protect you."

I sighed wearily as the sounds of his retreat receded into the blackness. I didn't have the slightest doubt he was right.

As we left Ixil, the city was dark except for a few smoldering fires glowing a dull red among the silhouettes of the dead buildings. The smoke was thinner, but still formed a veil across the moon as we walked. At night, Ixil had pulsed with life and sparkled with hundreds of small cooking fires and torches. Now it was only a row of shapes slightly darker than the sky beyond.

When we were several miles out of Ixil, we stopped to rest. We were finally free of the smell of the smoke and the sight of the rubble of our city, so the weary party gathered together to discuss the next move. Zazil Ha and I had already discussed it and we knew what we must do.

"We have escaped Ixil," I said to them, "and we cannot return. The Ixil we knew is no more. In the morning, Ixil will become a possession of Pom Tzec and placed under the rule of Cuac Caan. Zazil Ha is the only heir of Chan Oc and his line. Pom Tzec will not rest until she and I are either captured or dead. In another day's journey, we will be in Tulum. From there we shall go by canoe to Chetumal."

Everyone looked at each other uncertainly, then Akbal Dzib spoke. "We are all that remains of the Ixil we knew, and we have a duty to the memories of the ancestors. Let us go to Chetumal and take along the memory of Ixil."

As we began to walk again, Chuen tugged at my mantle.

"Father," he said, "isn't Cimi coming with us?"

Chapter 21- Chetumal

In which we become refugees, forced to start anew

A few days later, we found ourselves in several canoes heading south along the coast on the 180 mile journey to Chetumal. The sea was the blue green color common to this part of the world and the shoreline was mile after mile of palm trees and white sand beach. The journey took almost two weeks and we watched the scenery gradually change as we went south. The forest on the shore became thicker and the beaches became narrower. Low areas and swamps became more frequent. Even with a thatch canopy on the canoe, the heat from the sun was oppressive. Finally, the canoes turned toward shore on a stretch of land that looked the same as any other. When we got close to shore, however, we saw a narrow canal that led inland.

"The city of Chetumal lies at the head of a bay that opens several days further south," one of the boatmen said. "This ancient canal leads to that bay."

The canal was so narrow in some places that two canoes could barely pass, though it had probably been wider once. The jungle growth crowded the sides and overhung the water like a tangled canopy of leaves and twisted vines. Monkeys scampered and shrieked overhead, and birds flew up as we flushed them from their nests. The drone of insects was loud and constant, and the air was so heavy and humid that breathing almost seemed like drinking. Soon we emerged to what looked like another sea. In two more days, we were in sight of Chetumal.

The city was about half again as large as Ixil and stood on a bulge of land protruding into the bay so that water stood on two sides of it. Behind the city were several lakes. Here was a city that would be easy to defend, I thought as we drew nearer. The land was low lying, giving the impression that Chetumal was floating on the water. Several fast canoes came out to meet us to find out what our business was and who we were.

As we beached the canoes on the shore near the foot of a small pyramid, a delegation stood waiting for us, no doubt alerted by the messenger canoes. Nachan Can was greeted warmly by the elders.

"You are all welcome in Chetumal," he said to us. "Ixil is no more, but the line of Chan Oc will continue where it is already strong."

"But Pom Tzec must pay for what he did to Ixil," insisted Zazil Ha. "He has the blood of my people on his hands and must be punished. We must do what is RIGHT!"

"We must do what is POSSIBLE," said Nachan Can. "I too grieve for Ixil, but my duty is to Chetumal and its people. Let time and the gods deal with Pom Tzec."

Zazil Ha considered this for a moment, then said "You are right, lord Nachan Can. If Chetumal is to be my home, then it is also to be my concern."

"Come," said Nachan Can, smiling and sweeping his arm towards the city, "let us talk of the future."

In spite of the great tragedy that had befallen the city we had called home, we soon adapted to life in Chetumal. Nachan Can was an affable man with a bright sense of humor and an open, friendly manner. Under it all, though, he was shrewd and rational; two qualities I admired.

Akbal Dzib was made a scribe in the house of the memories in Chetumal. He brought the books we had saved from Ixil and carefully catalogued them and added them to the books already kept in the house.

Can Pec continued to recover, though his powers of

recuperation had somewhat diminished with age. The other warriors were made part of the holcom of Chetumal. As I had trained them in weapons, they soon became well respected among the Chetumal warriors.

Chuen, Imix and Etznab adjusted quickly, as children do. They soon had friends in their new home and seemed happy and content. Occasionally, however, I would find one of them, usually Chuen, sitting quietly, deep in thought. When I asked what was wrong, he would say how much he missed Cimi. Of course, we all missed Cimi, but with Chuen, it was the incomprehensibly arbitrary injustice of it that he had trouble understanding.

"Why did Cimi have to die?" he said once, his eyes brimming with tears, "She never hurt anybody. She never even got her adult name."

"In war, everyone suffers," I said, "the innocent most of all. She beat the sickness only to fall to Pom Tzec."

"I miss her," he said.

I placed my hand on his shoulder. "So do I."

Zazil Ha became an advisor to the elders and soon became a popular figure among everyone in Chetumal, especially the men. None of this surprised me in the least. If Zazil Ha had been placed in a desert, I had no doubt she would soon have the camels bringing water to her.

As for me, I was placed in the holcom as an advisor with no real power, but with responsibility for helping with training and strategy. The holcom of Chetumal was organized in a similar way to the holcom of Ixil, except that the senior Nacom had recently died and the holcom was under the command of the junior Nacom, Zotz Bacal. In contrast to Nachan Can, Zotz Bacal was a serious, somber individual. He was an eternal pessimist and worrier, often repeating an exercise several times to make sure it was flawless. He would consider every possible alternative, endlessly turning over different scenarios in his mind. He had little battle experience, since Chetumal was at peace, and I wondered how he would do in a situation that called for quick thinking.

When I say that Chetumal was at peace, I exaggerate somewhat. There was no open warfare, and few raids. The other cities in the area, however, were in an uneasy alliance with Chetumal; and it was only the control of the trade routes and the threat of Chetumal's holcom that kept them that way. Towns such as Macanahau, Yuyumpeten, Bacalar, Chequitaquil, and Chable were reluctant allies at best, and I wondered what would happen if the Spaniards arrived and started playing their familiar game of divide and conquer.

So I continued to train the holcom and advise the Nacom to be ready for a revolt of the other cities, or an invasion by the Castilians, and prayed these events didn't happen simultaneously. I began by preparing maps of the area and gathering as much knowledge of the other cities as possible. Next, I planned various defensive points against invasion or attack. All the while, of course, I taught fencing and pole fighting weapons technique.

Zazil Ha and the boys and I settled down in our new home. Nachan Can gave us a house that was somewhat bigger than the one we had in Ixil, and had lots of shade provided by both the surrounding trees and several thatched canopies. Zazil Ha, Of course, missed her parents and her life in Ixil. She had a smoldering desire to retaliate against Pom Tzec, but knew the limitations of our present position. Nachan Can was a widower, so his 10 year old son, Eb, was in the care of an aunt named Cab Mut. Her name means Honey Bird, and it fit her well. She was thin and nervous and was constantly making abrupt, bird like motions as she flitted from here to there. Eb enjoyed playing tricks on her and setting off another round of her nervous activity. But she had a good heart, and loved Eb as her own. Soon, Chuen, Imix and Etznab joined Eb

191

and were away from the house much of the time.

Chetumal was, on the whole, a pleasant place, relatively free of the intrigues of Ixil, and quite lax in the matter of sacrifices of captives. Because of the canoe trade, Chetumal had more contact with the outside world than Ixil had. Chetumal was a center of honey production, and bee hives made from hollow logs with their ends stopped with mud could be seen everywhere. There were so many hives that I was grateful that the bees were stingless. The honey was part of a thriving trade, with canoes calling at Chetumal from all around the Mayab, as they called the Maya world and even from Tabasco on the edge of the Mexica empire. Zazil Ha and I would often stroll down to the canoe landing and the nearby market to see the travelers from distant places and hear their stories.

Soon after we arrived, we started to hear rumors of an invasion of the land of the Mexica by Spaniards. Only a few had claimed to have actually witnessed this invasion, so reports were sketchy. I was troubled to imagine just what sort of storm was brewing over the horizon, but it was more than a year before I learned anything for sure.

It happened while we were idly watching the canoes come and go one day, and a large trading canoe arrived. The messengers said the canoe had come all the way from Tabasco and Campeche on the other side of the Yucatan. As they approached, we noticed that, unlike most merchants, these were ragged and poor looking. As the canoe touched shore and the merchants alighted, I saw a familiar face. There in a worn, plain mantle was Tolotl, the Mexica merchant from Coba. I greeted him and he thanked the gods we were both alive.

"Tolotl," I said, it is good to see you again, but what has happened? You look as if misfortune has befallen you."

"Misfortune?" he said, "Calamity is a better word, and even that does not fully describe what has happened. The

Spaniards came to Tenochtitlan, just as you warned they would."

"What happened?" said Zazil Ha, "Were they driven off?"

"After their victory over the Tabascans at Cintla," he said, "the Castilians continued up the coast until they finally landed and began to march inland towards Tenochtitlan with 500 of their own men and 400 Totonacs from the coast. Totonacs were vassals of the Mexica and joined with the Spaniards. Before he started inland, the Spanish commander burned all of his great canoes, so there could be no turning back."

I nodded. Cortes was following his plan of joining with one faction to fight another. Burning the ships was a bold and ruthless touch. It indicated that Cortes was probably exceeding his authority and feared revolt.

"The great lord Moctezuma heard of these strangers, but feared they might be might be the god Quetzalcoatl who was to return from the east and rule over the Mexica, so he waited, hoping one of the allies would stop them. But as the Spaniards crossed the mountains and plains, they fought battle after battle and were always victorious. As each town was conquered, the inhabitants joined the invaders against the Mexica, until soon, the Spaniards arrived at the gates of Tenochtitlan itself. With them were thousands of warriors from Cholula, Tlaxcala, and other states that were eager to strike at the Mexica."

Divide and conquer works best when the target is an unpopular tyrant state, I thought. "How did the Spaniards communicate with the Mexica and the other peoples?" I asked.

"They had a woman from Tabasco who spoke the language of the Mexica and the language of the Maya. They also had a man of their own country who also spoke the language of the Maya. He would translate the language of the invader into the language of the Maya so that the woman could then translate into the language of the Mexica." Tolotl said.

De Aguiller, I thought. He is speeding the conquest just as I had worried he might.

"Still fearing the leader, Cortes, might be the god Quetzalcoatl," continued Tolotl, "Moctezuma welcomed him to the city. Soon, Cortes took Moctezuma prisoner and hostage. The people turned against lord Moctezuma, thinking he was helping the Spaniards, and stoned him when he tried to speak to them. The people then rose in revolt and drove the invader from the city. But Cortes soon returned with more warriors of his own and of his allies. While he had been gone, sickness had spread and soon the people of Tenochtitlan were dying by the thousands. There was a great siege of the city by the Spaniards and terrible fighting. Death is now lord of Tenochtitlan. The city is in ruins. In the sacred precinct where the great pyramid stands, the white temples are black from smoke and stained red from the blood of the Mexica who died there. These Spaniards are like demons; they are not content with killing thousands and destroying the empire of the Mexica. They are even destroying the very buildings that are left. The great temple is being demolished to build a city for the conqueror. All is done; all is lost. The empire of the Mexica and the sacred city of Tenochtitlan are no more. "

His voice had trailed off and he had buried his face in his hands. He bore the stunned look of one who had seen a whole world and a whole way of life swept away in a storm he couldn't understand or control. I looked at Zazil Ha and could see she was thinking the same thing I was; is this our future?[10]

Tolotl tried to pick up the pieces that were left to him, but the rich trade with the Mexica was gone forever. Between the destruction of the war and the ravages of the disease, the former empire of the Mexica had gone from a series of large, prosperous nations to a wasteland. I soon had a meeting with Nachan Can, and Zotz Bacal to discuss the fall of the Mexica and its implications for us.

"Is it possible that the fall of Tenochtitlan could work in our favor?" said Nachan Can, "If the Spaniards are so far away and enjoying the riches of the Aztecs, then surely they will have no time for us."

"I have no doubt it will distract them for a while," I said, "but I also have no doubt that they will not rest until every land that can be conquered, has been. If a man sees two jade necklaces lying on the ground, will he pick up one and leave the other? They will come here."

"Then we must devise strategies to deal with them," said the leader of the holcom, Zotz Bacal, "but if the mighty Mexica could not stand before these men, what chance do we have?"

"Your question is well put, Zotz Bacal," I said, "and I have given this matter much thought already. I believe we have several advantages over the Mexica. First, we know these are men and not gods; second, we have no gold or treasure that would make great sacrifices on their part worthwhile; third, we have no central capitol whose fall would cause the fall of everyone; we are many independent states; fourth, our land has heavy undergrowth to slow the enemy and to give us cover; fifth, the swamps and lagoons in the area make it difficult to use horses effectively; and finally we have someone among us who speaks the invader's language and knows his ways."

"And that person is you, I presume," said Zotz Bacal.

"Of course," I said, "I know the Spaniard's weapons, his tactics, and I know what makes him brave and what makes him afraid. Make no mistake; you will be facing an enemy unlike any you have ever encountered. They are smart, they are tough, they have better weapons, and they are completely ruthless. The Spaniard does not fight to take captives; he fights to kill as many of the enemy as possible, and he is very good at it. To defeat him, we must use every weapon we have;

especially our minds. The most basic Spanish tactic is to join with one group to defeat another. They exploit old hatreds and rivalries, especially among vassal states," I explained, "So the first thing we must do is to make sure we are on good terms with our neighbors so they won't turn against us when the time comes to unite."

"Well, there's no problem there," said Nachan Can, "Our relations are good; we tell them what to do and they do it."

"With respect, my lord," I said, "that is not what I meant by good relations. The Mexica probably said the same thing about their neighbors."

"Then what do you mean?" he asked.

"We must make sure our relationships are mutually beneficial." I said. "They must be our allies because it is to their advantage, not because we force them. If they are satisfied, they will be less likely to join with the Spaniards."

Nachan Can was silent, so I barged ahead. "I propose that we meet with each Batab and review the terms of the alliance to see what we can do to make it advantageous to each of them. We have to see to it that we offer more than the Spaniards."

Nachan Can and Zotz Bacal looked at each other, then Nachan Can started laughing.

"Gonz-lo," he said between chuckles, "you truly bring a fresh perspective. We would never have thought of that."

"Then...then you agree?" I said, unsure of what the laughter was about. "You will do it?"

"Do it?" said Nachan Can, "Oh, no; of course not, but the idea is refreshing. The Batab of Chetumal haggling like a common merchant; it is really most amusing."

"But, why..."

"Gonz-lo," he continued, "you are wise in the ways of warfare and your counsel regarding the Spaniards will be invaluable, should the time come. The ways of statecraft, however, are my domain. Chetumal thrives as the dominant member of the local alliance. We have advantages in trade, agriculture, and taxes. I cannot give up these things in the hope that the other states will become so happy that they will suddenly become our true friends. What will I say to my people who will suddenly find their lives harder? What will I say to the families of those who died in wars that preserved the alliance? No, my friend, we will not give away what we have earned with our blood."

"Nachan Can," I replied, "your concerns are certainly important to the people of Chetumal, but so is unity in the face of an invasion. Force can bring obedience, but not loyalty. If the Spanish come, the other states could turn against us."

"If the time ever comes, they will see where their true interest lies. If the time does not come, we would have thrown away our advantages for nothing. Now, let us speak of it no more; there are other matters to plan."

We went over the state of the holcom and discussed where we could improve our defensive abilities. I was disappointed that we would make no effort to win the loyalty of our allies, but Nachan Can had political considerations to satisfy. Still, I worried that our neighbors could become our enemies overnight.

Chapter 22- The Bravery of Can Pec

In which we settle in Chetumal, but watch for the Spaniards

I walked home with Can Pec that night. He was enjoying life in the holcom of Chetumal. Being a warrior was his whole life. In fact, when the subject of women came up, Can Pec would make a gesture with his mantle, as if tying the end in a wedding ceremony, and say "I am Can Pec. My wife is the holcom and my children are the jaguar warriors!"

When we reached the front of the courtyard of my house, I invited him in for a drink of chocolate. He said he couldn't, but would stop just long enough to pay his respects to Zazil Ha and the boys. This was an old ritual that had started in Ixil, so I thought it was time to start it again.

In the house were Zazil Ha, the boys and Cab Mut, the aunt who watched them along with the Batab's son, Eb.

"...and that Imix," she was saying in her rapid, bird like talk, "he just never sits still. He's not at all like his brother Chuen. Chuen is so smart, he keeps asking questions that I can't answer. Yesterday, he asked why Batabs were always men. Can you imagine? And Etznab is just too intense about knowing the details of things. Today, I was making a stew, and Etznab burned his hand by sticking it in. He was trying to take out the pieces to see what was in it. And then, later in the afternoon....""

Zazil Ha seemed relieved to see us. "Ah, here is Gonzalo," she said, cutting off Cab Mut's stream of chatter. "And he has brought our old friend from Ixil: Can Pec. Can Pec, this is Cab Mut."

Cab Mut and Can Pec looked at each other and mumbled

a greeting, but their eyes locked together as they stood there in silence. Finally, I could bear it no more.

"Er...I asked Can Pec to stay for chocolate, but he must be going."

Still looking at Cab Mut, Can Pec said "Oh...well, I think I could stay a little while."

Strangely, Can Pec stayed for chocolate and remained for almost an hour afterwards, something he had never done before. He said little, and amazingly enough, Cab Mut was also subdued. Finally, Cab Mut got up to leave and Can Pec stammered an offer to escort her home. She said she didn't need an escort, but if he were going in the same direction, he might as well. They departed together into the night, leaving Zazil Ha and I looking at each other in silent bewilderment.

"What just happened here?" I said finally. "Are they under a spell?"

"In a way," she replied, "In fact, I recall something quite similar happening some years ago."

"Where?" I said.

"At the house of the memories," she replied.

The new training schedule started the next day. Zotz Bacal and I worked out patrols to afford early warning of any approach of the Spaniards. I believed that the approach would surely come from the sea, but Zotz Bacal, with his usual thoroughness, insisted on landward patrols as well. He also wanted to have an entire battle plan worked out in advance. The day was long and tedious and I was weary at the end of it.

Zotz Bacal relaxed a little and told me of his background as we were putting the plans away. He was from a warrior family, and his father had been Nacom before him. His father had been killed in a poorly planned attack, and Zotz Bacal had been obsessed with thoroughness in planning since then. I told him that planning was important, but once the heat, noise and confusion of battle begins, the plan seldom fits the way things develop. I didn't change his mind, but perhaps gave him something to think about.

Several days later, I found that my suspicion of Can Pec had been correct. He had come by the women's school where Zazil Ha taught and waited for her afterwards. Zazil Ha told me of their conversation:

"Zazil Ha," he said, "may I speak with you?"

"Of course, Can Pec," she replied, "There is a shady spot beneath that tree."

They sat down and Zazil Ha waited for Can Pec to begin. He fumbled for words and seemed embarrassed. He made a few remarks about the weather first and that told Zazil Ha that something important was on his mind, because it is impossible to hold an intelligent conversation about the weather in Chetumal. Everything there is to say about the weather in Chetumal can be contained in one phrase; it's always hot and sometimes it rains.

Finally, Can Pec said, "Zazil Ha...this woman Cab Mut...."

"Yes? What about her?"

"Well,...you're a woman...and .."

"And.....?"

"Do you think she likes me?" he finally stammered.

"Didn't you escort her home a few nights ago? What did she say then?"

"She just said good night," he said, miserably.

"You escorted her home and all she said was good night?" Zazil Ha said, amazed, "Why didn't you talk to her?"

"I didn't want to push her," he said, "Don't you think she might like me?"

"Well, why don't you ask her?" Zazil Ha replied. "She would certainly know better than I would."

"But, I mean...has she said anything to you?"

"Only about Imix's latest prank, I'm afraid. Why don't you go see her and talk to her?"

200

"Do you think she would?...talk to me, I mean?"

"Of course she would. Why not?" Zazil Ha replied, getting a little exasperated.

"But she's a relative of a Batab," he replied.

"Can Pec, I am a relative of a Batab!" she said, somewhat louder than she had meant to.

"Well, yes, but ..."

"Now listen to me," she said, taking charge of the conversation, "You're a warrior; attack! You go over to her house and talk to her. Do it now and do it until she either likes you or throws you out. There is no other way. Now, go!"

Thus began the slow and sometimes painful courtship of Can Pec and Cab Mut. The remarkable thing about it was that neither of them had ever shown any interest in the opposite sex before. Although you would never have guessed it, they were wildly attracted to each other from the moment they met; but they were each so shy that their courtship was a series of fumbles and mishaps. Can Pec, who had been known to singlehandedly attack an entire holcom, was utterly terrified of talking to a woman he was interested in as a possible mate. He could talk to Zazil Ha or any other woman, but Cab Mut paralyzed him. Cab Mut, in turn chattered like the bird she was named for on most occasions, but froze up around Can Pec. Perhaps each of them had waited so long to find a mate they were afraid of saying the wrong thing and spoiling everything.

Their clumsy antics helped take my mind off the steadily rising tide of Spanish conquest that crept closer each day. But several more years passed with no further word of invasion, and we all relaxed a little.

As in any Mayan city, there were many ceremonies in Chetumal to placate the many gods, but there was only one that is unforgettable; the fire walking ceremony of 1527. Chuen was 14 at the time and had begun training to be a scribe. Imix, at 13, wanted to be a warrior, and Etznab, at 11, simply wanted to know every detail of how things worked. Meanwhile, Zazil Ha, ever in search of new knowledge, had charmed the local astronomer into showing her how to observe the stars and chart the heavens. Although the astronomer was a somewhat withered old man, I was a little jealous of the amount of time he was spending with her in the evenings. She would come home late and talk of the path of some star across the sky and I would try to be interested, but where she saw the majesty of the universe, I saw only specks of light.

Can Pec and Cab Mut were still proceeding by inches in their courtship; so much so that everyone was losing patience with the whole business. One day, when we were out on a patrol in a canoe, he started rambling about the glories of Cab Mut for what must have been the hundredth time. Being in a canoe, there was no escape, and the sun had made me hot and irritable. Every man has his limit, and that day, I reached mine.

"Can Pec, if you don't stop babbling about Cab Mut, I will throw you over the side!" I finally shouted, almost swamping the canoe. "That's all you talk about; Cab Mut this and Cab Mut that. Well, if she were really that wonderful, you would do something about it besides talking! So don't bother telling me about her any more because I don't believe you."

"What do you mean?" he said in a hurt tone of voice.

"I mean that if you really loved her as much as you say, you would marry her! But you won't, because you can't. You have no romance in your soul. You're just an old warrior who doesn't know how to impress a woman."

"I have romance in my soul," he said defensively, "I'm just waiting for the right time."

"Look at that water, Can Pec," I said. "There are fish in that water that have more romance in their soul than you do. And do you want to know when the right time is? It was two years ago! The cycle of time won't come around for another thousand years; that should suit your romantic soul perfectly!"

We sat in sullen silence for a while. Finally he spoke, almost to himself.

"I could ask her to marry me. I don't know why you think I couldn't," he said.

"For the same reason I don't think you can fly through the air;" I said, "because you have shown absolutely no talent for it so far."

"Well, you're wrong. I could ask her any time......I will ask her!"

"When?" I said.

"I'll ask her."

"When?" I pressed.

"When the time is right."

"When?" I almost shouted.

He paused, looking out at the water. "At the fire walking ceremony next week," he said, finally.

The fire walking ceremony was one of those strange things I encountered, like the predictions of Chilam Balam, for which I could find no explanation. The purpose was to convince the ever fickle rain god Chac to send his rains for the corn crop. Zazil Ha, the boys and I arrived at the main plaza by the pyramid early. The crowd was just arriving and the area was starting to fill up. There were people from the entire region, including the vassal cities. The audience at a Mayan ceremony is as colorful as the ceremony itself. People wear the most fantastic array of intricate featherwork, jewelry and headdresses. The entire plaza, and much of the adjacent space was a riot of multicolored feathered finery and rattling jewelry. The first time I had seen such a gathering, I was thrilled and repelled at the pagan splendor of it all. Now, after almost two decades living among the Maya, these ceremonies seemed normal and unremarkable to me.

Directly at the foot of the pyramid, a large fire of wood had been burning for several hours and the area was even hotter than usual. The red hot glowing embers that remained had been spread out to form a glowing bed of coals about 30 feet long.

The ceremony started with the usual Mayan music that sounded like an orchestra falling down a long flight of stairs.

"If the gods were angry before," I remarked to Zazil Ha, "that music is likely to make them downright hostile."

She playfully smacked me on the arm. It was a longstanding, and by now rather humorous area of disagreement with us.

"Quiet. The priests are coming," she said excitedly.

From the temple at the top of the pyramid, the chief priest emerged dressed in red and wearing a huge monster mask that covered his entire head. He was to represent the rain god of the east as he slowly descended the steps of the pyramid. Then three more priests emerged dressed in white, black, and yellow to represent the rain gods of the north, west and south. Each of the priests carried a stone ax in his right hand and a crooked piece of wood to represent lightning in his left. Over each priest's shoulder hung a gourd filled with water. At the base of the pyramid, the priests halted, said some prayers, and sprinkled incense and water in front of them. Then each in turn, took off his sandals and walked barefoot across the glowing coals and then back again! I had seen this ceremony before, but it never failed to intrigue me. There was more to the ceremony, but the fire walking was the best part.

As the ceremony was breaking up I saw a messenger from one of the fast canoes work his way through the crowd and say something to Nachan Can who looked upset by whatever it was. At almost the same moment, Can Pec emerged from the crowd with Cab Mut in hand. They marched up to Zazil Ha and me, looked at each other for a moment, then turned to us smiling and said simultaneously; "We're getting married!"

While the congratulations were still filling the air, and Zazil Ha was hugging Cab Mut, a servant tapped me on the shoulder and said that Nachan Can wanted to see me. I excused myself, threaded my way through the crowd and approached Nachan Can, who was still sitting in the Batab's seat at the base of the pyramid.

"I have just received word from one of our messenger canoes," he said, "The Spaniards have landed just to the north of Tulum. And they are on their way south towards Chetumal."

Chapter 23- Montejo

In which I must deal with a new Conquistador

"The Spaniards have come ashore at Xelha, a coastal town north of Tulum," said Nachan Can. "If you were still at Ixil, they would be only two days away."

The invaders had landed on Cozumel, conferred with Nahan Pat, then crossed over and landed at Xelha several months ago. They had come ashore with the flag of Spain unfurled and shouted "Long live Spain!" to the astonished Maya of Xelha. The Spaniards promptly set up a small town as a base of operations. This was alarming news; a passing party of adventurers searching for gold was bad enough, but these apparently intended to stay permanently. The town could become a magnet that would attract invaders from all over. In addition, it was within a day's journey of Cozumel, Tulum, and Coba. If the Spaniards took those cities, trade would be seriously disrupted throughout the Yucatan. The expedition had struck out northwards and fought several battles. Then, when they were down to less than 100 men, they were reinforced and resupplied. Now they were heading towards us.

The next morning, Nachan Can considered the situation and its implications for Chetumal. I met with him, Zotz Bacal and the chief elder in the house of the Batab. Outside it was raining and had been doing so all morning. The chief elder said it was proof that the fire ceremony had been effective. The room was hot and humid as we sat on ledges built into the side walls.

"I know of this place called Xelha," said Nachan Can, "There is a sheltered lagoon that could hold hundreds of canoes. The Spaniards will have a good harbor. They can be reinforced easily."

The elder, Kukul Batz, was a short, thin man who walked with a limp from some long forgotten battle. There was no doubt where he stood. "We must send the holcom to exterminate the invader, before he arrives." he growled.

"I agree that the Spaniards must be driven out," I said, "But I don't think the holcom of Chetumal can do it now. We would have to move hundreds of men a great distance and leave the defenses of Chetumal weakened. In addition, we would also be seen as an invader by the local people, and we might have to fight them as well."

Nachan Can nodded. "It is so. We must wait and stay on our guard. If the Spaniard comes, we must find a way to throw him back."

Afterwards, I told Zazil Ha of our plans. She was silent at first, then spoke softly.

"Gonzalo....There will be blood and death before the Spaniard is driven out. You will be in danger. You will come back to me, won't you? "

I turned to her and gazed into the velvet brownness of her eyes. There were tears starting to form.

"I have lost so much in the last few years," she said, "I could not bear it if I were to lose you also."

"There are not enough Spaniards in this world to keep me away from you," I said.

The boys were away with Cab Mut for the day, so we had a long leisurely hour together in private. Soon, I would finally face my countrymen as an armed enemy. All over the Yucatan, thousands of people were about to play a part in a great drama that could only end tragically for the Maya and their children. But at that moment, as we lay entwined in the familiar warmth of each other's arms, there was only Zazil Ha and I in the whole world.

As I helped prepare the defenses of Chetumal, I thought

207

of my children and at my wife, and I knew I had to do anything I could to protect them from the fate of the Arawaks. Zazil Ha was older now, but as stunning and regal as the day I first saw her. Chuen was tall and gangly with black hair and green eyes. He reminded me of his mother most of all with his intellect and his easy poise. Imix was also tall, but a little heavier. He had reddish hair and a restless energy that reminded me of myself in Castile. Etznab was shorter and thinnest of all. He was focused and intense about everything he saw. Someday, I thought, much of the Yucatan might be populated by people who looked much like these boys. I hoped this new race would be able to capture what is best and noble about its parents and not what is worst.

Soon, we received more information from merchant canoes. The Spaniard leading the invasion was not Cortes, but Francisco de Montejo. He had headed south along the coast in the ship while his lieutenant, a man named Davila, had taken a column of men overland on a roughly parallel course. This was ominous news. If Montejo and Davila could coordinate their efforts, they could encircle Chetumal and attack from both land and sea supported by shipborne artillery.

"We must take the holcom north to meet Davila's column and destroy it, then we will have only the great canoe to deal with," said Kukul Batz when we met to plan our response.

"We must scout this column and assess its strength," said Zotz Bacal. "Then we can plan how to defeat it."

"While he marches, Davila will be out of contact with the ship," I said slowly.

"Of course:" said Kukul Batz, "they will not even be able to see the ship."

"Then what we must do," I said, "is to send warriors and spies north to delay Davila's column and lure it farther and farther from the sea so that they can be isolated and destroyed. Our warriors will drive them from the coast, and our spies will tell them of rich cities to be found further inland."

"But what of the ship?" said Nachan Can.

"With the delays to the Davila, the ship should arrive long before the column," I said. "We will attack it with warriors in canoes to try to harass Montejo. Without Davila's column for support, he may give up the fight."

Nachan Can thought for a moment.

"Let it be done," he said.

The next day, we organized a group of warriors and spies under the command of Can Pec to head north to intercept Davila's column. Now we could only wait, looking anxiously out over the water. We did not have to wait long.

A few days later, a speck on the horizon slowly grew larger until it resolved itself into a Spanish ship. It was of medium size and looked to mount at least eight guns. The ship was a dirty grey in color and had the faded red crosses of Catholic Spain on its sails. The Spaniards cautiously approached to a few hundred yards offshore, then furled the sails onto the yardarms, and dropped anchor. After the splash of the anchor striking the water, the ship became still. There was no move to send a party ashore; they were probably waiting for Davila to make an appearance. Many people of Chetumal came down to the shore to gaze in wonder and fear at the silent ship.

I went out with some other warriors in a canoe to scout the ship. It was named the *La Gavarra*, out of Seville. The Spaniards crowded the rail watching us and some called to us, but they made no other move. I tried to estimate their strength, and from the men I could see, there seemed to be very few on board, perhaps 20 or so. I couldn't be sure, however, since more could be below decks. As I looked at those dirty, bearded faces peering over the rail, I looked for some familiarity or recognition in any of them, but they were all strangers. Nothing seemed familiar but the look of greed.

By the next day, there had still been no move from the ship, but we had reports that a landing party had come ashore during the night and captured two people from Chetumal. The next night, one of the captives was put back ashore. The captive asked to be brought to me and handed me a scroll with the arms of Spain on the top. The Spaniards had been told of my presence by the captives and had sent a message, much as Cortes had done 10 years before.

I took the document and hesitated before opening it. The scroll felt alien and dangerous in my hand, as if I had been holding a snake. I sighed and unrolled the parchment. There was the same vivid black ink I had seen before, and a message that was more personal this time. It read;

Gonzalo, my brother and special friend;

I count it my good fortune that I have arrived and learned of you through the bearer of this letter, so that I can remind you that you are a Christian, bought by the blood of our Redeemer. You have a great opportunity to serve God and the Emperor in the pacification and baptism of these people, and more than this, you have the opportunity to leave your sins behind you, and to honor and benefit yourself. I shall be your very good friend in this and you shall be treated very well. I beseech you not to let the devil influence you not to do what I say, or he will posses himself of you forever.

On behalf of his majesty, I promise to do very well for you. On my honor as a noble gentleman, I give you my word and pledge my faith to keep my promises to you without any reservations whatsoever, favoring and honoring you and making you one of my principal men, and one of the most select and loved.

Consequently, I request that you come to this ship, or to the coast without delay, and help me carry out, through your

counsel and opinions, that which seems most expedient.
  Francisco de Montejo

So now the religious argument was to be used; mixed with a liberal amount of self-interest. I had to admit, it was clever. Religious fervor combined with the prospect of self enrichment had tempted better men than I. There was no chance of my being seduced by this appeal; the only thing to decide was how to answer. I thought that it would be best to appear friendly so that I might be able to deceive him or negotiate concessions later. Still, I couldn't resist some irony in my reply. Montejo's claim to be my very good friend was especially irritating, since he really wanted to use me for his benefit. It seemed that, to him, a very good friend was someone who was able to deceive another. So I found a piece of charcoal from a cooking fire and wrote a reply on the back of the parchment.

Capitan Francisco de Montejo;
  Senor, I kiss your grace's hands, but as I am a slave, I have no freedom to join you. I do remember God, and I will remember you, my lord. The Spaniards will find in me a very good friend.

Gonzalo Guerrero[11]

I sent this reply and contemplated the next move. Wanting to keep them off balance and disoriented, I sent 25 canoes of warriors out to attack the *La Gavarra*. They fired arrows and spears from a position too low for the cannons to hit. They did little damage, since the thick wooden sides of the ship might as well have been a fortress against our light missiles, but they kept the Spanish confused and on edge. Meanwhile, I was overseeing the fortification of Chetumal.

The Maya were aware of fortifications, of course, and had

used them long before I arrived. For defending against mounted and firearm wielding troops, however, a different approach was needed. Stopping a bullet or a cannonball required thicker barriers than merely stopping arrows and spears. The horses were another problem; they could get around most barriers. For this, we needed trenches dug with branches covering them to trap the horses and riders.

We made two lines of mounded fortifications encircling the city. I had learned about the best way to fortify against the attack of European troops from my uncle, and carefully laid out the angles and entrapments. I put the entire holcom to work on the task of digging the extensive earthworks, and the project went rapidly, although many of the warriors grumbled about doing slave work. But I wanted the warriors to do the work so they would be familiar with the fortifications and comfortable fighting from them. I had another reason, as well; I thought they would fight harder to avoid being driven from a place if they had worked to build it.

I stood with Nachan Can watching as hundreds of warriors dug at the earth to throw up the long fortifications of dirt and rubble. Other groups were digging pitfalls for the horses in locations I had specified. It was a scene of massive, ant-like activity, and I wondered what the Spaniards were thinking of this effort, which was clearly visible from the ship. Nachan Can had a similar thought.

"Surely, the Spaniards must see what we are doing," he said.

"I want them to see," I said, "I want them to worry about the reception they can expect. Most of all, I want to upset their plan."

"How will you upset their plan?" said Nachan Can.

"If they intend to attack, they must do so soon," I said, "before we are finished. They realize that every minute they wait will make their task harder. But if they attack now, they must do so without the support of Davila's column which has not yet arrived. So they must either attack now with a weaker force, or attack later when we are strongest."

"I do not think they will attack without the others," said Nachan Can shading his eyes with his hand as he gazed towards the *La Gavarra*, "there are too few on the ship."

"You are probably right," I said, "If we can destroy Davila's column, Montejo will never attack on his own. But look over towards the pyramid. A messenger approaches."

In a few moments, the messenger I had seen arrived to report from the warriors I had sent to intercept Davila. He was breathing rapidly and was shiny with sweat. He carried with him a battered Spanish helmet.

"Can Pec has been luring the enemy farther inland as instructed," he began.

"Good," I said, "that is exactly what we want."

"But Can Pec reports that the Spaniards are too strong to be defeated by his forces. They have over 150 men and 10 of the great deer-men (mounted men). He has sent this Spanish headpiece to show Nachan Can the protection that makes the Spaniard difficult to kill."

Nachan Can examined the helmet and tapped the hard surface with his finger. "Where are the Spaniards now?"

"About five days journey."

"Five days!" Nachan Can said, "If we could destroy one group, the other would probably turn back on its own."

"Yes," I replied in frustration, "but we can't destroy the ship because it is too sturdy and well defended, and we haven't the strength to destroy Davila. So in five days' time the Spaniards can launch a combined attack."

I paced back and forth in agitated thought, while Nachan Can and the messenger watched me. I looked out at the ship, calmly riding at anchor in the heat haze on the surface of the oily looking calm water, waiting for Davila to arrive. On the ground was a flat stone and a piece of charcoal from an old fire. I picked them up and wrote on the rock. Then I turned to the messenger, and handed it to him.

"Take this to Can Pec," I said, "Tell him to have a spy take it to Davila and to tell him that a party of Spaniards was ambushed along the coast and every one was killed. Tell Davila that the Spaniards were in a great canoe that had these symbols on it. Now, go quickly!"

On the rock, I had written the words *La Gavarra*.

That afternoon, as the second part of my plan, we sent two canoes laden with food and water jars to the ship, and I went along to listen to what was said in Spanish. The canoes hailed the ship and asked to come aboard. One of the Spaniards was reasonably fluent in the Maya language, and was the translator. He said we could approach, but not come aboard. Cautiously, the canoe bumped against the side of the *La Gavarra*, as suspicious, bearded faces peered down from the rail above. I reached out and grasped a metal hull fitting to steady the canoe. It felt cool and familiar in my hand.

"I bring greetings from Nachan Can, Batab of Chetumal," shouted the elder. We waited while this was translated. The Spaniards reaction was interesting.

"Greetings, he says," said one, "Treacherous heathens...are the cannons loaded?"

"The food's probably poisoned."

The translator spoke; "If you come in peace, then tell us what you want." This last word he mistranslated, causing confused looks among the canoe men. I whispered the correct word to the elder.

"My lord has commanded me to bring these gifts as a sign of our sympathy for the loss of your countrymen," the elder said smoothly. "We have received word that a great battle was fought to the north and the man called Davila and all his companions were killed. And this," he said, holding up the Spanish helmet, "was brought back from the battle ground by a messenger."

The flourishing of the helmet added just the right touch of

authenticity and drama to the false tale, and I was pleased to see the Spaniards gasp and go pale when they saw it. One Spaniard, a tall, bearded one that I took to be Montejo himself said, in Spanish;

"Holy mother of God! Davila and all of his men....gone! This is a grave calamity."

Others were crossing themselves and praying. Several shook their heads in stunned silence. Others spoke in voices that were a mixture of fear and awe.

"Davila and all his company; slain to a man."

"This is Satan's own country!"

They were convinced. As we were pulling away, I heard Montejo say that their mission in Chetumal was now hopeless. Of course, this was exactly what I wanted them to think.

The *La Gavarra* upped anchor and sailed slowly out of sight. A few days later, we received word that Davila, believing the spy's false report that a disaster had befallen Montejo, had also turned back. Chetumal was saved.[12]

Chapter 24- Celebrations

In which we enjoy a respite, for a while

The celebrations continued for three days, with huge cooking fires set up in the plazas. It was more like a festival than a banquet, with people coming and going constantly. A more formal feast was planned for when Can Pec and the warriors returned in a few weeks, but in the meantime, food and bowls of balche were everywhere, and Chetumal was a riot of noise and excitement, with the joy of the people filling every street along with the pungent smells of the cooking fires. While the city was still drunk with victory, however, Chuen came to me.

"Father," he said, "everyone is rejoicing because the Spaniards were defeated, but I know they are wrong."

"What do you mean?" I said.

"I have heard you and mother talk of Spain and the Spaniards." he said, "I have seen the maps you have made of the Yucatan and of Chetumal. The Spaniards are not defeated, only pausing. Soon, they will come and will return again and again until they overrun the land. We have to win all the time, but they only have to win once, for when they are established, they will never leave."

I was amazed at how perceptive Chuen was, at a time when everyone else thought the danger was passed. Chuen had always been the intellectual one; the one who saw the overall nature of things and was a step ahead of most people in understanding. His words were like a bath in cold water.

"Yes, Chuen," I replied, "I am afraid you are right. The others don't understand, but it is so."

216

"Father, I am your oldest son," he continued, "and it is my duty to do what I can to defend my family and my people. I wish to become a warrior."

"What?" I said, almost shouting, "You can't be a warrior. You are needed here. We have warriors already; but you are more than that. You are the future. You are the hope of the Maya. You must live on to help rebuild and replenish. I may not always be here to protect your mother and your brothers. You must be here for them."

"If the Spaniards come," he replied, "it will be too late to help. I must try to keep that from happening."

I looked at Chuen carefully. He was almost as tall as I was, and looked very much like a Maya except for his green eyes. Of all my sons, Chuen most embodied his mother; he had her poise, spirit and intellect. Some of his gestures reminded me of her and his laugh was almost identical. I had expected him to become a scribe or astronomer or mathematician, but never a warrior. He seemed all wrong for such a brutal calling. Imix, with his recklessness seemed much better suited.

"You will not be a warrior," I said, "There is far more to the traditions of the Maya than fighting. You must help to preserve the knowledge, the philosophy, and the spirit of a great people. You must live to keep the flame burning."

He was silent a moment. "I will respect your wishes, father," he said, "but at least let me be trained so that I can help preserve my life and that of our family if you are not here."

This seemed a reasonable and prudent request, so I agreed to let Chuen begin warrior training the next week. He thanked me and ran off. I watched him go with my heart filled with both pride and sadness.

In spite of an uncertain future, we had won the first battle in the war to keep Chetumal and the Yucatan free of the Spanish presence. Montejo and Davila had been turned back with little loss of life on either side. Of course, this victory was only temporary; Montejo and Davila were sure to meet up again and discover the ruse. What would happen then was anyone's guess. For the moment, however, the invader had been turned away, like Attila at the gates of Rome.

Once again, I was a hero. It seemed as if the Maya were either ready to canonize me or kill me, depending on the circumstances. For the moment, no one could do enough for me. When Can Pec and the warriors who had been north returned a few weeks later, there was a more formal great feast of rejoicing to welcome them back. The feast was held at night in the great torchlit plaza near the Batab's house. There was every variety of food and drink, including the ever present balche. The guests were seated at long wooden tables set in rows radiating out from the raised platform on which the Batab and the elders sat. Musicians passed among the crowd blowing, clanging, bashing and otherwise making the infernal racket that passed for music among these people. Small groups of feathered dancers cavorted in time with the noise and everyone was having a grand time. Zotz Bacal, who was reserved and stuffy any other time, managed have enough balche to get roaring drunk. He finally passed out on a table, much to the amusement of the diners seated there.

As I sat with Zazil Ha, Chuen, Imix, Etznab, Can Pec and Cab Mut, people kept stopping by the table to congratulate me on the brilliant campaign strategy. The boys beamed with pride and Zazil Ha lit up the night with her brilliant smile.

The feast had started with a ceremonial blood sacrifice by the Batab and the chief priest, but soon became a scene of revelry. If the Spaniards were to appear now, I thought, they could simply walk into Chetumal and take it.

"Zazil Ha," said Cab Mut, rushing up to our table, "my wedding to Can Pec has been delayed too long. But now there is nothing to stop us. We wed in three weeks time!"

"And this time," said Can Pec, "the Spaniards had better

not get in the way!"

The celebration was still going on as we made our way home. Zazil Ha hung on my arm contentedly while the boys followed at a short distance.

"I am glad you were able to get rid of the Spaniards, Gonzalo," she said, "It must be hard to fight your countrymen, but I know why you do it."

"Zazil Ha," I said, "we have been together for 16 years now. You know my thoughts and I know yours. This victory will not last forever. I think you realize that as well as I do."

"I know," she said.

"We can defeat them once or twice, but in the end, they will overwhelm us," I said. "I want you to promise me that, if anything happens to me and the Spaniards come, you and the boys will use your knowledge of Spanish to protect yourselves; even if you must cooperate with them to do so."

"I can only promise to do what I must," she said. "I cannot promise to cooperate."

"If...if something does happen to me," I said, "I want you to know that it was my love for you that made me do what I did. If the Spaniards call me a traitor, remember that I was loyal to what I loved most."

"I know that also," she said quietly. Then we stopped and kissed to the muffled snickers of Chuen, Imix, and Etznab walking behind us.

By the time the wedding of Can Pec and Cab Mut arrived, the nervousness and excitement of Can Pec was such that an invasion of the Spaniards would have paled by comparison. He had always been a worrier, of course, but now he fretted over details constantly and even Cab Mut was getting irritated.

"Gonz-lo," he said one day, "I have been thinking about the wedding."

"Really?" I said wearily, "I would never have guessed."

"What do you mean by that?" he said, defensively.

"Simply that every discussion we have had in the last two weeks has begun with you saying that you have been thinking about the wedding!" I said testily.

"And what is wrong with that?" he demanded, "A man should think about his own wedding. There are important decisions to be made."

"Oh, yes!" I said sarcastically, "Important decisions such as how many feathers to wear, or who will be the first to give a boring speech, or whether the tamales should be placed to the left or to the right of the chilies, or which mantle you should wear."

"Why shouldn't I be careful which mantle I wear?" he said.

"Can Pec, you only own three mantles, and they are all red! Why can't you be concerned with something important?"

"How do you know it isn't important when you won't even listen to me?" he snapped.

"All right," I sighed, "what is it this time?"

"Well, I've been thinking; which of my sandals should I wear?"

Meanwhile, Etznab was having troubles of his own. He had been down with the canoemen, and had been trying to study the design of the canoes to try to improve the speed, or ease of paddling. He had made several models at home with different hull shapes and had been anxious to try his ideas on a full sized canoe. One day, Etznab came home in a rage of frustration and threw one of his canoe models against the wall. I was astonished to see such a display from Etznab, who had always been quiet and not prone to excitability.

"The canoemen!" he said resentfully, "They won't try my design for a new canoe. I have worked for weeks with models and I think I have a way to make the canoes faster with no more paddling effort. I explained it to them and showed them the model, but no one will build a canoe that way. They all say that the canoes always have been built the same way, so they should not be changed."

Tradition again, I thought. It was both the strength and the curse of the Maya.

"Why can't they see that there could be a better way?" Etznab went on, "Why can't someone at least try?"

"Perhaps I can explain, Gonzalo," It was Zazil Ha. She had heard the conversation and had come up beside Etznab.

"The Maya are a people with a long and proud past," she began, "They cling to the old ways that have served them well. When invaders came in the past, they brought new ways also, but the Maya did not rush to change, and the invaders were absorbed. By holding to the old ways, the Maya have survived. So do not be quick to condemn; the canoemen are merely being Mayan."

Etznab was confused, as was I.

"Then should I not try to make things better?" he asked, "Should I not try to change anything?"

"Of course you must!" She almost shouted the words. "You must always try and always push the others to try also. For there are some changes that must be made. You have a great gift; you can look beyond tradition, and find the ways to make life better. You must nourish that gift, and never give up. Never!"

Etznab smiled and said, "Thank you mother, I will heed your words." Then he walked out with a new determination.

"Zazil Ha," I said, "you never lose the ability to surprise me."

She smiled slyly. "You should not be surprised, Gonzalo. I have always known the value of traditions, even when I have broken them. After all, I broke one of the oldest traditions of all."

"What tradition was that?" I asked.

"Never marry a dzul," she said mischievously.

221

When the day for the wedding finally came, I felt as much relief as joy. Can Pec had worked himself up into a frenzy of worry and maddening attention to insignificant detail. Several times, we had almost come to blows over some problem I thought was laughable but he thought was of critical importance. Now, finally, the day had come.

The wedding was a great success. Can Pec's nervousness evaporated when the ceremony began and the tying of the mantles together was complete. Cab Mut looked completely happy, Zazil Ha sat with that somewhat smug look that many women have at weddings, and everyone had a good time. The speeches were somewhat less boring than usual because every speaker made some joke about Can Pec's nervousness the past few weeks, much to the delight of the crowd. After the speeches and the banquet that followed, I realized that Can Pec was married at last. Now, perhaps, he would devote his full attention and energies to the holcom. When he had been on a mission, he had been the competent professional he always was, but at the warrior compound, he had been constantly distracted.

Late that afternoon, when all the guests had left, I walked with Zazil Ha along the beach. The water felt cool on our feet as we walked along the edge of the bay.

"I hope Cab Mut is as happy as I have been," she said.

"Oh," I said, "I think she will be fine. If Can Pec is not to her liking, she will no doubt tell him so, and he will adjust. The old warrior now has a new Nacom."

As we laughed, I noticed a commotion further down the beach. A group of men walked along the edge of the water towards us. They were very excited and were shouting and gesturing towards two canoes that were paddling side by side parallel to the beach. One canoe's occupant was large and muscular, and the other's was small and thin. Each man was paddling furiously, and the canoes were moving rapidly in our direction.

"It looks like they are racing," said Zazil Ha.

"Yes," I said, "and the thin one seems to be beating the big one. That is strange. The big one should be a much stronger paddler."

Zazil Ha eyes widened and she held her hand up to her mouth. "Gonzalo!" she said excitedly, "That is Etznab!"

In a second, I could see that she was right. Etznab was paddling rapidly and was widening the distance between himself and his rival. The men on the shore were cheering for one or the other. Zazil Ha and I suddenly found ourselves cheering for Etznab as he pulled ahead. They were racing towards a pole in the water about 30 yards away.

"Paddle, Etznab; you are winning!" we shouted. And as he reached the pole ahead of the other canoe, he stopped and the crowd cheered wildly. I asked one of them what the race was about.

"Etznab told everyone he knew how to make a canoe faster, but no one would build one his way because it was not the way we were used to," the man said, "Finally, Etznab built a canoe himself, and challenged our strongest paddler to a race. Everyone laughed at him, but no more. I will ask him to build a canoe for me, too."

Zazil Ha and I looked at each other.

"Etznab listened to you," I said. "He now knows when to break a tradition."

Chapter 25- Montejo the Younger

In which there is new trouble to the north

So Can Pec and Cab Mut settled down to married life, Zazil Ha continued to teach and study astronomy, Etznab continued to experiment and tinker, and I continued my routine with the warriors, all the while with one eye on the horizon watching for the return of the Spaniards. Chuen began warrior training and was an adequate, if not exceptional soldier. Later that year, he was taken on as an apprentice by the scribes who kept the records and did the calculations of the time cycles. If Chuen was a mediocre warrior, he was an outstanding apprentice, often seeming to be one step ahead of his teachers.

Imix, on the other hand, only seemed to excel in trouble. His episode with the wounded boar was typical of his habit of jumping into something impetuously, and suffering for it later. He asked to begin warrior training, but I told him to wait a year because I knew he would rebel at the discipline. During that year, Imix spent half of his time trying to get out of the trouble he had gotten himself into the other half.

By 1530, it had been two years since the LA GAVARRA departed and there had been no further intrusions in our waters. We heard from passing merchants and canoe men that Montejo had met up with Davila and they had abandoned Xelha and reestablished themselves in Tabasco on the other side of the Yucatan. They were probing outward from that area through the desolate brush and swamps to the few settlements in the interior, and to Campeche and

Champoton on the northern coast. Cortes had taken an expedition across the country to the south, from the land of the Mexica to Honduras, which is over 100 miles south of Chetumal. I had even heard a rumor that Montejo had reappeared at the sacred city of Chichen Itza in the interior. The Spaniard was nibbling around the edges of our world. How long could it be until he was ready to take a bigger bite?

By the end of the year, the old astronomer that Zazil Ha had been studying with died suddenly, leaving a void in this most important of positions. The astronomer was vital to daily life since he, along with the mathematicians and scribes, determined the time for planting. This was critical since an error of even a few days could result in a crop failure and famine.

A controversy soon developed because it was generally accepted that Zazil Ha was now the most able astronomer in Chetumal. It was also generally accepted that the post could never be held by a woman. There were all sorts of religious and social reasons for this, most of them nonsense in my opinion, but the prohibition was strong. In addition to being a woman, of course, Zazil Ha had the additional handicap of not being born in Chetumal. I had a lot of fun with her about this since I had suffered the same problem in Ixil.

At any rate, some of the more practical people in Chetumal thought that Zazil Ha should be made astronomer, or at least assistant to the astronomer. They argued that in such troubled times, Chetumal must have the best astronomer it could find, no matter who. But just when the tongues were starting to wag in earnest, Zazil Ha publicly recommended a younger apprentice for the post, and declined to even be an assistant. Nachan Can and the elders agreed and the matter was settled. Later, when we were sitting in front of our dwelling listening to the sounds of the tropical night and smelling the wisps of smoke from the incense and cooking fires, I asked her why she had done it.

225

"There will be enough for the people of Chetumal to concern themselves with soon," she said philosophically, "They must not waste their energies on trifles."

"Trifles?" I exclaimed, "This is one of the most important posts in the city. You are the best they have."

She smiled. "Perhaps," she said, looking off into the distance, "but their faith in the traditions of the Maya will be shaken soon enough. The Spaniards will turn their world upside down, and I will not be a part of that. Let the people of Chetumal keep what traditions they can....for the moment."

"But what about you? What about what you want?" I said.

"Gonzalo," she replied, turning to me, "I do not have to tell you that there are things in this world that are of more importance than you or me; things that are bigger."

When Imix finally joined the warriors, he settled down, somewhat. The discipline was a burden, but he put up with it for the opportunity to have an outlet for his energy and destructive tendencies. When the warrior trainees sparred with padded weapons, Imix was a terror. Several times he was punished because he kept flailing away at an opponent who was already defeated. Even so, the commanders were happy at the prospect of turning Imix loose on an unsuspecting enemy.

After the fall of Tenochtitlan, Tolotl had shifted his trading activities to Chetumal, Tulum and Coba. He had prospered, though not as he had under the Mexica. I saw him again about a year after Montejo had left. He had recently been to Chichen Itza.

"Oh, yes," he said, "I travel to Chichen Itza frequently. There are still enough pilgrims there to create a good market in small bits of gold or jewelry for offerings to the gods."

"But I have heard that Montejo is at Chichen Itza and has established a settlement there as he tried to do at Chetumal several years ago."

"No, that was the father," said Tolotl, "His son, Montejo the younger is at Chichen Itza. He has about 200 or 250 men and 20 or 30 horses. They have gotten the support of the Maya of the Ceh Pech and Ah Kin Chel alliances to the west. The Batab of Chichen Itza has allowed the Spaniards to settle there for the time being, but it is said he will turn on them soon."

"Why do they think so?" I asked.

Tolotl sighed. "I'm afraid the Spaniards are like a guest who stays too long. He is welcome at first, but soon becomes a burden. The Spaniards established a town at the holy city and call it Ciudad Real de Chichen Itza. Soon after establishing themselves, they tried to apply the *Repartimiento* system."

"I know of the *Repartimiento* system." I said, "It starts with a declaration that the people acknowledge the sovereignty of the Spanish king."

Tolotl nodded. "Indeed. But when Montejo read this to the Batab, he answered by saying, 'We already have kings, oh noble lords. We are the Itza!' I was told that Montejo was quite disappointed."

"Who are the Itza?" I asked.

"They were invaders long ago, but are Maya now, and among the fiercest of the Maya at that." he said. "Chichen Itza was once their capitol. At any rate, I left soon after, but have been told that resistance is building to the *Repartimiento* system and that the Spaniards have divided the land among themselves and are attempting to take food and labor by force. I would not be surprised if the pilgrim trade is not disrupted as a result. I may have to avoid the place until this is settled."

As I spoke with Tolotl, I realized that what happened at Chichen Itza would have a much greater impact on the Yucatan than what happened at Chetumal. Chichen Itza was a sacred pilgrimage city that held high religious and historic significance for all the Maya. The occupation of Chichen Itza would have a greater impact than the occupation of Chetumal ever would, as if a Moorish army were to occupy Rome. Montejo would have to be stopped at all costs. I also came to realize that I would have to go there to help the Maya in the fight, for their sake and my family's. All the years of fights, skirmishes and deceptions led to this one struggle in a far off, holy city. The fate of the entire Maya world might well depend on what happened at Chichen Itza.

I talked to Zazil Ha about going to Chichen Itza. Her quick mind instantly grasped the strategic and symbolic importance of the city and the necessity for ejecting the Spanish settlement. That didn't make the prospect of separation any easier. She nodded silently, and bit her lower lip, a sign of internal anguish I had seen before.

"I will go with you," she said.

"No," I told her firmly. I seldom tried to order Zazil Ha to do anything, but this was too important. "There will be great danger there. Our sons could lose a father. They must not lose a mother as well."

"All right, Gonzalo," she said finally, "I understand why you must go to Chichen Itza alone, but my heart is sad at the thought of being apart."

That night, I told the boys I was going to Chichen Itza. Imix wanted to go with me to fight Spaniards. Imix was now 19, and was clearly suited to be a warrior. His place was with the others. I put my hand on his shoulder and wished him luck.

"Thank you, father," he said as he turned to leave.

After a hug from Zazil Ha, he was gone.

Chuen wanted to come with me too, but I made him stay along with Etznab and Zazil Ha. She would need them in the months to come, and the Mayan people would need their knowledge and skills to survive. We said our goodbyes and I told them to never forget who they were; that they were a new race, a blending of two great peoples with the blood of

Spanish knights and Mayan kings in their veins.

Finally, I was alone with Zazil Ha for what might be the last time. We looked at each other silently for a moment in the now empty house, then I took her in my arms and held her tightly. "I will always return to you," I said. "Remember that."

"If you are able," she said, almost choking on the words.

"Zazil Ha," I said, trying to reassure her, "I..."

But she put a finger to my lips to stop me.

"Gonzalo," she said softly, "if you return to me, then we need no words. If you do not return, then there are no words. Go now, and do what must be done for our people. Remember that no matter how dark the night, how hot the sun, or how terrible the battle, you will carry my heart with you always."

I kissed her and held her close without speaking. We clung together tightly, taking refuge in each other's arms against a world that was pulling us apart. I drank in the familiar warmth and feel of her as a man will drink deeply before crossing a desert. Many times in the weeks to come, I would return to this one bittersweet moment and hold it close to me as I held her close to me now.

Finally, I whispered a few final words in her ear, took one last long look into her deep brown eyes, and was gone.

Chapter 26- Chichen Itza

In which I meet a new enemy and an old friend

Montejo had landed on the western shore with 200 men and 40 horses. They had marched through the land of the Ceh Pech Maya and formed an alliance with them and with the Ah Kin Chel Maya. With auxiliary warriors from these allies, Montejo entered the land of the Cupul Maya in the center of the Yucatan. The Cupuls resisted, but the combined forces had no trouble defeating them. The expedition then founded a settlement at Chichen Itza, at the suggestion of the Ceh Pech, who no doubt enjoyed seeing their old enemies the Cupul humiliated.

It appeared that Montejo and Davila had planned to conquer the Yucatan by establishing bases at Chetumal and at Chichen Itza, from which they could strike at the entire area. These bases would have split the land down the middle and planted the flag of Castile in the heart of the country.

The Batab of Chichen Itza was initially friendly to Montejo, even taking him in to live in his house. He had hoped that the Spaniards were only to stay for a short while, and even provided them labor to build temporary houses in Chichen Itza.

Once he was established, however, Montejo promptly attempted to set up the Repartimiento system by giving large tracts of land to his men. Tribute from these tracts was demanded to supply the Spaniards with food, supplies and labor. The proud Cupul soon turned against the Spaniards because of these demands, and refused to cooperate. As the Spaniards increasingly used force to obtain the labor and supplies they needed, non-cooperation soon turned to active

230

resistance. At one point, the Batab himself tried to assassinate Montejo, but was killed in the attempt.

Now the Spaniards were increasingly isolated and had to rely on raids to obtain food. At one point, the warriors had attacked the Spaniards and killed several men and horses. The Spaniards were now under a blockade in their fortified settlement in the ancient city. The lords of the Cupul Maya had sent out a call to rally others to their cause. Now the Spaniards were being encircled as more warriors arrived.

I traveled with Can Pec and 20 other Chetumal warriors. Our journey took us through Coba and the lake where Zazil Ha had shocked me by bathing naked in public, and past the marketplace where I had first met with Tolotl and heard of the wonders of the Aztecs. Somewhere to the south was Ixil, now under the thumb of Cuac Caan and the loathsome Pom Tzec.

From Coba, the remains of an old ceremonial road, or sacbe, led almost due west and passed to the south of our destination. This was the easiest way through the forest so we traveled for several days along the partially overgrown surface.

Finally, as we approached Chichen Itza, we saw more warriors that had gathered to fight Montejo. As we came within sight of Chichen Itza itself, we found ourselves among warriors from all over the Yucatan. The Cupul Maya, wearing red and yellow mantles, were the majority since this was in their territory, but there were also warriors of the Chikinchel, painted all in red, who had fought a bloody battle with Montejo's father when he had marched north from Xelha several years before, warriors of Cochua, with their red and blue feathered armbands, and warriors from the alliances of Sotuta, Tazes, and Ecab. The western alliances of Ceh Pech, Ah Kin Chel and Tutul Xiu remained on the side of the Spaniards, though they were not active militarily.

The warriors had erected barriers and fortifications at

places controlling the roads in and out of Chichen Itza. A noose was being slowly tightened. There was an air of excitement among the warriors surrounding Chichen Itza. They seemed to sense that some great destiny was being played out and were determined to be a part of it. We were welcomed by the many warriors from all over the Yucatan who manned the barricades that we passed through.

I was gratified to find that I was known to many of these warriors as a leader of sorts. My role in fighting the Spaniards at Ecab and Chetumal made me accepted and even respected by many as a leader of Maya resistance. I was given a stone building to use as a headquarters and our warriors were given several wooden buildings that had been abandoned by the Spaniards as they had drawn their defensive perimeter inward. My headquarters was a small stone building with a decorative roof comb and was painted a dull red color. It sat on a raised terrace directly across from a round tower that had been used as an observatory.

The city of Chichen Itza was not occupied full time as Chetumal was, but was a place of pilgrimage and sacrifice. The capitol of the Cupul Maya was at Saci, some miles to the east. At the center of Chichen Itza was a pyramid dedicated to the worship of Kukulcan, the feathered serpent who was the god of wisdom and learning. Kukulcan was also the Mayan counterpart of the Aztec god Quetzalcoatl whose predicted return from the east in the form of a bearded man had helped Cortes conquer the Mexica nation. The books of Chilam Balam had a similar prophesy. I wondered if Montejo knew of the story and wanted to take advantage of it by coming to Chichen Itza.

Like the nearby Temple of the Sun, the pyramid had been built by a previous invader who had introduced human sacrifice.[13] There were the usual heart cutting sacrifices, and also the sacrifice of people and objects by throwing them into a large cenote near the pyramid. The city must have been extensive at one time, but now was reduced to a few score occupied buildings that were in various states of disrepair. Some buildings were almost indistinguishable from the vegetation that was slowly engulfing them; others were merely mounds of rubble and brush. Huge structures of indeterminate shape lay beneath tangles of vines and creepers.

The first thing I did after getting settled was to sketch a map of the area. I made several trips and talked to many people to get the feel of the place. The Spanish settlement of Cuidad Real de Chichen Itza was scattered throughout the city, but was centered around a massive structure that had been a ball court. I had heard of the ritual ball game called Poc Topak, but had never seen it played. The game consisted of two teams moving a ball around by hitting it with their knees, elbows, and hips, trying to score by bouncing or driving the ball through a heavy stone ring set high into one of the side walls.

The ball court at Chichen Itza had not been used for many years, but the massive complex of rectangular walls resembled a fortress, and, for this reason, Montejo had made the Spanish headquarters there. Between the side walls, a distance of perhaps 100 feet, the Spaniards had built a series of wooden structures that housed them and their horses. There were two walls about 25 feet high and over 300 feet long, and a detached short wall about five feet high at each end. The walls formed a rectangle about 400 feet long and 150 feet wide. This configuration gave the Spaniards an easily defensible fort with four gates. Men at arms stood guard on the tops of the walls, so that, except for the unusual shapes and the serpent carvings, the Spanish enclave resembled a medieval castle. There was even a square temple at the top of one of the high walls with a stone stairway leading up to it, reminding me of the tower keep that was a feature of European castles.   I saw several of the Spaniards pacing back and forth on guard duty and they appeared tired and nervous looking. Most had bandages, probably from wounds received in earlier skirmishes. They looked different from the Spaniards I remembered. They seemed dirtier and more world worn, as if their time in the Yucatan had made them harder, tougher, and more cynical. We had been young and optimistic; we were going to save the heathen and enrich ourselves at the same time. These men seemed to know that there were no riches and little room for Christian charity.

I was with Can Pec when I first saw the ball court. Storm clouds were massed in the skies behind the forbidding walls, giving the place an ominous aspect. I examined the fortifications from all angles, but could find no weak point. The Maya had built too well. Can Pec and I sat thoughtfully on an overturned stone and gazed at the foe. Here, Can Pec was absorbed by the responsibilities of being a warrior. Cab Mut would have to wait.

"This will be difficult," he said, finally.

I nodded, still looking at the ball court.

"It's a strange thing. I have been a warrior all my adult life," he continued, still with his eyes fixed on the ball court, "It's all I have ever wanted to be, ever since I was a boy in Ixil. There have been many battles, against many enemies, but this disturbs me greatly."

I looked at him. He continued looking at the ball court.

"I have never feared an enemy, but this time, it almost seems we are fighting fate itself."

He turned to me at last and said, "Gonz-lo, the Spaniards will one day rule this land, won't they?"

I didn't answer at first, trying to think of some optimistic reply, but I couldn't lie to Can Pec; we had been through too much together.

"Yes, my friend, I believe they will. But the Maya will endure."

For days, I studied the problem of getting at the Spaniards in their fortress. One day, I was in my headquarters pouring over some maps and sketches I had made when a guard came in.

"Excuse me, Gonz-lo," he said, "but there is a woman called Ix Kukum here to see you."

This was not unusual. Several times, I had been interrupted by people who wanted to see me on some pretense, but were merely curious to see the white warrior who fought with the Maya. As I said, I had become well known.

"I'm too busy to see anyone," I said, without looking up, "Besides, I don't know anyone by that name. Tell her to be gone."

"As you wish," said the guard and left.

Ix Kukum means Lady of the Quetzal Feather, and indicates someone who, like the Quetzal feather, possesses both beauty and great value. But I had more important things to do than to meet strange women.

I heard a faint murmur of voices outside, and the guard was back.

"I am sorry, Gonz-lo," he said, apologetically, "but Ix Kukum insists she must see you now. She won't go away."

"All right," I sighed, "I will see her, but tell her to be brief. I have much to do."

A moment later, I was aware of a woman standing in the doorway. Because I was busy and somewhat annoyed at the interruption, I continued examining the map without looking up.

"Yes, what is it?" I said gruffly.

"Hello, Dzul."

I snapped my head up, and there stood Cimi.

"Cimi!" I gasped, "Oh, my God, you're alive!" I stood up so suddenly I knocked the table over. I reached out and touched her face, hardly daring to believe it might be real. It was, and I embraced her so hard she gasped for breath.

"Cimi," I kept repeating, "we thought you were killed when Pom Tzec attacked Ixil, but you are alive. How did you find me?"

"I heard them speak of the dzul who fought with the warriors," she said, smiling, "and I knew it had to be you."

I looked at her. She was a mature woman now, but still had that look of curiosity and cheerfulness that I knew so well. Her face was attractive, but bore the scars left by the smallpox.

"But, what...how..." I said, confused, "how did you survive the fall of Ixil? And what of Balam and Ix Kutz, and Ahau?"

Her smile faded. "My mother woke me one morning and said that warriors were attacking Ixil. My father told us to leave immediately and go to Izamal where my aunt lives. He said to go to the north, but not to stop for anything and not to look back. He said not to wait for him. He would send for us or join us when it was safe. Then he went to fight.....I never saw him again."

She paused and I looked at her more closely. She was tall and intelligent looking, and was attractive in the delicate way Zazil Ha was. Cimi had lost the rapid chattering speech she had had as a child, and her cheerfulness and optimism had been dampened by a life of too much hardship and too much tragedy. She would be..how old now, 28? I was overjoyed to see her, but also a little sad to know that the Cimi I had known was gone forever.

"As we left Ixil," she continued, "we crossed the raised plaza on the north side and looked back at the city. There were warriors fighting from the milpas into the center of Ixil. There were so many, they covered the ground. Even from that distance, we could see that our warriors were being pushed back and Ixil would soon fall."

"We pressed on to the north of Ixil and made our way

through the tangled forests to Izamal. We seldom had enough food and never enough water. Mother found berries and we stole corn from small milpas and ate it raw. Ahau cut his leg on a thorn bush and Mother and I took turns helping him walk. We walked until our sandals broke and then until our feet bled. Finally, we reached Izamal and found my aunt. Weeks went by and we never heard from my father. Then two years later, my mother got the sickness and died. Before she died, she gave me my adult name...Ix Kukum."

"I'm sorry, Cimi," I said, "Ix Kutz was a fine person. And your father, Balam was the one who made me a warrior."

She stopped and suddenly cheered up as if dismissing the memories from her mind.

"But that was long ago," she said brightly, "I still live in Izamal....with my husband, Can Matz. Here he is now."

I looked around at a tall warrior who had appeared in the doorway.

"We have come to help drive out the Spaniards," she said, "We have left our daughter in Izamal."

Cimi was married and had a daughter; and her name was now Ix Kukum. I was still having trouble grasping it. We talked for another hour as her husband sat somewhat lost in the flood of news and memories he only knew second hand. She was delighted to hear of how I had saved Ix Chan.

"When we left, I couldn't find Ix Chan; there was no time," she remembered, "I have always thought she was burned. I should have known that my friend Dzul would save her."

I told Cimi...Ix Kukum... that Zazil Ha and the boys missed her terribly and that she must promise that if anything happened to me she would go to Chetumal and see them. She promised and turned to leave. As she started down the path from the house with Can Matz. I called to her and she turned around.

"Ix Kukum," I said, "You said you have a daughter. What is her name?"

She smiled with a smile as bright as those I remembered. "Her name is Cimi!" she laughed.

Chapter 27- An Unexpected Enemy

In which I suddenly come face to face with my past

I spent long hours scouting the Spanish fort at the ball court to find a weakness, but could only find a small gap in some thick vegetation that choked the northwest gate. The other gates were barricaded with stones, earth and debris, but this gate, because of a thick tangle of bushes, was only partly closed. I found a gap in the bushes and a vantage point from which I could see what was happening within the walls. We could never attack through so narrow a gap, but, at least I could spy occasionally.

The Spaniards came and went all day long. There were armed forays to outlying areas to take food and supplies. Often, they would bring back prisoners to labor for them. Occasionally, there would be an alarm raised by ringing a bell that was placed in the temple at the top of the high wall. Most of these alarms were overreactions to minor movements of the Maya outside the walls, and I thought it indicated that the Spaniards were getting on edge. In spite of sickness and several skirmishes and raids, there were still about 180 Spaniards within the walls and they were all well armed and ready to fight. This position would not be overrun.

Possibly because of my reputation, I was called into meetings of the war council that was attempting to coordinate the efforts of the accumulating warriors. The council was a breathtaking collection of tough warrior chiefs decked out in a Mayan splendor of multicolored feathers, paint, and ornaments. Seldom has organized death looked so impressive. They met under the trees by the side of the sacred cenote of sacrifices on the north side of the city. Nearby, there were several pilgrims dressed in white robes and standing by the edge of the cenote. Several of them were chanting and burning incense while several more threw sacrificial objects such as jewelry or small statues into the well. The objects turned lazily in the air, then splashed the surface of the dark green water at the bottom of the high limestone walls of the cenote. In spite of the war with the Spaniards, the religious rituals of Mayan life continued.

The council was headed by Namax Cupul, but the true leader was Nachi Cocom, lord of the Maya of Sotuta, the adjoining state and an ally of the Cupul. Nachi Cocom was a great warrior who had many victories against his blood enemies to the west, the Xiu of Tutul who were now allies with the Spaniards.

"We must attack the Spaniards!" he was saying, "We are many and we are warriors. The dzulob must be crushed!"

"Why waste our warriors?" said another. "Time is our greatest weapon. We have only to wait and the victory will be ours. The invaders will fall into our hands like ripe fruit."

Namax Cupul turned to me and pointed to me with his staff of office.

"The arguments weary me," he said, "We need fresh points of view. This is Gonz-lo, the warrior Nacom of Chetumal. He was once a dzul, but now is among the bravest of the Maya. He helped defeat the Spaniards at Ecab and at Chetumal. Soon he will help us drive them from the land of the Cupul Maya as well. Welcome Gonz-lo."

"Thank you, lord Namax Cupul," I replied with a slight bow, "I am honored to be among such brave warrior lords."

"What say you, Gonz-lo?" said another, "Should we attack the Spaniard or wait?"

"All eyes were on me. Nachi Cocom stood with his heavily muscled arms crossed across a large jade chest piece over his generous stomach. He wore a loincloth of spotted jaguar skin and a feathered headdress that was at least two feet high. His face paint was red and black, as was his embroidered mantle. He looked like the last person you would want to face in battle.

I considered my answer carefully. Balam had long ago taught me to consider the political consequences of my actions, and I was wary. I thought that waiting made more sense, but didn't want to openly oppose Nachi Cocom, who was a greater hero than I was.

"My lords," I began, "lord Nachi Cocom speaks from his warrior's heart and speaks with the fighting spirit of the Maya. We should all be ready to fight to the death for our land. But the Spaniard is a different enemy. I have fought against him and I have fought with him. With their weapons and their fortified position, they want you to attack. It is the only hope they have, for it could result in so many Mayan deaths that we would give up. If we do not attack, they will have no choice but to either try to escape, or to attack us outside the protection of their fortifications. I say we hold our fighting spirit against the day when we can meet the invader on our own terms."

There was a buzz of voices that seemed to be in general agreement, but a deep voice from the rear broke through.

"My brothers," it said, "are we to respect the voice of one who has betrayed his own kind?"

I looked around and saw the source of the voice. My blood froze when I saw it was Pom Tzec, his face painted black to match his red trimmed mantle. Like a field of corn waving in the wind, the other warrior chiefs parted before him as he walked through the crowd until he stood only a few feet in front of me. At his side was my old enemy, Cuac Caan, still wearing the tall quetzal feather headdress formerly worn by Chan Oc, and managing to look both glowering and smug at the same time.

"This man," Pom Tzec began, in his booming deep voice, "is himself a Spaniard. So either he is trying to help them, or

241

he has betrayed them. How long will it be before he betrays the Maya as well?"

Pom Tzec; the man who had killed my shipmates and who had killed my friends and attacked Ixil along with Cuac Caan. He stood there arrogantly with his fists on his hips. I had to restrain the urge to pounce on both of them with my dagger.

"Betray?" I shouted, "This man who has the blood of more of the Maya on his hands than any Spaniard speaks of betrayal? He has betrayed his allies and betrayed the people of Ixil by putting Cuac Caan on the mat of power. Mayan women and children lie dead because of this man, and a proud city...."

"Gonz-lo!" interrupted Namax Cupul sharply, "Pom Tzec is the Batab of Dzilpan and a warrior Nacom like yourself. Cuac Caan is Batab of Ixil, and a great warrior as well. All of us here are determined to fight the Spaniards, not each other. Your feelings about these men must be put aside. Pom Tzec raises a valid question; we are in a death struggle with the people you came from. Can we be sure of your loyalty?"

"Lord Namax Cupul," I replied heatedly, "my loyalty has been proven many times over. And I would ask the noble lords to remember one thing; of all the warriors here, I am the only one who is a Maya by choice!"....which was a highly inaccurate explanation of why I had become a warrior, of course, but it was effective. The entire assembly cheered and raised their war clubs and spears in salute. Pom Tzec stood stony faced and silent.

Several weeks went by and the pressure on the Spaniards mounted. The council heeded my advice to avoid a direct assault and limited action to a few scattered skirmishes. The bell in the temple on the wall rang often with alarms showing how nervous the Spaniards were. Can Pec remarked that the frequent alarms at night must be depriving them of much needed sleep.

242

I was inspecting a roadblock next to the Temple of the Sun one morning and generally marveling at the massiveness of that structure as well as the pyramid of Kukulcan a short distance away and the fortified ball court several hundred yards beyond that. I climbed the steep steps to the top platform of the sun temple. At the top of the stairs was a Chac Mool, a reclining stone figure that patiently awaited the next sacrifice. Behind it, monstrous stone serpents stood guard in front of a temple that was overgrown with trees and tangled vines. A large lizard scampered by my feet as I turned to look at the Maya barricades. As I was trying to picture what this city must have looked like when it was at its peak, Nachi Cocom and some of his warriors also climbed the stairs. He looked at me for a moment without speaking, then asked me what I thought the Spaniards were thinking.

"I believe they are getting desperate," I said, gesturing towards the ball court, "They are cut off from food and reinforcements. They have probably been hoping that we would grow weary of the siege and give it up, or would attack their fortifications and be massacred, but now they must know that we will not go away, and will not give them an easy victory."

He nodded. "Gonz-lo, you know the dzulob better than anyone. What do you think they will do now?"

I thought for a moment. "I believe they will attack us soon with all their strength in an effort to break out and reach their allies to the west. They know that if they wait much longer, they are doomed."

"Then we must be ready at any moment," he said, nodding in agreement. "This is the last group of the dzulob remaining in the Yucatan. They must be killed or driven off."

I hadn't realized it before, but he was right; if we could rid ourselves of Montejo, there would be no more Spaniards in our land. I smiled in satisfaction at the knowledge that we were near our goal. There would be more Spaniards later, of course, but for now, we had almost won.

"Look," I said, pointing toward the Spanish fortifications, "something is happening. They are moving the barricades that are sealing the opening between the walls."

"Yes," said Nachi Cocom, "and they are coming out!"

Just as he said the words, the Spaniards came pouring out of their fortifications, heading for the nearest Maya barricade. The mounted men led the way, and quickly flanked the first group of warriors while the rest of the Spaniards smashed into the Maya head on. The warriors were outnumbered, outflanked and out fought by the desperate Spaniards, and were soon left behind as the attackers swarmed to the next defenses. The Spaniards were trying to break out as I had predicted.

"Summon the others!" yelled Nachi Cocom, and in an instant the entire area was alive with warriors running to join the fight.

The Maya had set up barricades starting at about 100 yards from the ball court and several others at greater distances, so that the Spaniards, having overrun the first, now faced the second tier. But the second line of Maya barricades was anchored by the pyramid on one side, so the Spaniards were not able to turn both flanks with the horsemen as they had the first barricade. In addition, I could see that the Spaniards had already lost several men, and reinforcements were now swelling the Mayan defenses.

I scrambled down the steps and ran to summon the warriors of Chetumal, but Can Pec had already alerted them and I could see them emerging from a wooded area to the left.

"Can Pec!" I shouted, "This way!"

We passed a corner of the pyramid and soon reached the battle. Maya were coming from all over now, and for a moment, I feared it could be a feint. When I was close enough to see how many Spaniards there were, however, I knew that they were gambling everything on this one desperate throw of the dice. The fighting was fierce and merciless. Horsemen were hacking their way through living bodies and their horses were trampling warriors who got too close. Amid swirling clouds of dust, the Spaniards on foot were fighting like madmen, slashing, shooting and stabbing in a blur of murderous action. Once again, the air was filled with the sound of enraged men locked in a death struggle. The sounds of weapons striking flesh blended with the grunts, curses, oaths and screams of hundreds of men.

The Spaniards were now trying to fight their way through the second barricade and the battle still raged. I saw one mounted Spaniard wade into a crowd of warriors with his sword swinging frantically, only to be dragged from his horse and killed by Maya swarming over him. Warriors were falling everywhere and the bodies were several deep in some places. One horse lost his footing stumbling over bodies and fell, rider and all. The Maya speared the fallen rider in an instant. The crush of the fighting was so great with warriors crowding together to try to get to the Spaniards that I saw a Spaniard kill two warriors with a single sword thrust. The blade passed through one warrior and into the one pressing in from behind. The greater numbers of the Maya actually hurt their fighting ability as warriors to the rear, anxious to get into the fight, unknowingly pushed the ones on the front line directly into the Spanish steel like meat being fed into a grinder.

Just as Can Pec and I reached the second barricade, ten horsemen bore down on the flank with the riders yelling "Santiago!" and laying about them with swords. The attack sent warriors tumbling down like ninepins in the front ranks and sent survivors fleeing back through the others, spreading fear and panic. A few of the warriors tried to hold their ground, but were swept aside like leaves before the wind. In the jostle of close packed bodies, it was hard to maintain footing, and several fell and were trampled by the others.

I was not close enough to receive the initial shock, but the horsemen, along with crossbowmen and fusiliers soon were upon us as well. The fleeing warriors pushed past us followed by the Spaniards like an incoming tide. Horses closed in on all sides and their riders rained sword blows down on us in a storm of steel. Warriors held up wicker shields only to have a Spanish sword slice through them, sometimes slicing off the forearm as well. Warriors swung their war clubs only to have them strike the Spaniards' quilted cotton armor harmlessly.[14] I saw one warrior cleanly beheaded by a single sword stroke. Others were speared by lances or trampled by the horses. The height of the battle was an all-encompassing tumult of noise, blood, heat, and dust.

A fusillade of Spanish gunfire exploded with a cloud of smoke and a deafening roar, hitting a warrior next to me squarely in the head, and splattering me with blood, hair and feathers. A sword thrust cut down another on the other side. Out of this chaos, I was suddenly aware of a horse bearing directly down on me. Beneath the cotton armor, the horse was black as night, as if he had risen straight up from Hell itself. I braced myself with my spear extended as the horse thundered down on me, seeming to grow as he got closer. My terror mounted as I could feel the vibration of his pounding hooves through the soles of my feet, and as I stood quaking in the last few seconds, heard my own voice saying "Holy Mary, Mother of God, pray for us sinners now, and at the hour of our death, Amen...."

The world seemed to explode as the horse crashed into me, and I was thrown clear of the hooves and sword with such force that the air was expelled from my lungs and I couldn't breathe at first. Dazed and dizzy, I staggered to my feet. There was blood trickling from my nose and my spear was shattered, but I was still alive.

The battle raged on with terrible carnage on both sides. The Spaniards were determined to break through and the Maya were just as determined not to let them. Except for my father's dagger, I was now defenseless, and was almost trampled several times as I searched for a suitable weapon. I stayed on the flank where I would have room to fight in the fencing style I did best. Spying a dead Spaniard, I picked up his sword and felt its weight in my hand. It was sticky with blood, but felt natural and comfortable even after so many years. Now I had a weapon and could rejoin the fight. I turned around and found myself face to face with a tall Spaniard who was swinging his own sword directly at my head. Instinctively, I raised my sword and was barely able to deflect the blow. We faced off, each with a sword and a determination to live.

It is a strange thing, but in a tumultuous battle with hundreds of people fighting, you sometimes are so intent on the person you are facing that you are not aware of the others. So it was as I fought this Spaniard. My swordsmanship was still good because of my work with the spear and war club, and I felt that I was giving a good account of myself, but I could make no headway against this man. He parried every thrust and was not fooled by any of my tricks or feints. He seemed to know my every move and be ready for it. Not since Perez had I met someone who was so evenly matched, and even Perez wasn't able to seemingly read my thoughts as this one could. Finally, I tried a trick I hadn't used since I was a boy in Avilla, but the swordsman deftly sidestepped and with a backhand snap of his wrist, struck my sword from my hand. There was no other weapon within reach, so, in desperation, I pulled out my father's dagger.

I knew I was about to die. If I couldn't best this Spaniard with a sword, I would certainly have no chance with a dagger. But it was all I had, so I stood there awaiting the death stroke. The Spaniard looked at the dagger, then looked at me, then at the dagger again. He hesitated for a moment, then spoke in a voice filled with astonishment.

"G...Gonzalo?" he said, slowly lowering his sword.

I froze. I knew that voice, just as the Spaniard had known my swordplay and my tricks. No wonder.

In front of me stood Hectore, my brother.

Chapter 28- A Brother Warrior

In which I try to save a Spaniard

Amid the fury of the battle, we stood transfixed, staring at each other. He was heavier than before, and had a thick beard to go with the sun baked wrinkles in his face. He wore a crested helmet and a blood splattered brown cotton jacket and a blue cape. His knee length boots were scratched and cut from the thorny undergrowth he had traveled through and there was a bandage on his left arm. I stood wearing a loincloth and my red warrior's mantle. I wore the feathered helmet-headdress of the Jaguar warriors and had jade ear plugs, bracelets and necklace. My face was painted with a wide black stripe and I wore deerskin leggings. Each of us barely recognized the other. In childhood, we had fought make believe battles, now we faced each other as real enemies.

I was about to speak again, when I noticed that the Spaniards were falling back towards the ball court. Several warriors had noticed Hectore standing alone and were heading in our direction.

"Hectore!" I said, in Spanish, "They are retreating. You must go now or you will be cut off. Come to the northwest gate at dusk. Go!"

He hesitated, then turned and ran back to join the retreating Spaniards and was soon lost in the group.

The Maya were shouting and rejoicing all around me, but I could only think of one thing; my brother Hectore was here and he was now an enemy of my people. He must have joined the Montejo expedition just as I had joined the expedition of Juan de Valdivia.

"By the gods, we have stopped them!" It was Nachi Cocom again, surveying the human wreckage scattered from the pyramid all the way to the ball court and for 200 yards to each side. The dead and the dying covered the ground; singly and in groups. The Spaniards left over 40 dead on the field, including five horses. The Maya lost several hundred, but Nachi Cocom was delighted.

"You were right, Gonz-lo!" he said, "They tried to attack us with all their strength to break out. But we stopped them. Do you think they will try again?"

"I..I don't know," I said, "We will have to wait and see."

Actually, I was almost certain they would not try an all out attack again, but I needed time to think. My mind was swimming with this new factor. My brother Hectore, who I loved more than anyone except Zazil Ha herself was now one of the Spaniards I had sworn to destroy. I had fought the Spaniards to protect the ones I cared for, but my own brother was now also in danger. Mayan warriors that I had trained and fought with were now poised to take the life of my own flesh and blood. The bitter irony was almost too much to bear. I spent the rest of the day in quiet contemplation to decide what I should do. Was I to be forced once more to choose between my Mayan family and my Spanish family?

I thought of Hectore and how we had shared our secrets and dreamed our dreams together in Avilla. He had always been my staunch companion; he had never deserted me and would have never let anyone harm me. He knew my deepest thoughts and fears. Now he was facing death partly because of me. But how could I save him without betraying the Maya who trusted me?

At dusk, I was waiting in the heavy brush by the northwest entrance to the ball court. I had decided that I could not let Hectore die with the rest; I would smuggle him through the lines and west to safety. The Maya would never miss him and the Spaniards would think....well, it wouldn't matter what they thought.

There was a lot of activity in the ball court that night as the Spaniards tried to shore up their defenses. The air was filled with moans and cries of the sick and wounded. Food and water were short. Men with torches were coming and going and there was an air of desperation. After a while, I saw the figure of Hectore walking slowly towards me.

"Hectore...over here," I said in a loud whisper. He came closer and stood leaning against the stone wall by the edge of the brush. Anyone who saw him would think he was standing guard or brooding.

He looked at me in amazement, hardly able to believe that this savage standing in the bushes before him could be his long lost brother Gonzalo.

"It is good to see you, Hectore," I said quietly.

"Gonzalo," he said, shaking his head in amazement, "So you really are alive, but what happened to you?"

I told him of my life for the past years. If he was shocked or disapproving, he didn't say so. He had come to the new world in much the same way I did, but for a somewhat different reason.

"Mother died five years ago," he said, "Before she died, I promised her I would go to the new world and try to find you. I wanted to go anyway, for the adventure, but I never thought there was any chance of finding you, and certainly not at the other end of a sword. There were rumors you were alive and a renegade, but I never believed them. How can you fight with these savages against your own people?"

"How can you fight against those who are no threat to you or to Spain?" I replied heatedly, "Don't you realize what you are really fighting for? The enslavement of the innocent! Why can't you leave these people in peace?"

"Peace, you say? These people have never known peace. When they are not trying to kill us, they are killing each other. Gonzalo, you are fighting for a race that cuts out human hearts and feeds them to idols!" he said incredulously.

"Is that worse than burning so-called heretics alive? Castile cursed the Moors for being invaders; who is the invader now?"

He looked at me with a mixture of sorrow and exasperation.

"Noble words," he said, "but except for an opportune shipwreck, you might be fighting alongside me. You certainly were not concerned about the welfare of the Indians when you left Spain, as I recall."

"I suppose you are right, Hectore," I sighed, "but I have changed. This is the path I must walk now."

We looked at each other in silence a moment, and I was aware of the gulf that now separated us.

"What of father?" I asked, finally.

"He died the year before mother did. He also believed that you were still alive somewhere. Uncle Fernando died just two years ago. He had pieced together what had happened at Seville by talking to the dock master. That is why mother asked me to go to the New World to find you. Our sister Maria married a merchant, Pedro Gomezo, and has three children; the oldest is named Gonzalo."

I could feel tightness in my throat at the thought of all the lives that had been lived without me and all the people I had cared for and would never see again. I was glad that they knew I had sailed for the new world, but sad that I hadn't been the one to tell them. I took the jade necklace from around my neck and handed it to Hectore.

"When you return, give this to Maria. Tell her I will always remember her with affection."

"I will," he said, hesitantly, "...when I return."

There was another awkward silence, then Hectore spoke again.

"Someday, when all of this is over, I would like to meet Zazil Ha," he said, "She sounds like a vast improvement over

Consuelo, and is probably far better than you deserve."

"Yes, Hectore, she surely is. But what became of Consuelo?" I asked, and for the first time, I saw that wide grin that I had always known before.

"Ah yes, the good Señorita Arbenza," he said, obviously savoring the story, "She is now a nun in the convent of Santa Maria del Sevilla."

I felt oddly pleased. "You mean that she was so distraught at losing me that she took the vows of celibacy?"

"Hardly," he said, smirking, "Two months after you left, Don Arbenza caught her in her chamber with another young lover, only this time, matters had progressed too far for the suitor to make a retreat as you had done. The next morning, Consuelo was taken to the convent."

We both laughed. It was the first time I had laughed with Hectore in over 20 years and it was a feeling as delicious and heady as any balche.

"Hectore," I said, in a serious tone of voice, "the Spaniards are trapped here, and we both know it. The attempt to break out failed, and you will soon either be overrun or starved. I cannot save them, but I can save you. Come with me now and I will take you through the lines to the Ceh Pech Maya to the west who are loyal to Castile. You can tell them you escaped, but you must come now."

His gaze hardened. "If you were in my place, would you desert your comrades?"

"If you were in MY place, would you leave your brother to die?" I replied.

"The answer is no to both questions," he said calmly.

There was another awkward silence. Then Hectore spoke again.

"Remember when we were boys back in Avilla, how we would pretend to be soldiers and fight each other? You never wanted to be the Moor, only the Spaniard."

"Yes," I replied, "Back then, the choices were so simple;

good and evil; right and wrong. But now....." My voice wavered.

"Gonzalo," Hectore said, placing his hand on my shoulder, "we are all forced to make hard and bitter choices in life, and then must live with whatever results. You chose to fight for an adopted family and people, and I chose to fight for the glory of Spain. But I am still your brother and you are still mine. If I must die, then at least I have seen you one more time. We have each made our choices. Now we must follow where those choices lead us."

Then he extended his hand and I grasped it.

"Goodbye Gonzalo. *Vaya con Dios*."

"Goodbye Hectore, my brother."

We embraced tightly, then he turned away and disappeared into the Spanish camp.

Chapter 29- The Final Battle

In which there is a terrible reckoning in the darkness

The war council met the next day at the foot of the pyramid of Kukulcan, the site of the battle. This time, the mood was jubilant as the war chiefs, heady with the victory of the day before, tried to outdo each other in threats and ferocity. Pom Tzec and Cuac Caan were on the other side of the crowd, so I had no contact with them.

"The Spaniards are defeated!" shouted Nachi Cocom, standing on the head of a huge stone serpent at the foot of the stairway and raising his spear in the air, "The Castilians cower in the ball court and wait for the end. I say the end is now; I say we attack and finish them once and for all!"

This was met by cheers from the others, and a forest of feathered spears waving in the air. Everyone seemed ready to attack.

"Are we all agreed that we must attack the Spaniards at once?" said Namax Cupul, attempting to bring order out of this heady chaos. A collective cheer went up to indicate that everyone was ready to go.

Incredibly, it was at this precise moment that the Spaniards assaulted the barricades once again.

The bravado of the council was immediately deflated by the sight of the Spaniards emerging once again with firearms blazing and horsemen bearing down on the nearest warriors. Several of the council were on the pyramid steps and could see the Spaniards once again attack the closest outpost.

"Summon the warriors!" Nachi Cocom bellowed, "Now we finish them!"

255

We rushed towards the barricade that was under attack but just before we reached it, the Spaniards fell back to the ball court once again. The whole attack lasted less than five minutes, and I breathed a sigh of relief that Hectore was not in danger.

"By the gods," said Namax Cupul, "three of our warriors killed and the Spaniards retreat. They might not be as weak as we thought."

He turned to his nacom. "I want this barricade reinforced in case there is another attack. Bring men from the western barricades. We will show them. I don't know what they thought they could accomplish by that kind of attack."

I knew exactly what they had hoped to accomplish, and it appeared that they had succeeded: there would be no Mayan attack that day and the barricades to the west had been weakened. I had been certain there would not be another attack, but this was a feint, designed to bluff the Maya into delaying any attack and perhaps even rearranging their defenses. I was about to say so, but something held me back. For I had decided that I had to see Hectore again and persuade him to escape. I couldn't bear the thought of Hectore slain by one of my own warriors or worse yet, captured. If I had to witness my own brother taken to the sacrificial stone to have his heart cut out, I would go mad. There had to be another way. I would go again tonight and wait in the bushes near the gate, or perhaps even enter the camp to find him if necessary. This time, he would have to listen... he would have to.

"Well, Gonz-lo," said Nachi Cocom, breaking in on my thoughts, "it would seem that the Spaniard still has some fight left in him."

"The Spaniard is a tough and dangerous foe, my lord," I replied, "We must not underestimate him."

"And let him not underestimate us," he growled, thumping his massive chest with his fist, "Tomorrow at dawn we will gather all the warriors and wipe out the Spaniards. By this time tomorrow, Gonz-lo, if the gods smile on us, every man in the ball court will be dead or captured."

I waited until it was dark before making my way to the northwest gate through the underbrush as I had done before. Low clouds covered the moon and the humid darkness was thick and suffocating. I brought the sword I had taken from the battlefield; I was comfortable with this weapon and had decided to use it in place of the spear for close in fighting. As I crept through the brush, I rehearsed the words I would say to Hectore to persuade him. His presence could make no difference to the others; they would all perish with or without him. I had to save my brother before it was too late. The Spaniards must have sensed the closeness of their doom as well, I thought. The alarm bell was ringing almost constantly, showing how badly frayed their nerves were. Even Hectore would have to see the hopelessness of their position. My spirits rose as I convinced myself that I would be able to persuade Hectore to desert his fellows. I would save him and the Maya would never know. Surely it can't be betrayal to save your own brother?

But as I reached my vantage point and peered through the brush, an astonishing sight met my eyes. The Spaniards were silently filing out of the gate and disappearing into the darkness. The conquerors that had arrogantly divided the land up among themselves just a few months ago, were now sneaking away like thieves in the night. Both men and horses had rags tied to their feet to muffle any sound of footsteps. Similar rags were wrapped carefully around swords, stirrups, armor, and anything that could make a sound. The horses were being led carefully, not ridden, probably to lessen the chance of a guard seeing a tall silhouette. If they could avoid the depleted barricades to the west, they could be miles away by morning. I had to admire the boldness of the plan, and for a brief moment, I felt proud of my former countrymen.

As the Spaniards filed past, I strained my eyes for a last glimpse of Hectore. Finally, near the end, I saw him, walking tall and proud. He was in a group so I couldn't call to him. I wanted to yell. I wanted to wish him good luck. I wanted to tell him to tell Maria about me, but I could only watch in silence drinking in the last sight of him I would ever have in this life. Finally, just as he passed my hiding place, he turned his head and looked directly towards me. In the brush and darkness, he couldn't see me, of course, but he smiled, then turned his head back and disappeared.

There were about 100 of them and 10 horses. In a few more minutes, they were gone, on their way to the only chance of survival they had. When the last of them passed out through the gate, the compound took on a deathly stillness, and I was aware only of the sound of my own breathing as the silent black walls of the ball court towered above me.

Now I faced a new dilemma; my sworn enemies were escaping into the night. If they were not stopped, they might get away and regroup to return another day. I wanted to save Hectore, not all the rest of them. My duty was to sound the alarm among the warriors, and that is probably exactly what I would have done...if not for Hectore. If they escaped, I thought, they might return, so for the safety of the Mayan people, I should not let that happen. But if they were gone, had we not won? Why not let them return home? Why shed more blood? I debated with myself, but deep down, I realized I could turn against my country, but not my brother. I would sound no alarm, and I would say a silent prayer for Hectore and his comrades.

Cautiously, I entered the deserted ball court. The wooden houses were empty and the sidewalls towered above me blotting out the stars. I noted several fresh graves, no doubt from the battle. There was the usual assortment of debris and cast off baggage in the rooms of the ramshackle wooden huts that lined the walls. Crude furniture and barrels of supplies stood in otherwise empty rooms still dimly lit with flickering candles. A long building with hammocks had been the barracks, and another with straw had been the stable. I found a sword belt and slid my sword into it. In one building, I found what must have been the headquarters. There were scrolls of fine quality sheepskin with the records of land ownership recorded on them; the clerical aspect of the *Repartimiento* system. If you are going to seize someone else's land, you need to keep accurate records.

As I poked around the wreckage, I saw a familiar looking object in a corner. One of the Spaniards had abandoned a guitar brought all the way from Spain. Almost reverently, I picked it up and felt its smooth lightness in my hands. The rich color of crafted wood shone through gleaming varnish. Carefully, I fingered the frets on the rosewood neck and plucked the high E string. After all the years of Mayan music, the single crisp, clear note seemed to hang in the air like the song of an angel. I tried to remember how I had played in Consuelo's garden in Avilla so many years ago. But my fingers had grown rough and clumsy from life among the Maya and the chords were muffled and discordant with sharps and flats that grated on the ears. My ability to coax the soothing sounds I remembered had vanished along with my youth, my innocence, and the life I once led. With an overwhelming feeling of sadness and loss, I carefully placed the guitar back in the corner.

Through the open doorway, I suddenly heard the Spaniards' alarm bell ringing in the darkened temple on the top of the high wall. I couldn't believe it. They must have left someone behind to ring the bell periodically to make the Maya think they were still in the ball court. By God, I thought, there is a brave man.

As I approached the other end of the court, I heard the bell again, and decided to see the man who stayed behind to ring it. There were several ladders giving access to the top of the high walls and I climbed one. The wall was about 15 feet wide on the top and treacherous with loose stones and brush. As I stepped from the ladder on to the top of the wall, I saw the temple looming black against the night sky. The building was a massive square stone structure almost as wide as the wall it sat on and seemed to grow as I cautiously approached it. The front opening overlooked the ball court below and the roof was supported by two huge stone serpents. In the faint light, it looked like the gate of Hell. I carefully drew my sword as I got closer to the blackened opening. It occurred to me that there might be several well-armed Spaniards in there, but thought it unlikely. Only one man would be needed to ring the bell. Why sacrifice more?

My heart leapt as the bell rang again when I was only a few feet from the opening. The noise was shattering. As I was about to step in front of the temple to see who was inside, I noticed what looked like bowls of meat scraps placed in front of the opening near the ledge. Was this some sort of strange sacrifice? I stepped into the doorway, peered inside and saw....a dog. He was leashed on a rope that was tied to the clapper of the alarm bell hanging from the ceiling. Every time the dog tried to reach one of the bowls of meat scraps just out of his reach, he rang the alarm bell. As I walked back to the ladder, I laughed out loud at how simple and effective the trick was.

I was still laughing when I saw the warrior waiting for me on the wall.

"Gonz-lo," came a deep voice in the darkness, "you have betrayed the Mayan people just as I said you would."

"Pom Tzec!" I gasped, "What are you doing here?"

"In the battle, I saw you speak to one of the Spaniards, and I suspected treachery, so I followed you tonight." he said, "The Spaniards escaped and you did nothing to stop them; you did not even raise the alarm. You are still one of them after all."

"No, you are wrong, I...."

"You think your fellow Spaniards are safe now don't you?" he sneered, "But they have only succeeded in exposing themselves. When we attack them in a few minutes, they will have gone too far to be able to return to the safety of this place, and they will all die."

I felt a chill down my back at the thought of the doom my brother was heading into.

"You have not alerted the warriors," he continued, "but I intend to do so as soon as I am finished with you. You will die, Gonz-lo; not as slowly as I would have wished, but you will die."

"And this time, your words cannot save you," came another voice from behind me. I spun around and saw Cuac Caan holding a spear.

Pom Tzec's voice boomed again, a war cry this time, and I turned back to face him.

As I did this, he suddenly swung a war club out of the darkness striking the sword in my hand. I reacted a fraction of a second too late and the sword flew from my grip and clattered across the stones on top of the wall, disappearing into the blackness.

The club came out of the darkness again missing my head by inches. I heard the rushing sound and felt the air on my ear as the razor sharp obsidian blades sought my flesh. I fell backward and rolled along the rocky, weed choked surface of the top of the wall as Pom Tzec swung the club again and again, barely missing my face and clipping off small pieces of brush next to me. Off to the side, Cuac Caan moved beside me, waiting to get a clear shot with his spear. Frantically, I tried to find the ladder while ducking and twisting to avoid the swinging club.

"Don't bother looking for a ladder," came the voice of Pom Tzec again. "Cuac Caan pushed them over when we followed you. The only way down is over the edge."

There was another way; on the other side of the temple was a steep staircase leading down to the other face of the wall. But Pom Tzec had now placed himself between me and the temple, cutting off my retreat and making himself harder to see against the black bulk behind him. I strained to see the great club sweeping towards me in the darkness. One wrong move and I would be dead. A burning hot pain shot up my side as Cuac Caan's spear slashed along my ribs. A few inches the other way, and I'd have been impaled.

"I should have had your heart cut out when I had the chance," Pom Tzec said as he advanced on me swinging the club, "If not for you, Zazil Ha would be one of my wives, and borne me strong sons."

I tried to goad him as I had done with others, hoping he would react carelessly.

"You are a pot of lizard droppings;" I said, panting, my right hand was now sticky with my own blood. "Zazil Ha would spit on you! I am the one she craves; the one who knows the warmth of her embrace, the one who fathered her children. In her eyes, you are lower than the mud."

To my surprise, he laughed.

"You will not provoke me with such a simple trick," he said, "Your clever tongue is well known, but soon it will wag no more."

With that, he renewed his attack, swinging and slashing with two hands on the club handle as Cuac Caan readied his spear for another thrust and I desperately scrambled to get out of the way. For big men, they were both surprisingly quick and agile. Pom Tzec had been a great warrior and had never been defeated. Cuac Caan was his equal. Now they were systematically driving me to the edge to deliver the death blow.

I was hoping Cuac Caan would throw his spear, giving me a chance to grab it, but he slashed and thrust. Another blaze of pain told me he cut me on the arm, and I fell to the ground as the war club passed over my head. As I scrambled in the dirt, trying to avoid my attackers and get away from the edge of the wall at the same time, my hand touched something hard and cool.

"Pin him down with your spear, Cuac Caan. Then I will finish him."

Cuac Caan stood over me with his spear poised and thrust. With a quick parry, I struck it away with my newly found sword. Cuac Caan was surprised, but reacted quickly. He thrust again, and parried a thrust of my own. Fortunately, Pom Tzec was still behind Cuac Caan and couldn't see what was happening, so I didn't have his war club to contend with as I dueled with Cuac Caan.

"Finish him!" roared Pom Tzec, as Cuac Caan lunged and I suddenly felt the spear tip plunge into my thigh. I almost fainted from the pain, but with all my remaining strength drove the sword blade deep into Cuac Caan's massive chest. He staggered backwards, still clutching the spear, and made gurgling sounds. My blade must have become lodged between his ribs, because it was pulled from my grasp once more as Cuac Caan collapsed over the edge of the wall and plunged into the darkness below. My leg would no longer hold my weight and I fell to the dirt near the edge.

Pom Tzec bellowed in rage and raised his war club to kill me once and for all. But I still had one chance. I reached in my leggings for my father's dagger. Pom Tzec was a dark shadow looming above me. I carefully awaited my chance as I tried to avoid the deadly blows. Finally, as he raised his arms above his head for another swing, I threw the dagger directly at his chest. But the knife bounced off with a loud metallic clank as it hit his stone medallion. In the darkness, I could not find it again. Now, I was truly defenseless.

I picked up a small branch from the ground and tried to parry the blows, but Pom Tzec sliced the branch down to nothing as he drove me steadily towards the edge. The alarm bell started ringing again, adding to the hellish confusion and tension. A blow caught me on the back as I twisted and ducked to avoid the club, but my bunched up mantle protected me from anything worse than a bruise. I groped on the ground trying to grab a stone to throw, but they were heavy building stones that were too big.

Pom Tzec was relentless as I dragged and rolled through the brush trying to avoid the club. It whistled in the air over my head, then smashed through the brush next to me. I was rapidly running out of room to maneuver as Pom Tzec closed in, pressing me closer and closer. I wanted to scream from the pain in my leg. Finally, as I crouched near the lip of the wall, my hand felt loose stones and sand. But there was no place left to hide. Behind me yawned a chasm of blackness.

Pom Tzec, having driven me to the edge, held his club over his head for the final blow.

"Now you will die," he said in triumph.

As he started the final swing of the club, I grabbed a handful of the loose stones and sand and threw it directly at Pom Tzec's face. He grunted and stepped back for a second and it was all I needed. Using my good leg, I lunged at him, driving my shoulder into his stomach and we went crashing down in the brush together.

"You have killed enough good people," I said between gritted teeth, "Tonight you will breathe your last."

The club had been knocked from his hand, but with his great strength he grabbed me by the neck and started to strangle me as we rolled on the ground. I was weak from fatigue and loss of blood, and he soon was overpowering me.

"It is you who will die this night," he snarled, "It is better this way, for I will enjoy killing you with my own hands." His face was so close, I could feel his hot breath.

As I struggled to free myself and he continued to choke the life out of me, we rolled towards the edge. Closer and closer we came, locked together until we teetered on the edge over the empty depths below. I couldn't break free and I couldn't breathe; I was starting to feel lightheaded. Pom Tzec was winning. Finally, I strained to make a last effort to break free, but in one terrible moment, we both rolled over the edge of the wall and fell into the blackness below.

We each reached out in panic as we fell into the inky void, flailing our arms trying to grab some support. Suddenly, I stopped with a painful thud as Pom Tzec plunged past me headfirst into the darkness. I couldn't see what happened to him, but heard the sickening crunching sound when he struck the paving below. Then all was quiet once again.

At first, I was too stunned to realize what had happened. I was apparently suspended in the air somehow. My body was supported, but my legs dangled in the air over the empty depths below. As my head cleared, I felt that I was straddling some sort of hard rounded stone surface. Then I realized what it was; the large stone ring set into the wall that served as the goal for the ball game.

Wearily and painfully, I climbed back to the lip of the wall and dragged myself towards the stone staircase on the other side of the temple. Halfway down the staircase, with the alarm bell still ringing, I grew dizzy, and everything seemed to be swaying. That is all I remember.

Chapter 30- The Scrolls

In which my story comes to an end, and I nearly do as well

Can Pec was speaking to me from the bottom of a well. His voice was faint and echoed hollowly. I knew who it was, but couldn't see him or understand the words he was saying. The world seemed to be slowly spinning around me in a red fog. I was only aware of darkness and pain as I slipped into unconsciousness once more.

I was floating in the air. The sun was hot, but all I could see was a bright reddish glow. Now I was being carried on a litter, but I still couldn't see. There were more hollow voices somewhere off in the distance. I was dizzy, then slept once more. I don't know how long.

Finally, I heard a voice faintly.

"Gonz-lo," it said, "can you hear me?"

"Come on, Dzul," said another voice, "Wake up."

Another voice spoke, closer this time. It was a female voice that was speaking to someone else. The voice was saying "I think he's waking up." Slowly, I was aware of misty light glowing in front of me. I strained my eyes and could make out a shape slowly materializing out of the glow. The shape took form and resolved itself into a face. For a moment, I thought it was the face of an angel welcoming me to eternal rest. But as my eyes focused, I thought I was hallucinating, for it was the face of Zazil Ha, looking at me with concern.

"Zazil Ha;" I managed to say, "am I in Chetumal?"

"No, Gonzalo," she said, "you are still at Chichen Itza."

"But how..."

"A few weeks after you left, I went to the temple to pray for you. As I gazed at the smoke from the incense, I thought I saw your face, and I had a vision that you were in trouble and needed me. I persuaded Nachan Can to send another detachment of warriors and I came with them. They had just brought you here when I arrived."

"But there is danger here," I protested feebly.

She smoothed my hair back and gently kissed my cheek. "Gonzalo, I stood against the gods for you. What are a few Spaniards? My place is with you, and here I will remain."

"What happened?" I said, and winced in pain at the effort.

"You were found at the foot of the stairway to the ball court," said Can Pec. "When we investigated, we saw the Spaniards had escaped. Apparently you and Pom Tzec and Cuac Caan tried to stop them on your own. They were both killed; Cuac Caan had been run through with a Spanish sword. The Spaniards got you in several places, but the leg wound is the worst. You lost a lot of blood."

"I heard you were wounded and came to help," said Cimi, (I couldn't get used to the name Ix Kukum) "just as you helped me when I was sick in Ixil."

I decided I would wait until I was alone with Zazil Ha to tell the real story. "What of the Spaniards?" I asked feebly.

"Nachi Cocom gathered the warriors and pursued, but the Spaniards ambushed us in the land of the Ah Kin Chel a day's march from here. The battle made us pull back and content ourselves with merely following them until they were safely away from our land." said Can Pec, "We were fortunate they left when they did. Near the coast, the Spaniards met a relief column of reinforcements under the command of Montejo the elder. In two more days, they would have relieved the Spaniards in Chichen Itza, and we would never have been rid of them."

"Where are they now?" I asked.

"They are in a village on the northern coast in the land of the Ah Kin Chel. They will not return soon."

I smiled to myself. If I had alerted the warriors of the

escape, the Spaniards would have been prevented from leaving Chichen Itza. But they would have been reinforced in a few days and we would never have been able to dislodge them. I had done what was best for the Maya after all. But was Hectore all right?

"How many of the Spaniards died?" I asked, and held my breath awaiting the answer.

"None;" said Can Pec, "there were several wounded, but they were taken away by the others."

Thank God, I thought. Hectore is safe, and the Spaniards have been driven out at last.

For weeks, I lay under the watchful eyes of Zazil Ha, Cimi and Can Pec. My leg wound was festering and blood kept appearing, but I was getting better. I had seen Mayan medicines do wonders before, and hoped for the best. Although I felt that my wounds would not prove fatal, I fell into despair at the thought of dying. Thinking of Hectore, I wished I could communicate with my family in Spain so that they would know what happened to me and would understand why I did the things I did. My brush with death made me want to tie up the raveled ends of my life.

Zazil Ha stayed with me day and night. I told her of my meeting with Hectore and she was happy for me because I had seen him and briefly told him something of my life among the Maya.

We had long talks about our life together and our hopes for the future of our children. We had been together so long, we usually knew each other's thoughts even before they were spoken, so I was only slightly surprised when one day she suddenly said "It is good that you saw your brother, but you must write your story so everyone in Spain will understand."

"What?" I didn't know what she meant at first.

Zazil Ha smiled at me. Her face sparkled with light as it always had. "Gonzalo, I know your heart better than anyone on this earth. I understand your love for me, but I also understand your feelings for those you left behind. What you have done is courageous and noble; your family and friends in Spain need to understand that." Her voice was rising with passion and determination. She had obviously been thinking of this as much as I had. "Your story is a proud and a brave one; you must tell it. The rest of the world must know."

"But how could I...." I protested feebly.

"You told me the Spaniards left scrolls in one of their houses," she said, excitedly. "You can write your story in the language of the Castilians. When they return, as you and I know they must, they will find the scrolls and know the truth."

I still hesitated. "But there is so much to tell..."

She moved closer to me, until I could feel the warmth of her breath on my cheek and smell the flower scent of her hair. "After all our life together," she whispered, "I know the needs of your soul; this task is something that is calling out to you. You will find no peace until you answer."

I stroked her cheek and looked into those wonderful brown eyes. "If I write the story, I must write all of it, you know. I must tell the truth, even when it is ugly."

She smiled. "Of course you must. After all, knowledge is a gift of the gods...as is love."

An hour later, Can Pec and Cimi appeared carrying bundles of scrolls and quill pens, and several pots of black ink. I smiled when I saw them, then looked at Can Pec.

"Thank you both," I said, "Now there is something I must do."

Then I began to write.

Now my confessions are finished, and I can stand before God when my time comes with a clear conscience. With Zazil Ha's support, I have worked long hours as I healed, laboring to put a lifetime of extraordinary experience into words. I have tried to tell the truth as I saw it and lived it.

Anyone who reads these words may judge for himself whether I was a renegade and a traitor, or simply a man who found himself in remarkable circumstances, caught between two worlds locked in a struggle only one would survive. I never fought against Spain, only against Spain's threat to my family and my people. Even while I fought, I considered myself a son of Spain. Many times in these past years, I have thought of my former life in Avilla and fondly remembered the sound of church bells and the sweet taste of grapes still warm from the sun. The faces of the people I once knew have haunted my dreams and caused an ache in my soul.

But there are other faces in my dreams, the faces of the Mayan people with all of their achievements and all their shortcomings. I see the faces of Chan Oc, Balam, Cimi, Can Pec, and my sons. Most of all, I see Zazil Ha, standing in the doorway of the house of the memories, laughing as she bathes in the lake in Coba, raising her children and charting the heavens. I fear for her, for her people, and for their ancient way of life, poised on the brink of extinction.

And so, I made the choice to stand with the Mayans against the Spanish conquest that threatened to devour them. In the end, I believe our choices determine our destiny. Some are made willingly and some are forced upon us, and as Cimi once pointed out, we often have to choose when we don't know what the outcome will be.

It is all too easy to look back on my life and question these choices. What if I had not gone to Consuelo's room? What if I had not gone to the house of the memories where I met Zazil Ha? What if I had not stepped in to save de Aguiller or Can Pec? What if I had gone with de Aguiller to join Cortes?

I will never know the answer to any of these questions, but the answers really don't matter. The choices have all been made, and through them, I have lived a life with purpose. And as my Uncle Fernando said so many years ago, I have tried to keep the world from getting worse. Most importantly, I have known the companionship of friends, the smiles on the faces of my children and the love of Zazil Ha.

How could I have chosen otherwise?

The End

EPILOGUE

No more is known of Gonzalo Guerrero. He may have died as he thought, or he may have recovered and gone on to fight another day. There are accounts that he died in 1537 leading a group of 50 war canoes on an expedition to Honduras. But then, there were also false claims that he was killed at Chequitaquil. The complete story will probably never be known.

De Aguiller acted as interpreter for Cortes all through the conquest of Mexico, but died soon after. Cortes died of a fever at age 63. The Montejos, father and son, established another settlement on the northern coast after leaving Chichen Itza, but soon abandoned the effort. By 1535, a year after the retreat from Chichen Itza, there was not a single Spaniard remaining in the Yucatan, just as Guerrero had hoped. The respite was short, however, and in 1541, the Montejos returned with greater forces. Nachi Cocom, who had bitterly fought the Spaniards at Chichen Itza was finally defeated and forced to submit; he was even baptized and renamed Juan. Chetumal fell in 1545, never to rise again.

Elsewhere, the Maya fought on, but the ravages of famine and disease, coupled with the Maya propensity for fighting among themselves helped the Spaniards wear them down. Although formally conquered by 1547, the Maya of Yucatan still fought guerrilla actions from isolated pockets, had occasional revolts, and, at one point, requested aid from the United States. There was a full scale war in 1857 in which the Maya actually took back the Yucatan from the Ladinos. The Maya were on the verge of overrunning the capitol, Merida, when their troops drifted away because the corn planting time had come. They could always fight another day, but if the corn was not planted at the proper time, they would starve.

Isolated guerrilla actions continued even into this century. The final peace treaty wasn't signed until 1929. In 1994, on New Year's Day, the Maya again revolted against the Mexican government.

Today the great Mayan cities are either ruins, or razed to make way for Spanish cities. The resorts of Cancun and Cozumel provide the only glimpse of the Yucatan most people will ever see. Some visit the ruins of Tulum or Coba or a hundred other smaller sites and wonder what sort of people lived there. The Maya, meanwhile, go about their business, and in some places, still make offerings to Chac for a good rainfall.

The city of Ecab, where the Spaniards and the Maya first clashed, is a collection of broken and scattered ruins near the resort of Cancun, a few miles to the south. The pyramid was razed by the Spaniards and a large church built on its base. The rest of the stone was used to build a mission. Xelha, where Montejo set up the first Spanish settlement and near where he sank his own ships, is a national park whose lagoon is visited by thousands every year. Near the park entrance are a few stone ruins that many of the visitors fail to notice.

The ruins of the great city of Coba are only partly excavated, and are so extensive and overgrown that a visitor needs a guide to keep from getting lost. The lake where Zazil Ha bathed is located next to the parking lot and across from the restaurants.

Most of the shrines to Ixchel on Cozumel were destroyed by Cortes at the same time he was ransoming De Aguiller. A few ruins remain, but Cozumel is now a resort noted for scuba diving. Playa San Francisco, the beach where Guerrero and Zazil Ha made love as the sun set is a popular tourist site only a few miles south of San Miguel. In the capital itself, on the waterfront, there is a plaza and statue devoted to Guerrero. The statue includes his wife and three children. Fittingly, the Guerrero statue stands facing the Mexican city, with its back to the water.

Thanks to its good state of preservation, and its proximity to Cancun and Cozumel, Tulum is the most visited of all the Mayan ruins. The beach where the trading canoes landed still exists and is often featured in travel posters. The temple above the beach still overlooks the sea as it did the day Juan de Grijalva and his crew first saw it.

No trace remains of Mayan Chetumal. The present Mexican city of Chetumal may have been partially built on the ruins, but archeologists are not sure, since the Spaniards often dismantled existing structures for building materials. Here, too is a stature of Guerrero, along with his wife and children. A similar statue stands in Akumal, a beach town opposite Cozumel.

On the way to Chichen Itza, the tour buses from Cancun pass through the city of Valladolid, built by the Spaniards on the ruins of Saci, the capitol of the proud Cupul Maya.

Chichen Itza, itself, still stands and is a prime tourist destination. The site has even added an "interperative center". Near the Nunnery, where Gonzalo Guerrero lay wounded and wrote his confessions, a refreshment and souvenir stand is now located. Also near the nunnery is a small stone structure called the Red House, where Guerrero had his quarters and where Cimi reappeared.

During the day, the tour buses arrive, their diesel engines roaring and belching fumes. Hundreds of tourists swarm over the temple of Kukulcan sweating their way up the steep stairs that once knew the tread of sacrificial victims. The whole site is awash with tourists and vendors like some sort of Mayan theme park.

By late afternoon, however, the buses leave and the site empties. As the shadows lengthen, quiet descends on Chichen Itza once again. And if you were to stand between the ball court and the pyramid on a moonlit night, there is a haunted, alien feeling about the massive stone structures that loom in the ghostly gray half light. You can almost hear the echoes of the shouts of the crowd at the ball court, or hear the sounds of the Spaniards clashing with the Maya at the barricades, or smell the incense smoke drifting from the pyramid. On such a night, you can sense the presence of Gonzalo Guerrero, desperately fighting a fight he could not avoid and could not win for the woman he could not live without.

HISTORICAL BACKGROUND

The Confessions of Gonzalo Guerrero is a work of fiction, but it is based on actual events.

In 1511, 18 people of the Juan de Valdivia expedition were shipwrecked on the unknown shore of the Yucatan. Soon, because of sacrifices, disease and overwork, only Gonzalo Guerrero and Jeronimo de Aguiller survived. Over the next few years, de Aguiller remained a slave while Guerrero married and rose to become a warrior chief.

The name of the city where Guerrero was based is not known, only that it was two day's journey from the coast opposite Cozumel. There is a small ruin of a place called Ixil that fits this description. The cities of Dzilpan and Xcalampak are fictitious, as is Pom Tzec, but the warfare, rivalries and intrigues depicted were typical of Mayan life at the time. The name of Guerrero's wife is also not known for certain, but is believed to be Zazil Ha. The names of his children were also not recorded. The only Mayans whose names are known are Nahan Pat (the Batab of Cozumel), Tax Matz (De Aguiller's master), Nachan Can (Batab of Chetumal), and Namax Cupul and Nachi Cocom (of Chichen Itza). The prophesies of Chilam Balam are documented.

In 1517, another Spanish expedition under De Cordoba was ambushed after landing at Ecab, and again defeated at Champoton when they went ashore to refill leaking water casks. Although there has been speculation about Guerrero's possible role in these events, nothing is known for sure. However, the gold offerings Cordoba's men brought back from Ecab caused the Spaniards to send the Grijalva expedition the following year. About that time, the smallpox epidemic depicted became the first of many European diseases to ravage the Yucatan and weaken the Mayan resistance.

In 1519, Cortez led a third expedition that landed on Cozumel. There, he heard of two mysterious white men living two day's journey into the interior. Realizing the valuable intelligence these men could provide, Cortez sent messengers with the message depicted in the book. De Aguiller returned and told of Guerrero's refusal and the fact that he was now married and had three sons. De Aguiller also told Cortez that Guerrero was a leader in time of war. The battle of Cintla and the subsequent fall of the Aztecs happened as related.

Francisco de Montejo's settlement at Xelha, his subsequent problems, and trip north occurred as depicted, although Guerrero's involvement is not known.

The next Spanish contact with Guerrero was in 1527 when Montejo came to Chetumal and learned from a captive that Guerrero was in the service of Nachan Can. How or why Guerrero, who was near Cozumel in 1519, came to be at Chetumal eight years later is not known. Montejo's message to Guerrero, and Guerrero's reply occurred as related. The double ruse that caused both Montejo and Davila to turn back, each thinking the other was dead is a matter of historic record, and Guerrero is thought to be responsible by both contemporary historians and by the Spaniards at the time.

Montejo's son's actions at Chichen Itza, the Batab's attempt to kill him, and the subsequent siege happened as stated. The location of the Spanish fortifications is not known, but the ball court seems best suited. The Spanish escape and the ruse involving the hungry dog tied to the alarm bell are also true incidents, as is the ambush of the Mayan pursuers. Guerrero's role at Chichen Itza, as well as elsewhere, has been the subject of much speculation, as have his character and his motivations. Given the circumstances in which he found himself, the thoughts and actions attributed to him in this book could well be close to the truth.

NOTES

---

1. The Moors, Islamic tribesmen from North Africa, invaded the land that became Spain in 711, bringing a rich and relatively tolerant culture. A long series of wars and campaigns resulted in the expulsion of the Moors when they were driven from their last stronghold, Grenada, in 1492. The same year saw the expulsion of the Jews, and the first voyage of Columbus.

2. Although Spain was a united nation, it was formed of smaller states such as Arragon and Castile. As a result, many Spaniards continued to refer to themselves by the names of these states.

3. The Holy Inquisition was used to bolster the power of both the church and the state. The constant cycle of accusations, denouncings, trials, repentings and executions was similar to China's Cultural Revolution in our own time. Although the power of the Inquisition diminished, it wasn't officially abolished until the 18th Century.

4. The island of Hispaniola, just east of Cuba now contains Haiti on its western half and the Dominican Republic on the east. Santo Domingo is still capital of the Dominican Republic.

5. Hernando Cortes dropped out of law school to come to

Santo Domingo in 1504. He became bored with being a landowner and minor official and set out for adventure. In 1511, when he was 26 years old. Guerrero's description of him mentions his determination and his eloquence, two traits Cortes was to use with great effect 15 years later in Mexico. He conquered a feared warrior nation of several million with 500 men, some horses, and an extraordinary amount of courage, cunning, and luck. This is the first indication Cortes and Guerrero ever met, though it is doubtful Cortes remembered the incident years later when he sought Guerrero as a renegade.

6. The first Dominican friars had arrived the previous year. The sermon by Montesino resulted in protests back to Spain and demands for the expulsion of the Dominicans. Montesino went to Spain to plead the case for both the Dominicans and the Indians. As a result, the Dominicans remained in the new world and fought for the rights of the native population tirelessly and fearlessly.

7. This apparently conflicts with the account given by several sources, most notably by Diaz in his book The Conquest of Mexico. In these versions, the ship was en route from Darien in the south to Santo Domingo. However, both versions agree the ship foundered off the coast of Jamaica.

8. There is some disagreement over the extent of human sacrifice among the Maya, since its frequency varied from place to place in the small independent kingdoms that made up the Yucatan. It was certainly never practiced on a scale approaching that of the Aztecs, who reportedly sacrificed 20,000 victims to

dedicate the great temple in their capitol, Tenochtitlan, in 1487.

9. Guerrero is correct in his observation of a civilization in decline. By 1511, the Maya were well past their greatest days, and had been weakened by invaders, warfare, overbuilding, and fighting among themselves. Buildings erected during this period were smaller and noticeably inferior in craftsmanship. The Maya were living among the ruins of their past. The great cities were being reclaimed by the jungle.

10. Captives were the chief prizes of war. Noble or high ranking captives were sacrificed first, and others were made slaves.

11. Many writers have also commented on the similarities between Christianity and the religion of the Maya. This similarity made the work of Spanish priests much easier and resulted in a blending of the two faiths in a way that persists to this day. A farmer may pray to Mary in the morning and sacrifice a chicken to Chac in the afternoon.

12. Several versions of the prophesies of the Jaguar priest have been documented. Some, no doubt, were written after the fact, but in some places, the book caused the Maya to accept the Spanish conquest as fate.

13. The Spanish expedition of 1517 was under the command of Francisco de Cordoba. As Guerrero surmised, they saw the city from the sea and sailed to investigate. The Spaniards named this city "Great Cairo" because of the pyramids.

14. The Cordoba expedition continued along the northern coast until leaking water casks forced them to go ashore at the Mayan city of Champoton near Tabasco. They were attacked

and suffered great losses there. Guerrero is sometimes credited with planning or even leading this attack, but apparently he did not.

The expedition, suffering greatly from wounds and lack of water, made a horrendous voyage back to Cuba. Half the men had been lost and Cordoba himself soon died of his wounds. But just as Guerrero had feared, the gold impressed Governor Velasquez who formed a new expedition under Juan de Grijalva the following year. The conquest of the Yucatan had begun.

15. Smallpox, and later cholera and a host of other diseases killed far more of the native people than the Spaniards. The Indians had had no opportunity to develop resistance to the diseases and died in droves as a result. American diseases, however, had little impact on the Spaniards. Conditions in Europe were actually less healthy than in the Americas, with open sewers, domestic animals, body lice and general filth helping to build the immunity of those who survived.

As a result, diseases such as measles, which were minor to the Spaniards, became deadly killers of the Indians. As Guerrero points out, the psychological effects of the disease did as much to undermine the fighting spirit of the Maya as the physical ones.

16. Aside from Guerrero, Juan de Grijalva was the first European to see Cozumel and Tulum. He sailed around the Yucatan without landing until he came to Champoton where he landed and defeated the Maya who had done so much damage

to Cordoba the year before. As Tolotl indicated, the expedition then reached the edge of the Aztec empire and traded for gold objects they correctly assumed represented only a fraction of the wealth to be found among the Aztecs.

17. Guerrero's account of the message from Cortes and of his reply tally closely with the historical record. However, no one has previously discovered the full extent of the struggle between Guerrero and de Aguiller and its resolution. De Aguiller still had his Book of Hours when he finally joined Cortes on Cozumel.

18. With 500 men and a few dozen horses, Cortes conquered a feared warrior empire of several million. It was one of the most astounding feats of conquest in history, and seems impossible, even today. He was masterful at playing one group against another, and was aided by the Aztecs themselves, who were hated by the vassal states because of their constant demands for sacrificial victims. The Aztec emperor Moctezuma, fearing Cortes might be the returned god Quetzalcoatl, hesitated to act until it was too late.

In addition to these factors was the impact of diseases such as smallpox and cholera, as well as the weapons and prowess of the Spaniards themselves. Tenochtitlan was razed and Mexico City built in its place.

19. Guerrero succeeded better than he knew. After the double deception, Montejo left Chetumal and explored along the coast to the south. Davila, thinking he had to take over Salamanca de Xelha in Montejo's absence, returned to find it deserted. Montejo and Davila didn't meet up and discover the ruse until almost a year later, at which time they gathered a greater force and marched to the interior and Chichen Itza.

20. From Guerrero's description, this is undoubtedly the Temple of the Warriors, and can be seen at Chichen Itza to this day.

21. Popular depictions of the Spanish conquistadors usually show them in European plate armor, but in the Yucatan and other Mayan areas, it was seldom used. The Spaniards soon found this armor was too heavy and too hot for local conditions, and unnecessary for the relatively light weapons of the Maya, which had only a fraction of the penetrating power of European broadswords, halberds, crossbow quarrels, or firearms. So the Spaniards adopted thick quilted cotton armor similar to that of the Mayans, leaving only their helmets and gauntlets as steel protection.

Also by John Reisinger:

Historical Novels-

Nassau

Evasive Action: The Hunt for Gregor Meinhoff

Flanagan and the Crown of Mexico (Winner of Global eBook Awards Gold Medal for Best Historical Fiction 2014)

Nonfiction-

Master Detective: The Life and Crimes of Ellis Parker, America's Real-life Sherlock Holmes (Candidate for Edgar Award for Non Fiction 2006)

The Secrets Behind the Structures

Historical Mysteries (The Max Hurlock Roaring 20s Mysteries)

Death of a Flapper

Death on a Golden Isle

Death at the Lighthouse

Death and the Blind Tiger (Winner of the Global eBook Awards Gold Medal for Best Mystery 2014)

Death in Unlikely Places

Death across the Chesapeake

ABOUT THE AUTHOR:

John Reisinger lives in Maryland and is a former Coast Guard officer and a retired engineer. He is the author of a dozen books on historical themes, such as Master Detective, the Max Hurlock Roaring 20s Mysteries, and The Secrets Behind the Structures. He has appeared on a segment of the Travel Channel's Mysteries at the Museum.

His website is johnreisinger.com, and his blog is johnreisinger.net. He can be contacted by email at johnrbooks@yahoo.com

Author at Guerrero Monument in Cozumel